LAURA HONKEN

The Best Laid Lies

First published by Laura Honken 2022

First edition

ISBN: 979-8-9850791-2-8

This book was professionally typeset on Reedsy.
Find out more at reedsy.com

For my husband, Dean. Thank you for believing in me.

Contents

Acknowledgement

To Dean, thank you for your unwavering support and loving me no matter what.

To Tyler, Tylyn, Aleigha, MaddiLynn, Greysyn, and PaisLee; Jordan, Lauren, Liam, Brayden, and Autumn; Owen, Madison, and Capri; thank you for being my family, making me a grandmother, and always being there for me.

To Casey and Julie, thank you for being two of the best sisters anyone could have and for making Dan and Tony part of our family.

To Jessica and Michael, thank you for being such a huge part of my life.

To Jessica, thank you for allowing me to use your beautiful images and creating such a striking cover.

To Tylyn, thank you for your expertise in making the perfect promotional items.

To Pat, Casey, Rebecca, William, Brandie, Deb, Tanley, Christiana, Mallory, Ryan, and Brittany, thank you for being my alpha and beta readers. Your feedback was instrumental.

To William, thank you for listening to my ideas and giving your honest feedback. This wouldn't have worked without you letting me bounce those ideas off you.

To Rebecca, thank you for being you. Your guidance was appreciated beyond words.

To Christiana, thank you for your proofreading skills and always being willing to give me your opinion.

To Ally, thank you for your knowledge and formatting the cover.

To Mom, I miss you every day. Thank you for encouraging me and being as strong as you were.

To Bob, rest in peace, big brother.

To all of my friends and family, I wish I could name you all individually. You are all in my heart and I love you.

1

Chapter 1

If anyone watched her, Ella Dalton appeared to be singing the familiar birthday song. Her mouth moved along with the words, but no sound was exiting her mouth. Not because she didn't want to celebrate the little girl's birthday, but because she was uncomfortable in social situations. Ever since her father's death when she was young, severe social anxiety had ruled her life. Convinced she was not attractive enough or smart enough to bring any value to a conversation, she did her best to avoid interactions with other people. Now, at the fifth birthday party of her stepdaughter, Ava, she was trying her best to pretend she didn't want to crawl away and hide until it was over.

The song ended, and Ava happily blew out her candles with her beaming mother and father on each side of her. Ella looked at Ava's father and felt her love for him overwhelm her. It wasn't easy, though. She had married Matthew shortly after his daughter's birth and always felt she was in competition with Ava's mother, Adrienne.

Ella had tried to have a positive relationship with Adrienne, but felt the persona she presented to the world was completely fake. She was one of those people who tries to appear so friendly and sweet, but you know is actually insincere and talking about you the moment you turn your back. Unable to ever prove her theory of Adrienne's duplicity, she had to accept her as part of her life. Everyone else seemed to adore and admire Adrienne; she had been raised in abject poverty to a drug-addicted mother but had managed to overcome her obstacles.

Today, she had extra attention due to the walker she had been using for the past few weeks. Adrienne explained to everyone, even if they already knew, that she had multiple sclerosis and was experiencing a severe flareup of symptoms. She hobbled her way to Ava to help her blow out the candles. Once the candles were successfully out, she yelled at everyone there, "Look at the beautiful baby Matthew and I made together," before hugging Matthew to her. Ella saw her husband nervously glance toward her and gently pry Adrienne away, sensing her closeness to him was making his wife uncomfortable. Once he freed himself, he walked to Ella and drew her close to him.

"I'm so proud of you for being here for Ava and me," he told her before he placed a soft kiss on the tip of her nose.

"You know I love that little girl," Ella replied. "I would do anything for her."

"I know you do," Matthew stated. "Will you be okay if I go mingle with some of my friends?"

Reluctantly, Ella nodded. "I won't be gone long. When I get back, we can go home," he promised.

Watching her husband move from person to person with such ease, Ella couldn't help but feel jealous of his ability to be comfortable in any situation. They had been married a little over four years, but they had been together for five years. It might sound cliché, but the sight of him still took her breath away. Matthew had wavy chestnut hair and deep brown eyes. He stood six foot two inches, and his daily runs kept him in remarkable physical shape. Ella exercised to keep herself healthy, but she wasn't nearly as diligent as her husband. She knew she had married above her station for looks and couldn't believe someone who looked like him wanted to marry someone who looked like her. Ella had money, and she sometimes worried that Matthew had married her for that reason, but he had his own money. He was comfortable, but he was far from as wealthy as Ella. She couldn't believe that he loved her for her. Why would this smart, handsome, sexy man want someone not as attractive as him and who suffered from social anxiety? Yet, despite her misgivings, when they were together as a family, without any outside influences, she sensed he loved her. When she was able to be herself and wasn't worried about how everyone else saw them, she was able to believe every word he said to her. He laughed at her jokes, took care of her when she was sick, and was always interested in sex. She knew there was a genuine love between the two of them, despite their differences.

"Hi, Ella," said a familiar voice.

Turning, she saw the face she was expecting. "Hi, Jeff, how are you?" she asked.

"Enjoying this as much as possible," he replied honestly. "Are you as uncomfortable as I am?"

"I am," she replied. "But I know you love Ava too much to miss this."

"You definitely know me," Jeff replied.

Ella was grateful for the one person at the party who she knew felt as uneasy as herself. Jeff was the brother of Adrienne's husband, Jake. Neither Ella nor Matthew was particularly fond of Jake, but his brother was the complete opposite, soft-spoken and god-fearing. Jake never seemed overly bright or caring, but Jeff had always seemed to be intelligent and sensitive.

"Are you as anxious to leave as I am?" he asked her.

"I really want to be happy to be here, but I'm so uncomfortable. A small party would have been my preference."

"Adrienne never goes small when it comes to making Ava happy. She would do anything for her," Jeff replied with sincerity.

"Why are you keeping this beautiful lady all to yourself?" Jake yelled at his brother, inserting himself into their conversation. He walked to Jeff and faked a punch toward his crotch. Instinctively, Jeff moved his hands to cover his private parts. When he did this, Jake slapped his brother across the face and laughed. "You fall for that every time, wussy boy."

An embarrassed Jeff shook his head as his older brother's antics. "Come on, Jake," he pleaded. "Can you not be that way on Ava's birthday?"

"Aww, don't be so sensitive," Jake teased. "You need to man up and quit being such a pussy." He wrapped his arm around Jeff's neck and pulled him down into the familiar wrestling hold. Attempts to release himself failed as he squirmed and punched helplessly as his much stronger brother, his face growing redder by the moment.

Averting her gaze to try to spare Jeff the embarrassment being inflicted upon him, Ella ordered softly, "Just leave him alone, Jake."

Surprised by her words, Jake released his grip on Jeff and shoved him away. His attention was now squarely on Ella. "Well, look who has something to say. Why don't you come over here and give me a nice hello."

Instinctively Ella stepped back in a futile attempt to avoid the unwelcome attention of Ava's stepfather. He stumbled toward her before clumsily attempting to kiss her on the lips. Thankfully, she managed turned her face in time, so he missed and could only drool on her cheek.

"Hello, Jake," she said as she wiped his mark off her face.

"That's no way to greet family," Jake exclaimed. He pulled her toward him for a hug, and she felt herself physically stiffen at his unwanted touch. The hug lasted much too long to be friendly. His hand caressed the small of her back before he moved it down to cup her buttocks.

"Stop it, Jake!" Ella yelled.

"Leave her alone," Jeff yelled as he tried to push himself between them.

"Mind your own business," he hissed at his brother as he pushed him away again. Jake's fist was ready to strike at his brother, but a strong hand around his arm stopped him from striking.

"I saw what you did!" Matthew yelled. "Don't you ever put your hands on my wife."

"Matthew," Ella said while gesturing toward Ava and the other children, "this isn't the place."

Through gritted teeth, Matthew glared at Jake and said, "In the house, now."

Jake walked toward the house with his shoulders slumped, looking like a toddler about to be punished, with Matthew and Ella following closely behind. "What is going on?" Adrienne asked as she struggled to catch up to the angry group. No one answered; instead, Matthew pointed toward the house to instruct her to follow them.

Once the door closed behind them, Matthew immediately let his feelings be known. "I never want to see him come near my wife again."

Holding her hands out in front of her, Adrienne said, "Can someone please tell me what happened?"

"Your pig of a husband felt up my wife," Matthew replied angrily.

"I didn't do anything," a defensive Jake stated. "I just tried to give her a hug, but apparently, she's too good for that."

"It's obvious you're drunk. You promised that you were going to stop drinking. I never want to see you near my wife again. Is that clear?" he shouted as he moved closer to Jake.

"Is it clear to you I didn't do anything?" Jake shouted back as he moved close to Matthew until the two men stood nose to nose, both with clenched fists.

"Everyone needs to calm down. I'm sure there's a reasonable explanation," Adrienne stated. Slowly moving to her husband, she put her hands on his shoulder and whispered in his ear. Jake nodded and took a step back from Matthew. "I didn't want to tell you this today since it's Ava's birthday, but we received some bad news yesterday. Jake wasn't taking the news very well, and he had a little too much to drink. I'm sure he didn't mean to do anything to offend you or Ella."

"What's wrong, Adrienne? Is Ava okay?" Matthew asked nervously.

"Ava is fine," she answered before her tears fell.

"Adrienne's multiple sclerosis is getting worse," Jake finished for her. "The doctor said it's progressing faster than they expected and she'll be in a wheelchair soon. She didn't want to tell anyone because she wanted Ava to have her day."

Adrienne squeezed a few words between her sobs, "Please... Jake is just having a hard time. Don't take our daughter's special day from her. I just want her to have as normal of a childhood as possible."

Matthew and Ella looked at each other, not knowing what to say. She knew he was feeling the same empathy for Adrienne she was, but was still worried about Jake's behavior. "Look," said Matthew, "I'm sorry for what you're going through. I'm sure we all agree that we want Ava to have a happy childhood and a great birthday, but we need to know that she is taken care of. We'll agree to forget this ever happened only if Jake agrees this is the last time he drinks and he keeps his hands off of my wife." Ella looked at Jake and could tell by his face that he was contemplating a retort that would lead to another argument, but Adrienne held up her hand to stop him.

"I think that's reasonable. Don't you agree, Jake?"

"Sure," an obviously disagreeable Jake answered. "But..."

"But nothing," Adrienne interrupted him. "Ella has every right to her feelings. If she said you made her uncomfortable, then you need to own that and apologize."

"Daddy?" a small voice said in a whimper.

Ella turned to find Ava standing inside the sliding glass doors, her eyes widened in fear. Ava was a strikingly beautiful child, with her natural blonde hair and crystal blue eyes. She was tall for her age, with a slender build. She felt instant guilt when she saw the pain in Ava's big eyes. She knew Ava didn't need to see this, and she placed her hand gently on Matthew's arm. "Honey," she said and cocked her head toward the little girl. Matthew turned to see his daughter and instantly softened. He ran to her, scooped her up in his arms, kissed her cheek, then said, "Daddy loves you."

"Are you guys fighting?" she asked in a scared voice.

"Of course not," Matthew lied. "We're just trying to decide which of us loves you more."

"Which one of you loves me more?" she asked with an innocence only a child can have.

"We decided we all love you equally because you're so amazing," he replied.

Satisfied with his answer, a small smile formed on her lips. "Can you help me open my presents?" she asked.

"Of course I will," he said as he grabbed her hand.

The two walked toward the door, but Ava turned back, "Ella, I want you to come too," she stated.

"I will be right there; I just need to talk to your mother first."

"Do you promise?"

"I promise."

Appearing to accept her at her word, Ava nodded and happily skipped out the door with her father.

Ella focused her attention back to the couple in the room. She wanted to convey her sympathy for her plight, but she felt Jake's behavior still required an apology. "Adrienne, I'm so sorry about your illness, but..."

Her demeanor changed now that Matthew and Ava were out of the room. She interrupted Ella's sentence and snapped, "What's the matter, bitch? Upset that you're not the center of attention?"

"Wh...what?" Ella stammered.

"I know you want Jake," she accused. "And I know you're the reason this whole thing started. You think you're so much better than everyone else, but you're not. You're pathetic." Adrienne looked at Jake and said, "Let's go."

Jake followed his wife toward the door but stopped to grab Ella's backside once again. "Someday, baby, you're going to enjoy my touch," he whispered in her ear menacingly before placing a kiss on her cheek. "Coming, babe," he said as he hurried to assist his wife out the door.

Stunned at their actions, Ella stood in the room, unable to move. She was aware Adrienne did not like her; she obviously felt Matthew was the love of her life, and Ella had stolen her happily ever after. However, Matthew had clarified it was a one-night stand that resulted in an unplanned but much-loved daughter and Ella had not broken up anything. Adrienne and Jake had never acted this brazen before. How was she going to tell Matthew that Adrienne's husband had threatened her? He was always defensive of her because she was the mother of his only child and Adrienne herself had experienced such a difficult childhood. For the time being, she did what she could, which was to paste a smile on her face and fulfill her promise to watch her stepdaughter open her gifts.

When they returned home after the party, Ella told Matthew about the threat and what Adrienne had said to her, but she did not receive the reaction she expected.

"Are you sure that is what she said?" he asked. "Is it possible you misunderstood what she said?"

"How can I misunderstand being called a bitch?" Ella shouted. "Why do you always defend her? She called me a bitch and let Jake threaten me."

Taking her in his arms, Matthew said, "I'm not trying to defend her. Look, I know this can't be easy for you, but Adrienne has to be a part of our lives because of Ava."

Slumping her shoulders, Ella cried softly, "I know, but can't you see she has an ulterior motive? She wants you for herself."

Swallowing hard, Matthew whispered, "Even if she wanted that. I love you and I never want to lose you."

Raising her eyes, she tried to catch his gaze, but she could tell he was deliberately avoiding looking at her. "Why won't you look at me?"

"It's been a long day and I just want to put this behind us. Can you do that?"

"What about what Jake said to me?"

"I will talk to Adrienne about it. Jake was drunk, and maybe he didn't realize what he was saying. But if it makes you feel better, I will make sure that you're never alone with him."

"How can you guarantee that? They live in a house we own on the same property where we live, and there are nights that you're out of town."

"We'll put in additional cameras and security equipment, okay? I promise you, I will never let anyone hurt you. Jake will never get near you again."

"You just let Adrienne call me a bitch and you aren't going to do anything about it."

"That's not fair, Ella. You know I have to keep a good relationship with Adrienne for Ava's sake, and I promise that I would never intentionally hurt you. I love you, not Adrienne. In fact, I can show you how much I love you right now if you want."

Ella couldn't help but smile at her husband even though she felt this was his attempt to change the subject. Deep down, she knew he loved her and would do anything to protect her, but she couldn't help but feel uneasy about another woman coveting him. Instead of prolonging the fight, she decided her anger belonged with Adrienne and Jake. She reached toward Matthew and asked playfully, "What do you have in mind?"

"Let me show you," he said as he lay her back on their bed. "I could never love anyone as much as I love you. You are my world, Ella."

After they finished, Matthew left to go on his daily run. He planned to make it a longer run than usual so that he could work off the birthday cake Ava had insisted he eat. Ella stayed in their bed, still thinking of his touch before her thoughts returned to Adrienne. Ella couldn't call her unattractive, but she also couldn't call her attractive. Maybe her opinion of Adrienne's looks was jaded because Ella didn't like her as a person. One of those instances where the more you know someone, the more or less attractive they become. It was apparent that Adrienne would have a particular draw to men, though. She maintained a fantastic figure and dressed to show it off. She kept her hair long and blonde, which she claimed was her natural color, even though it was apparent she was born a brunette. She wasn't a natural beauty by any means but did the best with what she had, and Ella had to respect her effort. However, there was one physical characteristic of Adrienne's that Ella couldn't get past: her thin lips. She often wondered how someone with such thin lips could have such a big mouth, but she pulled it off—always using her voice to make herself the center of attention. The two of them were so different, not just in looks but also in personality. Ella had once asked Matthew how he fell for her since she was nothing like Adrienne. Matthew's reply was brief and powerful, "Isn't that the point? If I wanted someone like her, I would be with her." The response summed up why she felt as secure as she was capable of in their relationship. If Matthew had wanted Adrienne, he could have easily had her.

The sound of Matthew starting the shower startled her awake. She hadn't heard him come back into the house when he returned from his jog. "Matthew?" she yelled.

"I took a long run, so I'm going to take a quick shower," he shouted back.

Still naked from their earlier lovemaking, Ella crept into the bathroom and surprised her husband by joining him in the shower. She immediately saw the scratches on his body. "What happened to you?"

"I tripped over a root and fell into a bush," he quickly answered. "I'm fine."

"Are you fine enough for another round of showing me how much you love me?"

"Always," he said before he leaned over to kiss her. However, before their lips could touch, Matthew's phone rang.

"Don't answer it," Ella begged.

"It could be about Ava. I better see who it is." He opened the shower door to step out to answer the call. Although she tried, she could not hear the conversation over the sound of the water. Suddenly, Matthew yanked the shower door open, and Ella knew something terrible had occurred.

"What happened?" she asked in a scared voice.

"That was Adrienne. Jake has disappeared."

2

Chapter 2

Dumbfounded, Ella quickly asked, "What do you mean? Is he missing?"

Matthew threw a towel at her and replied, "I don't know. Adrienne said he went for a walk after the birthday party and never came home. She's been calling him, but he's not answering his phone."

"What does she expect you to do about it?"

"She needs help looking for him," he replied. "Adrienne said he likes to go to the grove when he wants to be alone. She can't go check because she can't get around out there with her walker and she's really worried about him, so I told her I would go look for him there."

"Why is it up to you to look for him? She can call his brother or the cops," Ella reasoned.

Matthew sighed, "I'd be fine if he never comes back, but Adrienne is crying and that is making Ava cry. She said she tried to reach Jeff to go look for him, but he's not answering his phone and the cops won't do anything since he's an adult." Matthew smiled at her before saying, "If you go with me, we can make it one of our adventures to the grove, just like we used to."

Knowing what he was implying, she decided an adventure in the grove sounded better than the shower she had planned. Giving her husband a wink, she said, "Let me throw on some clothes quickly, and we can go."

The grove was a grouping of trees between their house and Adrienne's house. Ella and Matthew had built their dream home on an acreage in southwest Minnesota. At first, she wasn't sure about building their house in this location, but she and Matthew had grown up in the area, Ella just over the border in northwest Iowa and Matthew in southwest Minnesota. Although they grew up close in proximity, they didn't meet until they were in their mid-twenties, but their relationship grew quickly. When deciding where to build their home, the most important thing was to be close to Ava, and Adrienne insisted Ava would live nowhere but where Adrienne herself felt the most comfortable. Both Matthew and Ella had envisioned a house in the country and they both loved the beauty and welcoming nature of the area. Although Matthew was an extrovert and Ella was very much introvert, they both agreed that house away from close neighbors was what they wanted. A house off the beaten path would allow Ella to maintain her preference of being removed from other people and allow Matthew to embrace his love of the outdoors. To realize their shared dream, they purchased six hundred acres and built their house. Matthew wanted his daughter as close as possible, so he asked Ella if she would build a separate house on the outside edge of their property where Adrienne, Jake, and Ava could live. Ella agreed because it meant keeping Ava close, and she would do anything to make her husband and stepdaughter happy. She had helped raise her since she was a baby and, to Ella, Ava was her daughter. To show he understood her sacrifice of having his ex-lover so close, Matthew had kept a large grove of trees between their home and Adrienne's home. That way, Ella would not feel as if Adrienne or Jake were right next door. The additional benefit of the trees was that Matthew could make a running trail throughout the woods. He could get in his daily run and stay close to home. Surprisingly, Jake had developed an interest in the outdoors and asked to use the trail for walking. Matthew had reluctantly agreed as long as Jake walked when Matthew was not using the path. His daily run was his time, and he didn't want to see anyone else, let alone Jake. Now, Ava's stepfather seemed to be missing somewhere on that trail. Ella wondered about the possibility of Jake encountering a coyote or other animal among the trees. The area they lived in was not known for wild animal attacks, but there had been reports of a misplaced mountain lion appearing in the area from time to time.

When they left the house to begin the search for the missing Jake, Matthew instead veered toward the shed, where he kept what he called his toys, such as his four-wheeler, snowmobile, and motorcycle. "Where are you going?" Ella asked.

Replying over his shoulder, he stated, "I'm getting my gun. Who knows what could be out there? I think we need protection."

Although she wasn't fond of guns, Matthew's reasoning made sense. She had insisted the gun be kept in the shed because she didn't want it in her house. If there were wild animals out there, it would be better to have protection. Matthew returned quickly with the gun and tucked it into the back of his waistband. "Okay, let's go."

They walked down the trail hand in hand, Matthew on the inside to keep Ella safe from anything that might jump out from the trees. They were coming up to an area that held a special place in her heart. She and Matthew had spent their first day at their new home in this area, where they had discovered a family of bald eagles living in the grove. A smile crossed her face at the thought of the memory, temporarily distracting her from their task. Suddenly, she felt Matthew's grip on her hand tighten. "Stay here," he ordered as he carefully removed his gun from its location and crept toward a clearing.

Holding her breath, Ella did as she was told, even as she lost sight of her husband. "Call 911!" Matthew yelled. No longer able to stand back, she ran toward the sound of his voice. Peering through the trees, she saw Matthew kneeling beside Jake's body. It was obvious he was dead; his eyes were open, and there was dried blood under his nose and mouth. Placing her hand over her mouth, Ella cried out with a gut-wrenching scream, causing a flustered Matthew to turn toward her. "Get out of here, Ella. You don't need to see this."

Frozen, she stood staring at Jake's vacant eyes. A frustrated Matthew came to her, placed his hands on her shoulders, nudging her back until she could no longer see Jake. "Ella, I need you to help me. Can you do that?" She silently shook her head. "Okay, you need to call 911 now."

Unable to find her voice, she nodded again. Matthew turned from her and walked back toward the body. Finally managing to speak, she asked, "Don't you think it's best that you don't touch anything?"

Her words caused him to stop. "You're probably right. You call 911 and I'll make sure no one else is here."

Still shaking, Ella pulled her phone from her pocket and dialed the emergency number. Dead bodies were not commonplace in their small town, and the dispatcher asked her to repeat herself to ensure she had heard correctly. After giving the address, Ella used an app on her phone to open the security gate that protected the property so the police would have no issues making their way to the scene. "They're on their way," she told Matthew.

Nodding his head, Matthew didn't move his gaze from Jake's body. Ella knew this meant he was deep in thought, and it was best to say nothing to him. However, for his own safety, she had to tell him to put his gun on the ground so he didn't get shot by the police. Unable to anything else, she stood frozen in place, waiting for the help that would soon be there.

After about ten minutes, police cars, with full lights and sirens, enveloped their once-peaceful trail. The officers separated Ella and Matthew and began putting up the yellow police tape. The young officer with Ella called her by name, but she did not know who he was. "Do you know what happened?" she asked him.

"Sorry, Mrs. Dalton," he replied, "but we can't discuss anything with you yet. I can only tell you that the BCA will be here soon."

"What is the BCA?" she asked.

"We're too small a town to handle a suspicious death, so we have to call in the Minnesota Bureau of Criminal Apprehension to investigate," he explained. "They will want to question you and your husband." Just then, his radio crackled, and he turned away from Ella to talk to the person on the other end. "Mrs. Dalton, the BCA agent is asking us to bring you to the station in Worthington for questioning. He will be there as soon as he can."

"Of course," she answered quietly. "Can Matthew and I go together?"

"Sorry, but no. I will drive you; I don't think it's safe for you to drive, given the traumatic experience you just had. Someone else will bring your husband."

Ella silently followed the officer to his car, where he instructed her to sit in the back seat. She had never been in the backseat of a police car before, and she did not enjoy the feeling. To help quell her anxiety, she asked, "What is the name of the BCA agent coming to question me?"

"There are two agents coming," he replied. "One is Agent Williams and the other is Agent Ulrich."

Her body experienced a physical jolt upon hearing the name Agent Williams. She had known a Dale Williams in high school, and she had an enormous crush on him. He was the captain of the football team, the homecoming king, and the most popular boy in school. However, it was clear Dale didn't feel the same way about her. He made it clear they were only friends and that he intended to stay that way. Insecure, Ella could never tell him how she really felt. When it was time for her to leave for college, Dale had begged her to stay in touch. He said her friendship meant so much to him, and he didn't want to lose her from his life. The thought of watching Dale date other women and someday get married and have a family with someone else was more than she could bear. She lied and told him she wanted to spread her wings and make a clean start at college. She thought back to the pained look on his face when she said that a complete break was for the best. "Please," Dale pleaded, "can't we stay friends? You're honestly my best friend. I need you in my life." Dale was emotional, but Ella was steadfast in her decision, and they had not seen each other since that day. Some people might have thought she was cold for cutting him out of her life, but she knew her feelings required her to maintain the distance. Ella had gone off to her college, and Dale had gone off to his college. Last she heard, Dale had pursued a career in law enforcement. Could this be the same person?

The officer parked in front of the police station and escorted her into the building and led her to a small room.

"Just wait here," said the officer. "They'll be in to talk to you as soon as they can."

Ella looked around the room and knew immediately she was in an interrogation room. There was no style to the room; only a lone round table in the middle of the room with plastic chairs around it, plain white walls, and no decorations. She took a seat in a chair and waited. Her mind was going a million miles a minute trying to figure out what was happening, what were they going to ask her and Matthew. Could they honestly think either of them might know what happened or worse yet, somehow be involved? Ella could feel the anxiety; her legs and hands were shaking, and she knew an anxiety attack had already started, and a full panic attack would surely follow if she didn't stop it. She knew the best thing she could do for herself was to feel grounded by using the 5-4-3-2-1 technique Dr. McGregor had taught her. Acknowledge five things around her, acknowledge four things she could touch, acknowledge three things she could hear, acknowledge two things she could smell, and acknowledge one thing she could taste. Unfortunately, the one thing she could taste was blood in her mouth. She must have been biting her lip without even knowing it. She was concentrating on stopping the bleeding when the door opened, and Dale Williams walked through the door, followed by a female officer wearing the unofficial female detective outfit of black slacks, a crisp white button-down shirt, and black jacket.

"Sorry to make you wait so long, Ella," said Dale. Ella looked at her watch, surprised to realize she had been waiting for over an hour. *I guess time flies when you're scared to death,* she thought to herself.

"Dale," she said, "long time no see."

Dale purposely ignored her and said, "Ella, this is Agent Ulrich. She is in charge of the investigation into Jake's death. We need to talk to you for a moment. You are not under arrest. Do you understand?"

Ella nodded her head and said, "Yes, but please tell me what happened to Jake."

Again, Dale ignored her. This time it was Agent Ulrich who asked, "Where were you this afternoon after you left the birthday party?"

"I was at home," said Ella.

"Did you leave at all?" asked Agent Ulrich.

"No," answered Ella. "We didn't leave until Matthew got a call from Adrienne that Jake didn't come home."

"We?" said the agent while lifting her eyebrows in a questioning manner.

"Are you saying your husband never left this afternoon?"

"No," said Ella. "Matthew went for a run like he does every day."

"What time was that?"

"He left around 2:00 this afternoon and returned around 3:30," Ella answered. "Please tell me what is going on! Where is Matthew?"

Dale looked at Agent Ulrich, and they shared a "why not?" look. "Ella," Dale said, "this is appears to be a homicide. We heard from Adrienne that you and your husband had a fight with Jake at the birthday party."

Ella couldn't believe her ears. This was not happening. She looked from Dale to Agent Ulrich, searching for more answers. She was having difficulty finding words but could finally mutter, "Wh... what?"

"He didn't die of natural causes," said Dale, "and you and Matthew were fighting with him today."

Ella instantly knew where their questions were heading, and she knew she had to protect herself and her husband. She wouldn't lie, but she didn't have to because she knew Matthew would never hurt anyone. "Yes," said Ella, "but Jake had asked Matthew if he could use the running trail because he wanted privacy sometimes. Matthew told him he could only use it when Matthew wasn't using it. They're never there together."

Agent Ulrich said almost gleefully, "How long have you known about the affair your husband is having with Adrienne?"

Ella blinked her eyes rapidly. There was absolutely no way this was true; Matthew thought Adrienne was a good mother to Ava, but he swore he would never want her back. "That's a lie," Ella said forcefully.

Agent Ulrich looked at Ella like she was a child who couldn't accept that Santa Claus wasn't real. "Let me read some of his text messages," she said. The agent began reading the messages to Ella, pausing between each one for dramatic effect and looking at Ella to gauge her reaction.

"Please don't tell Ella."

"I will tell Ella."

"I don't want to lose my family."

Ella was shaking her head the entire time Agent Ulrich was reading the messages, as if the denial would make it untrue. This wasn't happening, and there had to be a valid excuse. Matthew would not do this to her.

"This one from this afternoon is my favorite," said the agent. "Tell Jake to stay away or I will make him stay away."

Agent Ulrich looked at Ella again and smirked at her. "Sounds like your husband wanted to get rid of his competition."

"No," repeated Ella. "This is not true. There is no way he sent those messages. I would have known."

"Well," said the agent, "he gave us permission to search his phone and the messages are there."

Dale had primarily stayed quiet, and Ella could see on his face that he was feeling sorry for her. She looked at him and pleaded, "Please, Dale, you have to believe me; neither of us could do something like this."

Dale let out a heavy sigh and said, "I'm sorry, Ella, I am. But that's not all we found."

Agent Ulrich broke in, "Shell casings found at the scene match the gun you and your husband own. How do you explain that?"

Ella looked at Agent Ulrich and thought this woman was enjoying her pain way too much. "So?" she asked sarcastically. "Matthew has his concealed carry permit, and there have to be hundreds of guns using the same caliber in southwest Minnesota."

"That might be true," said the agent, "but I'm pretty sure not all of those gun owner also have scratches on their body and gunpowder residue on their hands."

"Matthew picked up our gun for protection. He could have easily gotten residue from that," Ella reasoned. "I know you think you're right, but you don't know Matthew."

"With all due respect, Mrs. Dalton, I would say you're the one that doesn't know Matthew," replied the agent. "Did you see him when he came back from his run this afternoon?"

"No," said Ella. "I was sleeping when he came home. He went to take a shower." Then she quickly added, "Which he always does when he returns from his run."

Agent Ulrich rolled her eyes and began another question when Ella cut her off. "I am done here," she said. "I will not sit here and listen to you tell lies about my husband. Tell me where my husband is. We're going home."

"Like I said," replied Dale, "you're not under arrest, so you're free to go, but Matthew isn't going anywhere. We're holding him."

"No, no, no," Ella protested. "You're wrong, you're wrong."

Dale looked at her again with compassion. "Ella, he volunteered to take a lie detector test." Dale paused before adding, "and it showed deception."

Ella again felt her breaths become labored, and the tunnel vision started. The last thing she saw was Dale and Agent Ulrich rushing to catch her before she hit the floor.

3

Chapter 3

Ella slowly opened her eyes and tried to refocus on the room. She could tell she was on the floor, her head supported by Dale's strong arm. It was evident that Dale and Agent Ulrich were too busy arguing with each other to notice she had regained consciousness.

"You didn't have to be so hard on her," said Dale. "If anything, she could be his next target."

"Sorry, but I'm not sorry," replied Agent Ulrich, "I can't stand weak women and their stand-by-your-man mentality. She's obviously had everything handed to her throughout her whole life and can't handle someone telling her no."

Dale was about to reply when the other agent kicked at him. She had noticed that Ella was awake. "You okay?" she asked with fake concern.

Ella looked at her sternly and said, "I am not talking to you anymore. Dale, I will talk to you, but I am not spending one more minute with her."

Agent Ulrich shrugged her shoulders and said, "It's not up to you. This is my case."

"And these are my rights," Ella answered with more force than she had ever used in her life. "I'm not under arrest and I have no obligation to talk to anyone. You might think I'm weak, but I am stronger than you think. Either you leave, or I do."

"Just go," Dale said to Agent Ulrich. "Send in one of the deputies if you don't think I can do this on my own."

Spinning on her heel, Agent Ulrich stomped out the room, making sure to slam the door behind her so everyone would know she was not in agreement.

"Ella," said Dale, "are you willing to answer some more questions?"

"Yes," she replied,, "but only to prove to you that Matthew would never hurt anyone."

"Okay," said Dale, "but we're going to have to wait for the deputy to arrive. Since you and I know each other, she's probably going to send another officer in here."

Ella half smiled. "Dale, we both know this is being recorded, but I will wait with you."

While they waited, Ella cocked her head to the side and studied Dale. He was still in great shape, just like he was in high school. Ella had always had a weakness for dark-haired, dark-eyed men, and Dale was no exception. He wasn't as classically handsome as Matthew, but he had rugged good looks similar to Vin Diesel or Adam Driver. He just exuded masculinity. When they had known each other in high school, Ella was sure Dale knew she had a crush on him, but he never tried to exploit that fact. Most high school boys would have used her feelings to try to get sex, but not Dale. Ella wasn't sure if it was because of her shyness, or if Dale just wasn't attracted to her. After all, her mother had always told her she was lucky to come from money because no man would want her for her looks and certainly not for her brains.

It seemed Dale could feel her studying him because he looked up at her and gave her a smile that seemed to say, "We have a lot to talk about," but he didn't say a word. Just then, the door opened, and the young officer Ella had seen this morning came into the room.

"Hello again, Mrs. Dalton," said the officer.

"Hello," answered Ella.

Dale slapped his hands on his thighs and said, "Okay, Ella, I have some more questions for you. Are you ready?"

"Yes," said Ella.

"First, will you consent for us to take your phone and download the contents?"

Ella wordlessly reached into her purse, pulled out her phone, and handed it to Dale. He stood up, knocked on the door, and another officer instantly appeared to take her phone.

"We'll have it back to you as soon as we can, Ella. Will you also consent to give a DNA sample and have your fingerprints taken?"

"Yes, I have nothing to hide." After hearing her words, Dale nodded as the officer, who quickly handed Dale a swab to collect her DNA.

"Open wide," Dale instructed her as he put on latex gloves. Doing as instructed, Ella opened her mouth so he could complete the swab. She watched silently as he placed the swab into a bag that was then sealed before handing it to the officer.

Apparently feeling emboldened by being trusted with the DNA sample, the officer added, "They're also searching your house and grounds. Mr. Dalton gave us consent to search."

Ella saw the look of frustration Dale made in the officer's direction. "That makes no sense, Dale. Why would Matthew give you consent to search if he had done this? He's not stupid."

"I can't comment on that, Ella," said Dale. "We need to do an easy test on your hands to see if you've fired a gun recently. Okay?"

"Okay."

Another officer entered the room and swabbed her hands. She wasn't worried; she knew she had not even held a gun.

"How did Matthew get gunpowder residue on his hands?"

Ella looked blankly at Dale, "I...I don't know," said Ella, "But, like I said, he grabbed his gun for protection before we went to search for Jake."

"When was the last time he shot that gun?"

"I don't know."

Dale sighed and looked at Ella again, not with sympathy or empathy but exasperation. "Ella, I'm only telling you this because we were friends. Adrienne admitted she and Matthew had recently had a sexual encounter, and he was seen fighting with Jake this morning. Adrienne said she called Matthew and asked if he had anything to do with Jake's disappearance. She said she didn't ask Matthew to look for him."

"She's lying," said Ella. "Matthew was just trying to help her because she wasn't able to look for him herself."

"If she's lying, why would she admit to having sex with Matthew?" Dale asked.

Ella replied, "I know what Matthew told me, and that was that Adrienne had called him to tell him Jake was missing and to ask for help."

"Fine," said Dale. "What did Matthew say Adrienne told him?"

"She said Jake had not come home from his alone time, and couldn't reach him," said Ella.

"Why would she call Matthew for help?" asked Dale.

"She always calls Matthew for help," said Ella. "She wanted him to check the grove because she wouldn't be able to navigate the trail with her walker. She said she couldn't reach Jeff and the police wouldn't help her because Jake was an adult."

"Has Matthew ever been violent with you?" asked Dale suddenly.

"No," Ella answered firmly.

"Was he ever violent toward Jake?" asked Dale.

"No," Ella answered again, with more force. "I have never seen him violent toward anyone."

"That's not what Adrienne said. She said Matthew almost punched Jake at her daughter's birthday party," Dale replied.

Ella was amazed at how Adrienne was manipulating everything that had occurred. "That's not true," she answered. "Jake was inappropriate toward me and Matthew just stopped him."

"Did he ever say anything about not wanting Jake around?" asked Dale.

"Well, I mean," said Ella, choosing her words carefully, so she could be truthful without implicating her husband. "He has said before that he wasn't the type of person he would have picked for Ava's stepfather. But he never once said anything about hurting him."

"Was Matthew having an affair with Adrienne?" asked Dale.

"Absolutely not," Ella said adamantly.

"Were you having any marital issues?" asked Dale.

"No," said Ella, "Matthew and I have a strong relationship. He was not cheating on me."

"How did he get the scratches on his body?"

"He said he tripped and fell into a bush when he was on his run. That has happened before. He tries to see the eagles while he's running and doesn't pay attention to his footing."

"Okay," said Dale. "Ella, I am going to lay this on the line for you. Number one, Matthew has no alibi for when Jake was killed. Number two, he put himself in the same location where Jake was killed at the time Jake was killed. Number three, text messages show that Matthew wanted Jake out of the picture. Number four, a weapon was found that matches the shell casings. Number five, according to Adrienne, Matthew looked for Jake on his own and went straight to his body. Number six, he showed deception on the lie detector test. Number seven, he has scratches on his body. All of these are adding up to show that Matthew killed Jake."

"I need to talk to Matthew," said Ella, feeling the nausea returning. She thought, *Can this be true? Is Matthew the man I think he is, or is he a lying, cheating murderer?*

"You won't be able to talk to him today," said Dale. "He's in booking right now, and since it's a Saturday, he won't be able to make his first appearance before the judge until Monday. You can see him after that."

"Dale," said Ella. "I have had enough. Please return my phone, and I will be contacting an attorney for Matthew. I don't want him talking anymore until he has representation."

Dale nodded toward the young officer, who had remained silent the remaining time he had been in the room. "I'll see if they're done," he said and got up and left the room.

He looked at Ella and whispered, self-conscious about the conversation they both knew was being recorded. "Ella, I know this is hard for you, but you might need to face the truth. Do you know your husband as well as you think you do? Does anyone ever really know what another person is capable of?"

Ella looked at Dale and could tell he was worried about her, but for some reason, she became angry. "Is that what this is about, Dale?" she asked. "Do you want to solve this case, or are you more concerned at getting back at me for refusing to stay friends with you?"

Dale shook his head. "Ella, this has nothing to do with you. No matter what you read online, there are good cops out there, and I am one of them. My only purpose is to find a murderer."

"Then you need to look harder," said Ella. "None of this makes sense. I have told you that Matthew is not stupid, but he would have to be beyond stupid to have made it this easy."

"Crimes of passion are rarely well thought out," said Dale.

Just then, the officer returned to the room and handed Ella back her phone. He whispered in Dale's ear, and Ella saw Dale's eyes grow wide.

"You need to take some time and think about everything. The officers at your house found your husband's blood-stained shirt hidden in a woodpile behind your garage," Dale told her. "We'll send that off for testing. If that comes back as Jake's blood, then you'd better find him one hell of a lawyer."

Ella took a deep breath and steeled herself. "I'm leaving, and I'm going to call an attorney. We are done here."

"You're free to leave," said Dale. "Just think about everything you have learned today."

Ella got up on her still shaky legs and left the room without saying another word to Dale. Who was she supposed to trust now? Her husband? Dale? She just knew she had to find out the truth, even if it led her back to Matthew.

"Don't forget to stop and have your fingerprints taken," Dale reminded her as she opened the door to leave the room.

4

Chapter 4

Ella walked out of the police station, trying to figure out what to do next. Dale had told her she couldn't go home until the crime scene technicians finished their search and she had been driven to the station by the police officer. She had no home to go to and no vehicle to go anywhere. Most people would call a family member or a close friend for help, but Ella had neither. Her parents were dead, her husband was sitting in a jail cell in the building behind her, and her stepdaughter was only five. If only she had made an effort to meet new people, she might have at least one friend to rely on for support. For a moment, she thought about calling Dr. McGregor, but she remembered the doctor was out of town for the weekend. She pulled out her phone, which no longer felt like hers, and searched for the only public transportation available. Ride shares, like Uber and Lyft, had not yet made their way to this area, so her only option was the local taxi service. She asked the dispatcher, Melody, if she could send a taxi to the police station. After she hung up, she thought, *Melody sounded so lovely. I bet she's the kind of friend you could call when you need help. If only I knew her. If only I knew anyone.*

She needed to find the best defense attorney available, so she placed a call to the only person she thought could help, her personal attorney. She knew he couldn't handle the case, as he wasn't that type of attorney, but he would refer her the right person. Even though it was a weekend, he picked up the call quickly. "Ella, what a pleasure to hear from you."

"Max, I need your help," she said bluntly. "Matthew has been arrested for murder. I don't have time for specifics, but I need you to recommend a defense attorney."

"Did you say Matthew has been arrested for murder?" he asked incredulously.

"Yes, that is what I said. I don't mean to be rude, but I need someone right away and you're the only one who can help me."

"Of course, Ella," he replied. "There's a great attorney in Minneapolis by the name of Casey Klein. She's a fighter and extremely intelligent and she helped another client of mine. I will call her for you right away."

"Thank you," she replied. She knew the lawyer would most likely have to come from the twin cities, the same place she found Max. Worthington had murders occur in the past, but not regularly, so there were no attorneys in the area with the experience Matthew would need. She was ending the call when the taxi pulled up. "Where to?" the driver asked. Ella almost started to cry at the simple question because she had nowhere to go. Doing her best to control her emotions, she decided to head to the closest hotel to wait for a return call.

After checking into her room, she studied her surroundings. The hotel was nice enough. It was clean, with a king-size bed and large bathroom, but it wasn't home, and she was alone. She wanted a shower to wash the police station and the remnants of the day off her but couldn't risk missing a return call from the attorney. Ella lay on the bed and turned on the TV, absent-mindedly flipping through the channels, not paying attention to what was on. She had always loved watching *Law & Order: Special Victims Unit* and true crime documentaries, but now the thought of watching anything like that made her sick to her stomach. However, she found herself wishing a detective like Olivia Benson was working on Matthew's case because she knew Olivia would discover the truth. *If only I had a fraction of Olivia's strength,* she thought to herself. She turned onto her side and hugged the pillow tightly against her. How could this be happening? Matthew and Ava were the only people she cared about in her life, and now she could lose them both. Dale's words echoed in her ears, "He volunteered to take a lie detector, and it showed deception." No, not the man she knew.

Ella was twenty-six when her mother passed away. Her mother had never been the loving, sweet mother Ella wanted and needed, and they had never been close, but she was the only family Ella had, and her passing was difficult for her. When her mother died, she had not left a will, which was unbelievable considering the size of her estate. Ella thought there had to be a will somewhere, but her mother's attorney didn't have one. Was her mother so disappointed in Ella that she couldn't bring herself to write a will that would leave the estate to Ella? She knew that her mother was not the type of person to leave anything to charity. Either there was a will with the entirety of the estate left to her, or her mother purposely didn't write one to cause more legal headaches for Ella.

Her only chance to find any documentation was to get into her mother's laptop. Ella had a court order to break into the machine to make sure everything was done legally. Her mother's attorney was present when the computer technician, who called himself an ethical hacker, came to complete the break-in.

The ethical hacker was Matthew. He was beautiful. His chestnut hair was longer then, about shoulder length, but his tall and muscular frame had not changed since the first time she saw him. He was wearing a tight t-shirt, and Ella could see the defined muscles of his abdomen under his shirt. He was built, but not too built. She was amazed at her physical reaction to him. Ella had never before felt a jolt like the one she felt when she saw him, not even for Dale. She was attracted to Dale, but she had never felt the type of electricity she was feeling now. Ella had done the college experience and the obligatory losing of her virginity, but she had never felt drawn to anyone as she felt drawn to this stranger.

He looked at her and simply said, "Hi, I'm Matthew, and I'm your ethical hacker."

Ella started to reply, but the attorney interrupted her. Believing, as most attorneys who cater to wealthy clients do, that he was smarter than everyone else in the room and his voice was the only one needed, he said matter-of-factly, "This is the laptop. We need to be able to log into it and see if there are any important files."

"No problem," replied Matthew. "This shouldn't take long." He sat down at the desk in front of the laptop and moved his fingers quickly over the keyboard.

The attorney leaned over Matthew with one hand on the desk and one hand on the back of Matthew's chair. He was trying to tell Matthew how difficult this was and how he knew so much about computers, and had Matthew thought of doing this or thought of doing that? Ella couldn't contain her giggle when Matthew said after a few minutes, "I'm in."

"Wow, that was impressive," said Ella.

"Well," said the attorney, "it's easier with a Windows operating system."

Matthew winked at Ella and said, "Sir, this is a MacBook."

"Whatever," said the flustered attorney. "Just do your job and look for the files."

Matthew again moved his long fingers over the keyboard and began pulling up files. There were documents, but no will. He searched for hidden files and encrypted files, and again there was no will. He looked at Ella and said, "Sorry, there's nothing here."

"Well, Ella," said the attorney. "I'll start the probate process for you. As the lone heir, you will be a very wealthy young woman."

Ella had never felt strong in her life. Her mother had always told her she was weak, but for some reason, Matthew's presence helped her find something buried deep inside her. She looked at the attorney, who she knew was more concerned about his salary than assisting her, and said, "You know what? I think I need to find my own attorney to represent my best interests. I won't be needing your services."

The attorney gave her a startled look and looked toward Matthew for support. Seeing none, he said, "Suit yourself," and stormed out of the room.

"I'm sorry for your loss," said Matthew. "I lost both of my parents in a car accident about two years ago."

"Oh, I am so sorry," Ella replied sincerely.

"I don't mean to pry but is your father still living?" he asked.

"No," Ella replied. "He passed away when I was five."

Ella saw compassion wash over Matthew's face. "Wow, that must have been so hard for you."

"I don't remember too much about him," she replied truthfully. "But from what I remember, he was a very sweet, caring man. I miss him."

"Would you like to search through anything else on her laptop?" Matthew asked. "Maybe we can find some family pictures."

Ella turned back to Matthew and thought that there was no way her mother had saved family pictures. Her mother made it clear she had married Ella's father for his money. That's why she was so disappointed Ella took after her father. But Ella didn't want her time with Matthew to end so soon. "Sure," she said.

Matthew stood up, pulled another chair close to his, and motioned for her to sit down by him. Ella sat down, accidentally brushing her leg against his. She felt the electric current go through her whole body, and it made her gasp.

A visibly startled Matthew looked at her and said, "Did you feel that too, or was it just me?"

Ella was surprised that he said that to her out loud, but that was Matthew. She didn't know it at the time, but Matthew was the type of person to tell you exactly what he was thinking and feeling. She couldn't find any words to reply and just nodded her head.

Matthew looked back at the computer screen and said, "Sorry, I just don't see any reason not to say what I think."

Ella just stared at him, amazed at this man sitting right in front of her. So, she said the only thing she could think of. "Did you find any pictures?"

Matthew sensed she was nervous, so he winked at her and said, "I found some pictures, but I don't think they're family pictures. They appear to be pictures of one person."

Again, Ella was surprised. Did her mother keep pictures of her? Maybe Ella was wrong, and her mother cared about her more than she thought. She eagerly moved closer to Matthew to get a better view of the pictures. Every single picture was of her mother. All the hope she felt was gone, and she felt defeated again. Her mother was a beautiful woman and was never shy about telling Ella how disappointed she was that Ella looked more like her father than like her. Apparently, Ella wasn't even attractive enough to warrant a picture in the hundreds her mother had kept. As she scrolled through, she couldn't even find a picture of them together. Every single picture was just her mother.

Matthew seemed to sense her disappointment and said, "Hey, I would like to take you to dinner. Since it's already 6:00, we could go out now."

Ella smiled at him. Typically, this is where she would say no because she wasn't mentally prepared to face the public, but she bit her lip and said, "There's food here. We could make something here if that works for you."

"Just the two of us. That sounds perfect to me," said Matthew.

Ella was interrupted from reliving that night in her mind by her ringing cell phone. It was a 612 area code – Minneapolis. She grabbed the phone and eagerly swiped to answer, "Hello," she said.

"Is this Ella Dalton?" asked the voice on the other line.

"Yes, this is Ella," she replied.

"Hi, Ella. My name is Casey Klein, and Max asked me to call you about your husband. Why don't you fill me in."

Ella started to let everything pour out of her. She was talking so fast that Casey had to ask her to slow down, "I'm taking notes, hon," she said.

After telling Casey everything she knew so far, she exhaled loudly. For some reason, just letting it out seemed to release some of the weight she had been feeling all day.

Casey chose her words carefully and said, "Hon, I have been doing this for over fifteen years, and I have lost cases, but I have won more than I've lost. I'm not going to lie to you. The one thing I will promise you is that I will never mislead you. It doesn't sound good, but I will fight for your husband, I will fight for you, and I will fight for Ava."

Casey's voice had a calming effect on Ella, and she knew immediately she liked this woman. More importantly, she trusted her, but she still needed to ask some questions. "How long have you been a defense attorney and how many murder cases have you defended and how many have you won?

"I've been a defense attorney for twenty years," she answered. "Of the cases I have defended, there have been twelve murder cases, of which I have won ten."

"When can you be here?"asked Ella. "I can wire you any retainer you require, and I will pay for any travel expenses."

"Well, hon," she said, "they are required to have Matthew make his first appearance on Monday. If you want to retain me, I will drive down on Sunday so I am ready to represent Matthew on Monday morning at the appearance."

"You're hired," said Ella. "Just let me know what you need to help Matthew."

"Ella," said Casey, her voice much more serious now, "do you believe he's innocent? Don't worry, I am representing you too, and I will never reveal anything you tell me."

"Honestly, Casey," said Ella, "I don't know who or what to believe anymore."

5

Chapter 5

Adrienne Griffin lay down on her couch and placed a cold washcloth on her forehead. She had never experienced a more emotionally draining day than she had today. She thoughtfully rubbed her fingers over her lips and wondered how Matthew was faring with all the questions the police must be throwing at him. She still considered Matthew the one that got away. There was a time when she thought Matthew would be hers, but then Ella had come along and had taken him from her.

There was no person in the world Adrienne hated more than the woman who stole Matthew. Ella was one of those breathtakingly beautiful women who always pretends she doesn't know she's gorgeous. Adrienne hated everything that makes Ella so attractive: her auburn hair, her green eyes, her full lips, and her skin undamaged by sun exposure. She hated her naivety. She hated her sweet personality. She hated how easily Ella maintained a perfect figure, while Adrienne struggled daily to keep her figure. She hated how much money Ella had. She hated how much Ava loved her. But the main reason Adrienne hated Ella is that Matthew chose her.

They had only spent one drunken night together, but Adrienne was determined to keep him. She was sure Matthew would dump Little Miss Perfect once she told him she was pregnant with his child, but Matthew had done no such thing. Any thought Adrienne had that Matthew would propose and they would be a family ended when Matthew told her his plan that all three of them would co-parent together. She had been so sure he would choose her so he could be with his child, but she was wrong. Matthew said he and Ella would love the child and wanted to share custody. They had offered her ten thousand dollars a month in child support and to find her a lovely home and cover all living expenses. She had pretended to be happy with the arrangement and told Matthew they would make it work, but inside she was seething. There was no way that bitch was going to be a mother figure to her child. Adrienne realized she needed to play the game to keep Matthew in her life and keep the financial support.

Once she knew Matthew wouldn't leave Ella, she decided to go on the prowl to find another man to marry her before she gained weight from the pregnancy. She usually only had two rules for picking a man, but she updated it to three after losing Matthew. Her new rules were: one, he must have a ripped body (because she worked hard to keep her body tight); two, he must be well hung (she wasn't going to waste her time on someone who couldn't fulfill her sexually); three, he must be pliable. Adrienne added the third rule because of Matthew. He had checked off her first two requirements, but he was too intelligent for Adrienne to control, and she wouldn't make that mistake again. Matthew never had street smarts and could be gullible, but he always followed his heart and her ideal man would make decisions with another organ.

She needed a husband, and she needed one quickly. Of course, she had a young lover on the side, but he was not what she considered marriage material. Jake, however, was perfect.

She arranged to meet Jake one night while out at a local bar. Adrienne knew of him before that night, but he was three years younger than she, and they had never socialized before. She knew he wasn't brilliant; gossip in a small town moves faster than a politician can tell a lie, and word around town was that Jake was always falling for get rich schemes. He sent money to a phantom prince in a foreign county and honestly thought he would receive millions of dollars in return. That meant he was pliable and she could easily manipulate him, but she also knew he worked relentlessly on his body, meaning he most likely considered sex to be the most important part of a relationship. That meant he had already checked off two of the requirements. Making a point of walking by him, she dropped her purse before bending over strategically so her backside would be right next to his face. She smirked when she heard Jake say in an aroused voice, "Don't I know you from somewhere?"

"No," she said as she seductively sat in his lap and wrapped her arm around his neck, "but you can get to know me."

Jake gave her a smile that said he knew he was going to get laid that night. He asked, "Ready to get out of here?"

"Ready and willing, baby," replied Adrienne. "I'm going to do you so hard that you'll want me around forever."

Jake's eyes grew wide. He quickly grabbed his keys, not even bothering to tell his friends goodbye. Adrienne stood in front of him and pushed against him as he ushered her toward the door. Jake reached under her skirt to rip her underwear off the moment they were out of the bar. They were both too worked up to wait to even get in the car; he just bent her over the trunk and entered her right there, neither of them caring if someone saw them. Feeling him inside her, Adrienne was ecstatic to discover Jake more than checked off the last of her rules. Maybe even a little bigger check than Matthew.

That night was all it took for Jake to be under her spell. After the quickie in the parking lot, Adrienne took him home, satisfying him over and over. She remembered the only advice her mother had ever given her, "Find yourself a man, lay him just right, and you'll be able to walk all over him forever." Jake was that man for Adrienne. He proposed to her that night, and they were married the following week. He was a little surprised when Adrienne told him she was pregnant with another man's baby (after the wedding, of course), but he was in so deep with her, she knew he would do anything for her and do anything she said, which was precisely what she wanted.

Now he was gone, and Adrienne had to figure out what to do next. She knew she had to plan a funeral, but she had never done that before, and she had no idea when the cops would release Jake's body. Jeff had agreed to let her and Ava stay at his house while the police processed the home she shared with Jake. She was starting to doze off when she heard Jeff yell from the other room, "Cops are here."

"Shit," said Adrienne. "Can't they just leave me alone? I told them everything already."

Jeff came down the hallway and looked at Adrienne still lying on the couch. "Just calm down. I'll let them in."

Adrienne rolled her eyes at him once he turned his back and could no longer see her. She really didn't like Jeff. He was always quoting the bible to her and telling her she would find true happiness by turning her life to God. Unfortunately, she was going to have to put up with him for now. She needed his help because there was no way for her to get through this alone.

Jeff opened the door before the agents could knock. "Hi, officers, do you remember me? I'm Jeff, Jake's brother," he said while enthusiastically extending his hand to shake theirs.

"Hello," said Dale. "Of course we remember you. Is Mrs. Dwyer here?"

"Griffin," said an annoyed Adrienne, without turning around to look at either agent. "I go by my maiden name of Griffin."

"My apologies," said Dale. "Do you feel up to talking to us for a few minutes?"

Adrienne reached up and took the cloth off her forehead and rubbed both hands over her face. "I'll do anything I can to help find who did this." She shifted her weight on the couch and picked up her legs with her hands to swing them over the front of the sofa. "Sorry," she said with closed eyes as if trying to hold back her tears, "with all this stress, my MS is really bad right now, and I need a walker to get around."

"Please, have a seat," said Jeff. Dale and Agent Ulrich accepted his offer and sat down on the couch opposite Adrienne.

Just then, a soft voice was heard from down the hall. "Mom," said Ava, "I'm scared."

"Jeff, would you mind?" asked Adrienne, her eyes still closed. "I need to speak to them."

"Of course," said Jeff, and he wandered off down the hall to tend to his niece.

Adrienne opened her eyes and looked at the agents across from her. She had already met the woman, but who was the man? Adrienne was intrigued.

He's hot, she thought. His clothing didn't hide the fact that he was definitely a hard body. Check off number one. She stared at his crotch, wondering if he checked off number two. Too bad he would never check off number three. He's most likely been a cop for a few years, so he was probably not easily manipulated. *Oh well, he might be fun for a ride or two*, she thought.

She could tell Dale had sensed her staring at his privates because he shifted in such a way to conceal the bulge. Adrienne did a hard blink and shook her head quickly as if she were coming out of a trance. "I'm so sorry," she said, "I was thinking about Jake and was lost in my thoughts."

"We understand," said Agent Ulrich. "Do you remember that we met this morning?"

"Yes, of course," said Adrienne. "You're from the BCA, right?"

"That's right," the agent replied. Adrienne thought she sounded like she was congratulating a child for remembering their address.

"I'm Agent Dale Williams," said Dale. "I'm assisting Agent Ulirch with the investigation into your husband's murder. I'm sorry we didn't get a chance to meet earlier, but I had to interview the main suspect's wife right away."

"Oh," said Adrienne. "Do you have a suspect?"

"Yes," replied Agent Ulrich. "We arrested Matthew Dalton earlier today. He's been booked into the county jail."

Adrienne started to sob quietly. "Matthew did it?" she said. "I knew he wanted me back, but I never thought he would take it this far. I just can't believe it."

"I'm very sorry to have to tell you this. He'll make his first appearance in court on Monday, but you do not need to be there," Agent Ulrich informed her.

Adrienne looked back at Dale because a new thought came to her mind. "Oh my gosh, I have to tell Ava. How am I going to do that? The father she loves killed the stepfather she loves."

"Do you want us to arrange for a counselor to come to help you talk to your daughter?" asked Dale. "We can certainly do that for you."

"Yes, yes, thank you," said Adrienne. "I'm so sorry. Where are my manners? Would you like something to drink?"

"No, thank you," replied the female agent. "We'll let you rest."

Dale and Agent Ulrich stood, thanked Adrienne for her time, and walked to the door. Dale stopped after opening the door and looked back at Adrienne. "Just one question," he said. "What did you tell Matthew when you called him this morning?"

"I asked him if he was responsible for Jake's disappearance," she replied quickly.

Dale looked at her and raised his eyebrow, "If you thought it was his fault, why did you just say that you didn't think he would take it that far?"

Adrienne looked back at Dale, and her hand fluttered nervously up to her head. "I'm sorry, I should have been clearer. I meant I never thought he would take it that far until I saw the text message he sent this morning. My mind is all over the place."

Dale pursed his lips, nodded at her, and said, "Okay." Agent Ulrich was pinching his arm, and she whispered, "Leave her alone."

"Thank you for your time," said Agent Ulrich, as she moved Dale out the door. Jeff came back down the hallway and watched them out the window. "He keeps looking back at the house," said Jeff. "What did you tell him?"

"Just the truth," said Adrienne. She lay back down on the couch and put the washcloth back on her forehead, but it was warm. "Be a dear and run this under cold water for me," she said to Jeff.

He took the cloth and walked to the kitchen to do as she requested. Adrienne knew that Jeff was pliable, so he had one rule covered. She knew he didn't check off rule number one because she could see the flab from his belly hanging over his pants, but she wondered about the other rule as she watched him walk back to her with the cold cloth. Maybe there was at least one physical characteristic he had in common with his brother.

"Thank you," she said. "I'm drained. Could you watch Ava for me while I get some rest?"

"Sure," said Jeff. He stroked Adrienne's hair gently and said, "You've been through so much. I'm going to pray for you."

Adrienne sighed and thought, *No matter how good of a lay he might be, I couldn't put up with him long-term.* Jeff was still stroking her hair, and she said, "Jeff, please check on Ava."

"Sure," he said and disappeared down the hallway again.

She found herself thinking about Jake again. It was hard for her to believe how much she missed him right now. Her only solace was the knowledge that Ella was probably having a worse day than her. Sure, Adrienne's husband was dead, but he was replaceable. How would Ella possibly replace Matthew? He was the type of man who would be kind to someone without expecting anything in return and was liked by everyone. By Matthew losing his reputation, Ella was losing the social acceptance she had and Adrienne so desperately wanted.

Adrienne again thought about how Ella had taken Matthew from her. Now Matthew had been taken from Ella. The delicious irony made a smile spread across Adrienne's thin lips.

6

Chapter 6

"Mom, I'm hungry," said Ava.

Adrienne opened her eyes to see her daughter standing directly over her staring at her with those big blue eyes. "Ava," Adrienne said as she turned away from her daughter and closed her eyes again. "You know to let me sleep. Have Jake make you breakfast."

"Jake isn't here," said Ava.

Hearing those words caused Adrienne to jolt back into reality. *No, Jake wouldn't be here, would he?* Adrienne relied on Jake to take care of Ava. He wasn't a great stepfather by any means, but he would make sure Ava was fed so Adrienne wouldn't have to be bothered.

"Where is Uncle Jeff?" asked Adrienne.

'I don't know," said Ava.

Dammit, thought Adrienne. *Where is Jeff? How am I supposed to take care of this kid by myself?* Adrienne was trying to think of anyone else to call to take over so she wouldn't have to deal with her child.

"Mom, are you listening to me?" asked Ava.

Adrienne took a deep breath and angrily replied, "Yes, I am listening to you. Can't you see that I am tired and having a hard time? Can't you ever consider my feelings?

Ava's big, blue eyes filled with tears. "I'm sorry," she said. "Maybe I can go stay with Daddy until you feel better."

"You can't stay with Daddy," snapped Adrienne. "He's not home."

"Ella will take care of me," Ava said hopefully.

"You can't stay with Ella either," Adrienne said with a raised voice.

The tears in Ava's eyes now fell down her cheeks. "Why?' she asked.

"Because I said you can't, and I'm your mother," said Adrienne.

At that moment, the front door opened, and Jeff walked in carrying bags of takeout. "Morning," he said. "I brought breakfast."

Ava's face instantly brightened, and she ran to her uncle. Jeff was kind to Ava, and she latched on to the affection he showed her. "Uncle Jeff," she said excitedly. "What did you bring me?"

Jeff knelt down to Ava, looking through the bags, and pulled out a to-go container. "Well," he said. "I had them make an Ava special. Pancakes with extra syrup."

"Yay," said Ava. "Will you eat breakfast with me?"

"Of course I will," said Jeff. "Why don't you take yours to the kitchen table, and I will be there in just a minute."

"Okay," said Ava as she happily took her pancakes and skipped to the kitchen.

"Why do you spoil her?" asked Adrienne. "She has to learn that life doesn't work that way."

Jeff looked at Adrienne with sympathy and said, "Adrienne, she's only five years old. I don't think a special treat of pancakes is going to hurt."

Adrienne rolled her eyes and said, "You're probably right. I'm just so tired. You'll watch Ava, right?"

"You know I will," he said, "but you need to talk to her about everything that has happened."

"I just can't right now," said Adrienne. "I'm afraid I won't be strong enough, and it will cause Ava more pain than necessary." Adrienne managed to make her eyes fill with tears and looked at Jeff hopefully, "Maybe it would be best if you talked to her. You're better at that type of thing than I am."

"I don't know, Adrienne," Jeff said. "Don't you think she should have support from her mother?"

It was now Adrienne's turn to burst into tears. Between her sobs, she said the words she knew would guilt Jeff the most. "I never had a good mother, and I don't want to mess up with Ava the way my mother did with me. What if I say the wrong thing and make things worse?"

Adrienne looked at Jeff and saw the instant guilt on his face. She knew he couldn't handle tears from a woman or a child; she had him right where she wanted him.

"Okay," said Jeff, "I will talk to her. "Try to get some rest."

"Thank you," said Adrienne. "You're too good to me."

Adrienne turned her back to Jeff and hugged the pillow. Her tears stopped the moment she had what she wanted.

She had fallen asleep on the sofa the night before, so she could hear Jeff and Ava laughing from the kitchen. She realized that sleep would not return, and she let her thoughts drift back to Jake.

They had only been married a few days when Jake met Matthew and Ella. They were there to talk to Adrienne about their plans to build a new house for themselves and one for Adrienne and the baby, but Adrienne was concentrating on the look on Jake's face that told her he was attracted to Ella. He had purposely dropped something on the floor behind Ella so he could get a closeup of her backside while he picked it up. Adrienne saw his eyebrows raise appreciatively at what he was viewing.

"You know you could never have her," said Adrienne the moment Matthew and Ella left.

"What are you talking about?" asked Jake.

"Ella," said Adrienne. "I saw how you were looking at her. That stuck-up little bitch would never have anything to do with a guy like you."

"Oh, really," said Jake. "I could have her if I want. I have my ways."

"You're delusional," said Adrienne. "What makes you think you could get her? She would never let you touch her."

"She doesn't have to *let* me do anything," said Jake. "I told you that I have my ways."

"What are you talking about?" said Adrienne with genuine curiosity.

Jake looked Adrienne up and down as if deciding to trust her with a secret. "Come here," Jake said while motioning toward their bedroom, "and I'll show you."

Adrienne followed Jake to their bedroom and watched him rifle through one of his dresser drawers. He pulled out a small bottle and held it up for her to see. "This is what I'm talking about," he said.

"What is that?" asked Adrienne.

"It's what I use on women who think they're too good for me," said Jake.

"Holy shit," said Adrienne, "is that one of those date rape drugs?"

"Yep," said Jake. "I guess I don't need it anymore because you and I both know that you'll never say no. You enjoy sex more than I do."

"Have you ever used it?" she asked.

"Sure," said Jake. "When I had to."

Adrienne looked at her husband. Sure, she had married him without really knowing him, but she wasn't expecting a surprise like this. She knew she should be angry. Her husband had just admitted to being a rapist. But instead of anger, she felt excitement. She looked at her husband and said, "Let's go out tonight. I want to try something."

Jake looked at her and asked, "Like what?'

"I want to see if this works," she said. "A college bar full of girls who think they're better than me should do."

Jake stared blankly at his wife. "Are you serious?"

"Yep," said Adrienne. "It sounds exciting."

"You are the best wife ever," said Jake. "Just when I think you can't get any sexier, you say something like that. What do you have in mind? A threesome?"

"No," said Adrienne. "I'm not into women that way, but it would be fun to watch." Adrienne could see an erection starting and quickly added, "We could record it too."

Adrienne looked at the surprised look on her husband's face and wondered if she had gone too far. Instead, Jake pushed her onto the bed, pulled down both their pants, and thrust in and out of her as hard as he could.

"I guess that's a yes," said Adrienne after they both finished.

"You bet it is," said Jake. "Let's get dressed and find us a woman."

Jake and Adrienne went to a local bar and scanned the room. Adrienne quickly focused on a beautiful young woman with dark hair and eyes, sitting with a group. She could tell the girl felt uncomfortable and didn't appear to be the type to hang out in bars. Even the bulky sweater and slacks she was wearing could not hide her trim figure. Adrienne eyed her the way a lion observes an injured gazelle. *Yes, this will be the easy one to separate from the herd and takedown,* thought Adrienne.

Adrienne elbowed Jake to get his attention, using her pinky finger to point out the girl she had chosen. "How about her?" asked Adrienne.

She could see Jake eye the girl carefully before he replied. "Oh, she looks good. I like her."

Jake started to walk toward the girl when Adrienne stopped him. "We have to wait for the right time," she said.

"How do we approach her then?" asked Jake.

"We rely on Minnesota nice," replied Adrienne.

Adrienne patiently waited for the other girls at the table to leave one by one. They were leaving their friend for an anonymous dance or game of pool with a random guy. When the girl was all alone, Adrienne knew it was time to strike. The gazelle was now separated from the herd. "Let's go," she said to Jake.

They walked up to the table, and Adrienne said sweetly, "Do you mind if we sit here? There are no other open tables, and we just want to get off our feet for a moment."

"Sure," said the girl. "I guess that's okay. My friends have deserted me anyway."

"Thank you so much," said Adrienne. "This is my husband, Jake, and my name is Adrienne. We're newlyweds."

"Congratulations," said the girl. "My name is Justine."

"What are you doing in town, Justine? I don't think I've seen you before," said Adrienne.

"Just in town to visit my dad," replied Justine. "I'm on Christmas break from college, and I don't get to see my dad that often, so I decided to visit him. Dad talked me into going out tonight, but I don't know the girls I'm with very well. They're not really my friends."

"Well," said Adrienne, "we'll be your friends. Won't we, Jake?"

"Sure we will," said Jake.

Adrienne could tell Jake was still sizing up Justine, and she kicked him under the table so he would stop staring at her. She was just what Adrienne wanted, and she couldn't take a chance on Jake scaring her away. A pretty college girl. The type of girl that Adrienne felt always looked down on her.

"Hey, honey," said Adrienne. "Why don't you go get us all some drinks. Let's make Justine feel welcome."

Justine said quickly, "No, thank you. I'm not a drinker."

Adrienne was perturbed. Another Little Miss Perfect. She wasn't going to let her ruin this. "How about a diet pop or something?" asked Adrienne as she rubbed her stomach affectionately. "I can't drink either because we just found out we're expecting our first baby." When Justine failed to answer, Adrienne added, "Please? We want you to feel welcome, and it will be nice to be around someone else who's not drinking alcohol."

"Okay," said Justine. "Thank you for being so nice to me."

"Of course," said Adrienne.

Jake quickly got up and went to the bar to order the drinks. Adrienne observed him from the corner of her eye and watched him surreptitiously place drops into the drink he ordered for Justine. He walked back to the table carefully so as not to spill anything. "Here you go," said Jake.

"Thank you," said Justine as she took her first drink from the glass.

Adrienne watched Justine for signs the drug was working. It didn't take long before Justine's eyelids began to appear heavy. Jake signaled to Adrienne that it was time. He helped Justine stand, Adrienne grabbed her purse, and they walked/carried Justine to the door. No one noticed the young girl in trouble. Jake placed Justine into the backseat of their car and looked at Adrienne with a devilish grin. "Let's do this, babe."

They grabbed each other for a deep kiss, then placed their foreheads together, saying, "I love you" simultaneously.

The following day, Adrienne stood in her kitchen watching the young woman sleeping on her couch. As she watched, Justine started to stir awake. Adrienne walked over to her with a cup of coffee at the ready. "Morning, sunshine," she said.

Adrienne could see the confusion in Justine's eyes as she focused on the room around her. "Where am I?" she said.

"You don't remember?" Adrienne teased as she slapped at Justine's arm playfully.

"No," said Justine, moving to a sitting position. "What happened?"

"You got so drunk last night. Your friends left you, and you were depressed, so you started drinking. Apparently, you can't handle alcohol very well," Adrienne teased her.

"No, I can't," said Justine. "I don't drink."

"Yes, that's what you said, but you changed your mind last night," said Adrienne as she attempted to hand a cup to Justine. "I guess not being used to alcohol is why it hit you so hard. Here, I made you some coffee. You know, you're lucky we were there. We took you home and let you sleep it off on our sofa."

Adrienne saw Justine warily look at the coffee she was offering her. "I don't understand," she said. "I don't remember anything."

"That's because you drank so much, silly," said Adrienne as she reached out to touch Justine's arm. "Alcohol has that effect on people."

Justine snatched her arm away from Adrienne's touch and looked her dead in the eye. "Let me out of here," she said.

"Of course, you can leave," said Adrienne. "One of us will take you home."

"No," said Justine. "Where's my phone?"

Adrienne gestured toward Justine's purse that was sitting on the chair opposite Adrienne. "Your things are right there," she said.

Justine stood up, grabbed her purse, and ran out the front door, slamming it behind her. A naked Jake had emerged from the bedroom in time to watch her exit and said, "She might be a problem."

"I know how to take care of problems," said Adrienne, still staring at the front door. She turned her attention back to Jake, eyeing his manliness. "God, you're so hot," she said. "Do me right here, baby."

Jake smiled before joining his wife on the sofa. He was about to mount her when she pushed him off. "No," she told him. "You get on the bottom. Last night, you were in control. It's my turn to have control."

7

Chapter 7

Problems; everyone has them, but Adrienne had always known how to fix hers. The biggest problems she faced at this time were two men named Jeff and Dale. One problem she needed in her life and one she did not. Jeff was necessary. She needed him to care for Ava because Lord knows Adrienne had more important things to do than take care of her daughter. Dale was unnecessary and a thorn in her side. She could tell by how he looked at her during the brief questioning that he did not trust her. *I just need to find his weakness,* thought Adrienne. All men have a weakness, and no one was better at exploiting those weaknesses than she was.

Adrienne's cell phone began to ring, and she glanced at the caller ID – unknown number. *Why not?* she thought. *It might be fun to screw with a telemarketer or scam caller today.*

"Hello," Adrienne said in the sexiest, most breathless voice she could muster.

"Miss Griffin, it's Agent Williams," said the voice on the other side of the line.

Adrienne smiled to herself. He must have sensed I was thinking about him. She changed her tone to something more subdued and replied, "Oh, hello, Agent Williams, how can I help you?"

"Agent Ulrich and I would like to come to speak to you today," Dale replied. "Would it be okay for us to come over? We can be there in about thirty minutes."

"Of course," Adrienne replied. "Anything I can do to help."

"Great, we'll be there soon," he replied without saying goodbye.

Now I can find your weakness, thought Adrienne. "Jeff," she shouted, "where are you?"

"I'm right here," replied Jeff as he came down the hallway into the living room.

"The police want to come to talk to me," Adrienne said with tears in her eyes. "I think it's best if Ava isn't here. Can you take her to the park or something?"

"Certainly," said Jeff with a combined look of sympathy and adoration. "I am here to help you."

"Thank you," she said as she placed a kiss on Jeff's cheek. Adrienne thought she sensed Jeff's knees buckle a bit when she touched him. To gain more control over him, she stroked his arm and said, "You're the best."

Jeff exhaled slowly, looked at Adrienne as if he wanted to say something else, but shook himself back to reality. Instead, he called for Ava. "Let's go to the park, Ava."

"Yay," said Ava. "Can I bring Teddy?"

"Sure," said Jeff while winking at Ava, "what teddy bear doesn't love to go down the slides?"

Ava happily ran to the door to put on her shoes. "Uncle Jeff, let's go," she said excitedly.

Jeff looked back at Adrienne. "Are you sure you're going to be okay by yourself? I don't trust that cop. Something seems off about him."

"I'll be fine," Adrienne reassured him. "Besides, Agent Ulrich is coming with him."

"Okay," Jeff said hesitantly. He walked to the door to join Ava, turned back to her, and said, "Be careful."

Adrienne gave him a quick smile and nodded her head. She wasn't worried. "Ava, come give me a kiss goodbye," she ordered the little girl. Doing as she was told, she walked over to her mother to give her a hug and a kiss on the cheek. Knowing Jeff was watching them, Adrienne wrapped her arms around her daughter as tightly as she could and kissed her cheek repeatedly. "I love you so much, Ava." Sneaking a peek at Jeff, she saw him smiling at the two of them.

"I love watching you two together," Jeff said wistfully. "There's nothing as wonderful as a mother's love."

Smiling at Jeff, Adrienne finally let go of Ava. "Take care of my baby," she told Jeff as he and Ava were walking out the door.

"I will," Jeff promised.

"Ava, please take care of Uncle Jeff. I love him too." Jeff's eyes visibly brightened at her words and she never broke eye contact with him as he stumbled out the door.

Once they were gone, she went to her room to fix her hair, do her makeup, and put on proper mourning clothes. *The one who needs to be careful is Agent Dale Williams*, she said to herself.

Agents Williams and Ulrich arrived precisely thirty minutes after Dale's phone call to Adrienne requesting permission to see her. Adrienne had positioned herself comfortably on the sofa and muttered a soft "Come in" when they knocked.

Agent Ulrich came in first and saw Adrienne sitting on the couch with her walker nearby for easy access. She saw the sympathy in the agent's face and knew she already had this agent wrapped around her finger. Her focus had to remain on getting Agent Williams on her side.

Dale's reaction was the opposite of Agent Ulrich's. He looked at Adrienne, and his facial expression told her that he felt no pity for her. If anything, he looked perturbed at the presence of the walker.

"Please, sit down," Adrienne said sweetly. "Jeff was kind enough to take Ava to the park so we can speak openly."

As the agents were sitting down on the sofa across from her, Adrienne blurted out, "I think Ella had something to do with it. She made several unsuccessful passes at Jake. Maybe she wanted to get back at him."

Dale raised his eyebrows incredulously, but Agent Ulrich was the first to speak. "Was it Ella's habit to go after men who are involved with you?"

"Yes," Adrienne sobbed. "I didn't know her before she stole Matthew from me, but she seemed to take delight in causing me pain."

"Excuse me," said Dale, "what do you mean by her stealing Matthew from you?"

"You remember," scolded Agent Ulrich. "It was part of the interview I did with Miss Griffin on the day of Jake's murder." Adrienne looked at the agent, who appeared to feel even more sympathy for her than she did earlier. The agent had been cheated on by her husband, and Adrienne would use that to her advantage whenever she could.

"I do," Dale said while nodding his head. "But I would like to hear it from Miss Griffin."

"Well," Adrienne choked out, "it's a hard story for me to tell, but I will try." Her eyes filled with crocodile tears as she started to tell the story of Ella, the man-stealing whore. "Matthew and I have known each other since high school, and we always had feelings for each other. We started dating after we ran into each other one night, and we fell in love. Everything was perfect until Ella came around. Her mother had just died, and she needed Matthew's help with something computer-related, and she seduced him that very night. She made Matthew promises about helping him start up a computer business so he could be his own boss, but she would only help him if he married her and dumped me. I foolishly thought Ella would back down once she knew I was pregnant with Ava, but she had Matthew push me to have an abortion. Naturally, I refused, so then she tried to bribe me to go away. I told her I would tell Matthew what she was doing, and she just laughed at me and said she could make me disappear if she wanted. The only thing that saved me was Matthew. He wanted to be part of his daughter's life, so Ella had no choice but to accept Ava and me as part of his life."

"Really," said Dale. "That doesn't sound like the Ella I know."

Adrienne cocked her to the side to show her curiosity, "You know Ella?" she asked.

"Yes," Dale answered, "we grew up in the same town."

Adrienne stared down at Agent Williams. "Should you be involved in this case if you know Ella?"

"I assure you that I am impartial," Dale said defensively. "Please continue with your story."

Adrienne took a deep breath and proceeded to spin her web. "Matthew stepped in and told Ella she had to accept Ava and me if she wanted him in her life, so she finally backed off about the baby. But after I married Jake, she started hitting on him in front of me. It's like she was trying to get back at me for having Matthew's baby. Jake always rebuffed her, but that seemed to make her angrier. And she's a horrible stepmother. Ava is scared of her. I think that's why Matthew wanted me back. He wanted the family life that Ella wouldn't give him. He knows how much I love Ava and what a good mother I am."

Dale stared at Adrienne the entire time she spoke, his breaths becoming shallower with her every word. Her instincts told her that he did not believe her.

"Okay, Miss Griffin," Dale said to change the subject. "Can you tell me what time Jake left the house that afternoon?"

"It was around 2:00," Adrienne answered. "He wanted to be alone after what happened at Ava's party."

"What time did you expect him home?" asked Agent Ulrich.

"He's usually gone for less than an hour, so I was looking for him by 3:00," Adrienne stated.

"What did you do first?" asked Dale.

"I called Matthew to find out if he had confronted Jake and hurt him," said Adrienne. "Then I called Jeff to ask him to go look for Jake, but he didn't answer. There's no way I could get around out on that trail with this walker. My MS is really bad right now."

"Did you ever reach Jeff?" asked Dale.

"Yes, he said he tried to call, but couldn't reach me, so he decided to drive over to my house. He said he couldn't get on the property when he got there because of all the police cars blocking the entrances," answered Adrienne.

"Did you immediately think Matthew was involved?" asked Agent Ulrich.

"No," said Adrienne. "I didn't see the threatening text message until after Jake left. As soon as I saw that, I knew he had to be involved."

"Did Jake know about Matthew's text messages?" asked Dale.

Adrienne looked down. "Yes, he saw them after the party. He was angry and wanted to confront Matthew. Part of me thinks that Jake wanted to be on the trail to accidentally see Matthew on his jog. He knew Matthew runs every day," Adrienne said, using her fingers to make air quotes when she said the word accidentally.

"Why would he need to find a place to accidentally confront him if he knew he could see him by going over to his house?" asked Dale.

"Jake would never want to upset Ella at her home," said Adrienne. "He respects women too much."

"But confronting her husband on his run and possibly starting a fight wouldn't upset her?" Dale asked sarcastically.

"I don't know what he was thinking," said Adrienne. "I had just confessed that Matthew and I had slept together and I'm sure he had all kinds of emotions." She glanced at Agent Williams and Agent Ulrich before burying her face in her hands. "I feel so guilty for betraying him. It was only one time and Matthew had taken advantage of me."

Raising her face to read the expressions of the agents, she could tell she had Agent Ulrich, but not Agent Williams and that meant it was time for plan B. Adrienne brought her right hand up to her face and rubbed her eyes. "I'm sorry," she said, "I'm not feeling very well. Agent Ulrich, would you mind going out to my car and grabbing my prescriptions? I think Jeff forgot to bring them in when he picked them up for me."

Agent Ulrich looked at Dale, who nodded to tell her it was okay. "Sure," she replied. 'I'll be back soon."

Adrienne waited for the agent to exit the house before she turned to Dale. She leaned forward far enough to touch his knee, looked deep into his eyes, and with a single tear running down her face said, "I truly loved my husband, Agent Williams. I don't know how I am going to get by without him."

Dale's eyes widened before he moved her hand off his knee. "I'm sorry for your loss, Miss Griffin," he said. "But my job is to be one hundred percent sure we have the right person in jail."

Adrienne leaned back in surprise. He didn't know it, but Dale had made a significant mistake. She knew his weakness now. Normally, she could convince any man to take her side by using her charm and seductiveness, but it wasn't going to work with him. *It's not that he's not attracted to me; he's not attracted to any woman.* Plan B was to seduce Agent Williams, but now she had to come up with plan C. She would use this information to her advantage, but how to use it was still to be determined.

"Oh, I completely understand," Adrienne said. "I just want you to know that I want you to find out who is responsible for Jake's death, even if it is Matthew or Ella."

"I will," Dale replied. "Without a doubt."

The front door opened, and Agent Ulrich came back into the house. "I couldn't find any prescriptions in the car," she said.

Adrienne knew there were no prescriptions in the car, so she replied, "Jeff must have brought them in and not told me where they are. I'll have to ask him when he comes home."

Adrienne saw the look that passed between the two agents. Dale appeared to be telling Agent Ulrich that he had something to say to her. She knew he didn't trust her and it was time to end the conversation. "As I said, I'm not feeling very well. Can you both let yourself out?" Adrienne said in a tone to leave no doubt the interview was over.

Dale rose to follow Agent Ulrich out the door. He stood in the doorway and turned back to look directly at Adrienne. "You'll be hearing from us, Miss Griffin," Dale said without attempting to veil the contempt he had for her. He closed the door quickly to ensure Adrienne had no chance to respond.

Not if you hear from me first, thought Adrienne as she resolved to fix this problem. She would not allow Dale to ruin everything she had worked so hard to achieve.

8

Chapter 8

Adrienne sat back on the sofa, letting the thick back pillows absorb her body to create the illusion someone was hugging her. What was she going to do about Agent Williams? The more she thought about his secret, the more she realized no one would care. Being gay wasn't the taboo it once was. Sure, they lived in a small town in Minnesota, but Dale's sexuality would never be enough to tarnish his reputation as a police officer. Who would care? Maybe he'd be ribbed by fellow officers, but maybe not. Maybe he was already out, and there was nothing for her to expose. He seemed defensive but that could be just prickliness. What if she tried to out him, and instead, it backfired on her and made her look like the bad guy? *No,* she thought, *I need to come at this from a different angle.* She was deep in thought and realized the most straightforward answer was the best answer. The ruse that had worked the best for her in the past would work this time. After all, she only had to convince one person and he believed every word she said.

Jeff walked through the door with Ava to find Adrienne still sitting with her head in her hands as if on cue. "What's wrong?" he asked in full protective mode.

Adrienne raised her head, her eyes full of tears, and said, "Jeff, I don't know what to do. I need you to help me."

"I'll always help you," replied Jeff. He looked at Ava and said, "Ava, can you go play in your room?"

Ava appeared to be disappointed at being sent to her room again, "Can I just go to Daddy's house?"

Offering a half-truth, Jeff answered, "Sorry, honey, they're not home."

"But I want my Daddy and I want to go home," Ava cried. "That's not my room. My room is at our house and at Daddy's house."

Suppressing her instinct to belittle her daughter for crying, Adrienne pulled her to her instead. "I understand you want your Daddy, but he isn't home right now. Jeff was nice enough to let us stay with him while they're working on our house. We're both love you and will do our best to take care of you while he's gone."

"Where is he and why can't we go home?"

"He had to go away for a little while," she explained, "but, he loves you and he's thinking about you. Jeff told you that the workman have to fix our house. Until it's fixed, we can't go home."

"If I draw him a picture, will you send it to him for me?"

"Of course I will, but I have to talk to Uncle Jeff alone right now."

"Okay, Mom," Ava said as she wiped away her tears. "I'll go draw in the bedroom."

"I brought your colors over for you, Ava," Jeff said. "They're in the nightstand."

Ava nodded and walked down the hall toward her temporary room, dragging her teddy bear behind her.

When he heard the bedroom door shut, Jeff sat down next to Adrienne and gently took her hands into his. "Tell me what's wrong, Adrienne," he implored.

She looked at Jeff's concerned face and said the one thing she knew would make him feel the most needed. "Will you pray with me first?"

A smile spread across his face. "I would love to pray with you. Let's bow our heads, and I'll lead a prayer," said Jeff.

Adrienne nodded her head and closed her eyes. Jeff started speaking, "Dear God, please help guide Adrienne through this time of hardship. She needs you now more than ever, and only you can provide her with the knowledge she needs."

She didn't listen to the rest of Jeff's carefully chosen words. Instead, she opened her right eye slightly to see Jeff's face. She knew she had him exactly where she wanted him.

"Amen," said Jeff.

"Amen," Adrienne said quickly to ensure Jeff thought she had been listening to him the entire time. "Jeff, that was just perfect. Thank you so much."

"You're welcome, Adrienne. Now please tell what is wrong," he pleaded.

Tears formed in Adrienne's eyes. "I don't know what to do, Jeff. Agent Williams and Agent Ulrich were here and, and, and I'm just so scared," she cried as she reached out to hug Jeff close to her, burying her face in his shoulder.

Jeff wrapped his arms around Adrienne and pulled her closer to him. He removed one hand from her back so he could stroke her hair while planting butterfly kisses on the top of her head. "It's okay," he said reassuringly. "I'm here for you." He placed his hands on her shoulders and gently pushed her back until they were face to face. "Take a deep breath and tell me what happened."

"It's Agent Williams," Adrienne cried. "He threatened me!"

Adrienne felt Jeff's body tense at her words. "What did he do?" Jeff asked angrily.

"He... he... he... I can't even say it," she said as she turned her head away in despair.

Jeff put his hand on the side of Adrienne's face and brought her face back to his. He looked deep into her eyes, saying, "You know you can trust me. Now tell me what he did so we can figure out how to fix it."

Adrienne took a deep breath and quietly said, "Okay, but it's so terrible."

"No matter what, we will get through this together," Jeff told her.

"You're too good to me, Jeff," she said in an adoring voice.

She took another deep breath and said, "I'm ready to tell you, but only because I trust you so much."

Jeff nodded silently and motioned for her to begin.

"As I said," Adrienne began, "Agent Williams was here with Agent Ulrich, and at first, everything seemed normal. They both asked me questions, but Agent Williams told Agent Ulrich to go wait in the car because he needed to talk to me alone. When she left the house, he sat next to me and put his hand on my breast." Adrienne let out a loud wail so Jeff could fully understand the pain she must be feeling. "He told me that if I didn't have sex with him that he was going to make sure that I would be charged as Matthew's accessory."

"That son of a bitch," Jeff muttered under his breath.

Adrienne was shocked at Jeff's words as she had never heard him curse before. She had to suppress her smile because his choice of words meant Jeff believed her. He was too easy. She continued, "Jeff, I was so scared. I flashed back to the time I was sexually assaulted before, and I froze. I thought he was going to assault me right there on the couch. We were all alone, and he's so much stronger than me. I couldn't run away from him, and I think he used that to his advantage. The only thing that saved me was Agent Ulrich calling to tell him that they had to leave. But when he left, he told me he guaranteed I would see him again."

"That son of a bitch," Jeff said again, but in a much louder voice this time. He stood up suddenly and began pacing with his fists clenched at his sides. Adrienne decided to let Jeff seethe in his anger and not say a word. She would let Jeff think the newly created Plan C was all his.

Jeff stopped pacing and moved to sit down by Adrienne again. He pulled her to him and said, "I will take care of this. No real man preys on an innocent woman. Especially a woman with a disability. That type of man has no right to be a cop."

Adrienne nodded to signal her acceptance of his decision. "Whatever you think is best, Jeff. You're so much smarter and stronger than me."

"Don't say things like that, Adrienne," Jeff begged. "You don't realize how perfect you are. I can't imagine a better woman than you."

She could see the love in Jeff's eyes. *Well, he doesn't meet rule one, but he meets rule number three,* thought Adrienne. *I might as well see how well he checks off the other rule.* Adrienne leaned forward and gently kissed Jeff on the lips. She felt him pull back.

"Adrienne," he said. "You know I love you, and I would do anything for you, but I don't want to take advantage of you. You're in a vulnerable position right now."

I'm not vulnerable; I'm horny, thought Adrienne. She smiled sweetly at Jeff and said, "Jeff, you could never take advantage of me. I love you."

Jeff's entire face lit up at her words. "Are you sure this is what you want?" he asked.

"I am completely sure," she said. "You'll need to help me, though, because my muscles are so weak."

Jeff picked Adrienne up from the sofa and carried her down the hall to his bedroom without saying anything. Neither of them thought about the little girl in the room across the hall. Their only thoughts were of each other and satisfying their basest desires.

Adrienne began kissing Jeff deeply, but he pulled away and placed his forehead against hers. "Darling," he said, "you know I have never felt confident around women."

She nodded, not liking the direction of the conversation. "Of course."

"I always promised I would save myself for a woman I loved and you're the only woman I've ever loved. I've never made love before," Jeff admitted.

Holy shit, he's a virgin, thought Adrienne. There was nothing she enjoyed more than taking someone's virginity. She thought she was at an age where that wasn't possible anymore. She stroked Jeff's face with her hand and said sweetly, "I will help you through this. Just like how you have helped me with everything. All that matters is that we love each other. If two people genuinely love each other, like we do, making love will be natural and beautiful."

Jeff kissed her gently and said, "You are too good to be true."

Adrienne was tired of talking and moved her hand from his face to his crotch, causing Jeff to let out a loud groan. *Well, he finally has something in common with Jake. Check off number two*, she thought. *This is going to be fun.*

She guided him to where she wanted him to place his hands, and he groaned even louder. Jeff was eager to please her, but he was also careful not to hurt her in her delicate condition. He mounted her as gently as he could. When he entered her, she sensed his breathing stop for a moment before it became more rapid. Even though it didn't last very long, the experience was satisfactory since she hadn't had sex in at least three days. That was the longest she had gone without since she became sexually active.

When he finished, Jeff rolled off her and began softly crying. He pulled her over to him so her head would rest on his chest while he stroked her arm. "I love you so much," he said. "You are my everything."

"You're my everything too," Adrienne said in her most convincing voice. "Now, what are you going to do about Agent Williams?"

The question caused Jeff to snap out of his first-time bliss, stop crying, and become angry again. "I was planning to call his superiors and tell them what happened. He should be removed from the case and removed from the force."

Adrienne rolled her eyes because this was not the solution she had in mind. If Jeff called the agent's superiors and they knew he was gay, that would be the end of her credibility with the cops. She knew she had to convince Jeff to come up with a different plan. "Jeff," she said, "you know they're just going to protect him. It will be my word against his. Who do you think they're going to believe?"

"I hadn't thought of it that way," said Jeff while trying to think of another idea. "What if we had him come over again and secretly recorded him?"

Adrienne shook her head against his chest because she was fully aware that would never work. She raised her head to look him in the eye. "Jeff, there's only one way to deal with a predator like him. You and I both know that."

Jeff nodded. "Plus," Adrienne added, "what if he gets me alone before that? What if no one interrupts him, and he succeeds in assaulting me? Or what if he plants evidence to link me to Jake's murder?"

"You're right," said Jeff. "There's only one way to handle someone like him. Don't worry, I will take care of it."

"I know you will," said Adrienne, "because you're my knight in shining armor. If only all men were like you."

"Most men are good, Adrienne," Jeff answered. "Unfortunately, you've met some terrible ones during your life."

"I have," Adrienne said as she kissed Jeff again. "Ready for round two?"

she asked seductively.

Jeff smiled before kissing her back. "Definitely."

Adrienne hugged him to hide her smirking face from his view. *Some men are too easy,* she thought to herself. Maybe she would say a real prayer later to thank God for making men who are easy to manipulate.

After finishing with Jeff, she realized no one had seen Ava in hours. Deciding to check on her well-being, she used her walker to limp her way to where Ava had been coloring. She found her asleep on the small bed with the picture she had colored for her father lying beside her. Curious about what she had drawn, Adrienne picked up the picture. Her daughter had drawn three people, one labeled Daddy, one labeled Mommy, and one labeled Ava. She crumbled the paper in her hand when she realized the person Ava had labeled as mommy had red hair.

9

Chapter 9

Ella curled up on the hotel bed, hugging an oversize pillow, pretending it was Matthew. The emptiness was overwhelming, and she had never felt so alone. No more tears would fall as she lay staring at the wall, thinking about her life and the inconceivable turn it had taken.

The first date with Matthew was the best night of her life to that point. Ella never did enjoy big crowds, so staying in and fixing a simple dinner with him was the best first date they could have had. Their conversation never stalled and was never forced, and they had so much in common. Ella had to laugh when she remembered how Matthew was so concerned about the way he was dressed. "I feel like I'm under dressed," he said while looking down at his clothing and holding his arms out to the side to allow Ella a full view of his outfit.

Ella looked at him. He was wearing black sweatpants and a Minnesota Vikings shirt. She had never noticed his clothing because his face and personality so transfixed her. She tilted her head to the side and asked, "Why would you feel under dressed wearing a Randy Moss shirt?"

Matthew couldn't hide his surprise and asked incredulously, "You know who Randy Moss is?"

"Of course," she answered, "he's only one of the best wide receivers that ever played."

"Wow," Matthew replied. "You just keep getting better and better. But he's not one of the best; he is the best ever to play the game."

"Really?" she said with a raised eyebrow, knowing that Matthew was playing with her. "He was a great player, but let's not forget Jerry Rice."

Matthew dropped his mouth open in fake outrage. "Jerry Rice wasn't even a Viking! How could you say such a thing?"

"Okay, okay," Ella replied, holding up her hand to indicate her surrender. "You win. Moss was the best ever."

"Well," Matthew said, "it appears we've had our first fight."

"I guess we have," replied Ella nervously.

Matthew moved closer to Ella, his lips so close to hers, and asked, "Should we kiss and make up?"

Ella could feel his breath on her face, and she could not speak, so she slowly nodded. Matthew placed his lips on hers, giving her the sweetest kiss. No one had made her feel like this before; her knees physically buckled at the intense feelings she was experiencing.

"Whoa," Matthew said when he pulled his lips away from hers. "That was amazing."

Ella slowly opened her eyes and whispered back, "Yes, it was." She had never had sex with someone she had just met and never had a one-night stand, but she would have slept with him that night if he had asked. Her feelings and attraction for him were that strong. But Matthew was a gentleman and reached out to bring her hand to his lips and gently kiss her fingers.

"I've never felt like this about anyone," said Matthew. "I feel like I've known you forever."

"I know exactly how you feel," Ella replied.

Matthew grabbed her other hand with his, stared directly into her eyes, and said, "Ella, I told you that I believe in not wasting time and saying what I mean."

Ella held her breath and nodded at him, feeling excitement and fear at what he might say next.

"This is not a line," he said. "I think I am falling for you. Love at first sight never felt real to me before, but it does now. You're incredible."

Ella returned his feelings by saying, "So are you. I think I might be falling for you too."

"Well," he said, "it appears we are officially an item. Does that sound okay to you?"

She decided to answer him without words. Ella, who had never initiated a kiss in her life, leaned in and kissed Matthew directly on his beautiful mouth.

The ring from her cell phone pulled her back from her memory. The caller ID indicated it was Casey, and Ella was surprised. She thought they weren't going to talk again until Monday morning.

"Hello," said Ella.

"Ella," Casey said, "I'm here and have a room in your hotel. Do you have some time to talk, hon?"

"Of course," replied Ella. "But I look terrible."

"Hon, no one expects you to be holding yourself together right now. Tell me your room number, and I will be there in a moment."

"Room 215," said Ella.

"What do you know," replied Casey. "I'm already outside your door. My room is 214. Can you let me in?"

"Sure," Ella said. She hung up the phone and went to open the door for Matthew's attorney. Ella was scared to meet her; she sounded so reassuring on the phone, but what if she was different in person?

When she opened the door, the woman standing in front of her was not what she expected. Casey Klein was attractive, with curly dark hair and striking hazel eyes. A pair of glasses partially hid her eyes, but Ella could see kindness in those eyes. Casey was wearing simple black leggings with sandals, but Casey's shirt drew her attention. Ella half laughed and half cried – Casey was wearing a Minnesota Vikings jersey with number eighty-four on it, which was the number worn by Randy Moss.

Casey stood in the doorway, looking confused at the silence. "Are you going to let me in?" she asked.

Ella blinked her eyes hard to make herself stop staring at the jersey. "I'm sorry," she said, moving back so Casey could walk past her into the room. "You're wearing a Randy Moss jersey."

"And? You don't like Randy Moss?" asked Casey.

"That's not it," Ella said. "Matthew was wearing a Randy Moss shirt the day we met. I think it's a sign that you're the right attorney for us."

"Well," Casey said while surveying the room, "I'm going to accept that sign."

"Oh, hon," said Casey, changing into full mom mode. "You need light in here, and when did you last eat?"

"I don't remember," Ella said honestly.

"Let's get you something to eat," Casey said while Ella shook her head.

"It's not open for debate," said Casey. "Do you really want to argue with me? I get paid a lot of money to argue."

"I can't face anyone," Ella said. "This is a small town. Everyone is going to know what happened."

"Oh, pish," Casey snorted. "Who cares what they think? You need to take care of yourself. If you're not strong physically and mentally, you can't help me, and you can't help Matthew."

Unable to stand the thought of not being able to help Matthew, Ella reluctantly agreed. "Okay, I'll go," she said.

"Do you have any other clothes, Ella?" asked Casey, looking Ella up and down. "Sweatpants won't be appropriate for court tomorrow."

"No," Ella replied. "They haven't let me back in my house to get anything."

"We'll go get you some clothes, some food, and some necessities to get you through the next few days," Casey said in a way to let Ella know it was not open for discussion.

Casey drove Ella to the local super center in her Mercedes SUV. Ella was concerned the flashy vehicle would draw unwanted attention, but no one looked twice. Mercedes may not be an everyday vehicle brand in the area, but they were far from unheard of here. People outside of the Midwest tend to think everyone in Minnesota drives a beat-up pickup truck and speaks like they do in movies, but, like most stereotypes, they were exaggerated or just plain wrong. Granted, you were likely to hear someone say, "ope" or "you betcha," but Ella had never heard anyone speak with the exaggerated accent portrayed in the few movies set in her beautiful adopted home state. And a majority of the pickup trucks on Minnesota roads cost more than sixty thousand dollars. Not to mention the farm equipment that could run into the six figures, so no one was overly concerned by the appearance of a luxury car. When Casey pulled her vehicle into a parking spot and stopped the car, Ella felt her breath becoming more labored. *Not now,* she thought, *I can't have an anxiety attack now.*

As if sensing Ella's trepidation, Casey reached over and placed her hand on Ella's arm. "I am here for you, and you can do this," she said, "No one better try to mess with you while I'm around."

Ella turned to give Casey a look of gratitude, and she made her way toward the store with Casey close by her side. She had never been in the store before. Whenever they needed anything from here, Matthew would go in, or they ordered curbside pickup. Ella immediately felt out of place when they entered the store. She was amazed at how large it was; to her right was a deli and groceries; to her left, she could see a pharmacy and hygiene products, and almost directly in front of her was clothing. The lights in the store were so bright, and she felt as if everyone was staring at her. "I want to find some clothes and get out of here as fast as possible," she told Casey.

"Okay, clothes are this way, but you also need some basic hygiene products," Casey said as she directed Ella to the clothing racks. "You might be surprised at some of the nice outfits you can find in here."

The clothing racks were close together, and Ella squeezed between them to look through the pants, blazers, and blouses available. She was surprised at how much she did like the clothes. A smile came to her face when she thought how her mother would feel about Ella buying clothes hung up feet away from fruits and vegetables. Her mother insisted on wearing only designer clothing. She had told Ella when she was younger, "Dear, you need to dress nicely. It's your calling card. And you need something stunning to draw attention from your lack of looks and personality." When she was younger, Ella wondered why her mother stayed in the area after her father's death. She always seemed to think everyone else was beneath her, and Ella thought her mother would have been happier in a large city somewhere. But her mother was a big fish here. She would be surrounded by multi-millionaires in a big city and wouldn't have nearly as many people who she thought worshiped her for her beauty and philanthropy. Her mother always thought she was the most important person in the room. Thinking about her mother brought back her insecurities, and Ella thought she could feel someone watching her. She looked around but saw no one. Luckily, it was late at night, so the store wasn't full, but Ella kept her head bowed in an effort to conceal her face. She sped up her clothes hunting to end this shopping experience as quickly as possible.

Ella lifted her head to scan the store for her protector but didn't see her. She hadn't noticed that Casey had left while she was looking at clothes, and she had a moment of fear. Her breaths had started to become labored again when she heard laughter from behind her. She turned to see a group of teenage girls giggling and pointing at her.

One girl nudged another girl forward. The girl that had been provoked yelled across the store, "What's it like to be married to a murderer?"

Ella closed her eyes tight when she sensed the tunnel vision starting. She heard chants from the girls of, "You're married to a murderer." Ella was paralyzed until she heard a familiar voice.

"Hey," Casey yelled, her finger pointing directly at the group of girls, "what the hell do you think you're doing? Either get away from her, or you're going to have to deal with me. Trust me; you don't want to deal with me." The girls looked at Casey and then at each other and quickly decided this was a fight they could not win. They ran down an aisle and out of view.

Casey put her arm around Ella to hold her up. "I'm here," Casey said in her mom voice. "I'm so sorry. You were so engrossed in the clothes, and I thought I could sneak over to get you some makeup and a toothbrush."

"It's okay," said Ella. "Can we pay for this and get out of here, please?"

"Sure," Casey said, "let's get out of here."

After her experience inside the store, Ella made it clear she was not going inside any restaurant, and Casey agreed to go through a drive-through for food. They went back to Ella's hotel room to have their meal. Ella picked up the chicken sandwich on its flat bun and reluctantly took a bite. Not realizing how hungry she was she finished the sandwich quickly. She thought the food would make her sick, but surprisingly, it made her feel better.

"Hey," Casey said after Ella took her last bite, "look at you. Do you feel better?"

"Yes," Ella replied, "I do. Thank you for making me eat."

"As I said, I need you to take care of yourself," Casey told her. "I need your help, and Matthew needs your help."

"I don't know how much help I can be," Ella said softly. "I'm not very smart."

"Who the hell told you that?" Casey asked angrily.

"My mother," Ella replied.

"And why do you believe her?" Casey asked sincerely.

"Because my mother was beautiful and accomplished," Ella said. For some reason, she felt comfortable around Casey. "My mother had no problem telling me about my flaws and what a disappointment I was. She made it clear that I was stupid and homely."

Casey raised her eyebrows and looked directly at Ella, "With all due respect, your mother sounds like she's full of shit. I mean, have you ever looked in a mirror?"

"Of course, I have," Ella said quietly. "I know what I look like."

"Do you, though?" Casey asked sarcastically. "My God, you look like you walked out of the Jolene song."

Ella looked at Casey with a confused look, "The Jolene song?"

"Yes," said Casey. "The Dolly Parton song..."

"I know the song," Ella said a little defensively. "But I do not look like that."

"Hon, you're gorgeous," Casey said matter-of-factly. "Get that through your head. You're also intelligent. Quit listening to the crap your mother told you."

Casey didn't let Ella respond. Instead, she slapped her hands on her legs, giving Ella the Minnesota signal that it was time to call it a night. "I need to get some sleep before court tomorrow. You try to get some rest, and I will come to get you at 8:00. Goodnight, hon."

"Goodnight," Ella said as she followed Casey to the door to secure the deadbolt and place the chain. Sleep would be hard to come by; tomorrow would be such a big day. She would be allowed to see Matthew for the first time since his arrest.

10

Chapter 10

Ella's phone alarm blared at 6:30 AM, but she was already awake and had been for hours. Random thoughts had kept her awake: what would Matthew look like; what would he say; would he be happy to see her; what if he was guilty? She rolled from her back to her side and picked up the buzzing phone, its bright light hurting her eyes. Silencing the alarm, she again rolled onto her back to stare at the ceiling instead of the clock. After ten minutes, she willed herself to remove the covers, get out of bed, and take a shower. The shower did feel refreshing, something she needed to help her feel human.

She removed the makeup Casey had picked out for her from the shopping bag and marveled at how well Casey picked out colors Ella would choose for herself. The one thing her mother had taught her was how to apply makeup. With the precision of a makeup artist, Ella applied mascara and lipstick. She decided to forego any foundation except for concealer to hide the stress and lack of sleep evidenced by the dark circles under her eyes. She dried her red hair, pulled it straight back into a simple ponytail, and looked at her reflection in the mirror. *I look halfway presentable,* she thought.

The last task was to find the appropriate outfit. After selecting the basic black pants and blazer with a green blouse from her new clothes, Ella realized she had forgotten to buy shoes. They had left the store in such a rush that she had never even thought about only having sneakers to wear. She didn't know whether to laugh or cry at the oversight, which seemed to be the new normal in her daily life. With no other choice, she slipped on the shoes and sat on the edge of the bed to wait for Casey.

At precisely 8:00, Ella heard a knock on her door. Even though she was expecting Casey, she glanced through the peephole before opening the door. Gone was the motherly woman Ella had met yesterday; in her place was the high-paid attorney. Ella eagerly opened the door to get a better view of the metamorphosis.

She scanned Casey and mentally noted the changes: stunningly blue contacts replaced the glasses; a designer power suit replaced the leggings and Vikings jersey; four-inch designer heels replaced the sandals; sleek hair pulled into a bun at the base of her neck replaced the curly hair. Ella could not believe what an intimidating presence Casey had. Only when she spoke was Ella sure this was the person she'd met last night. "Let's go, hon," Casey told her.

Ella silently grabbed her purse and followed Casey out of the hotel to her vehicle. The courthouse where Matthew's hearing was being held was a short drive out of town, which they completed without speaking a word. When she parked the Mercedes in front of the building, Casey turned to Ella and said, "Okay, Ella, this is a brief appearance. They'll read Matthew his rights again, verify I'm his defense counsel, and set bail." Casey took a deep breath before she said the next part in a severe tone, "Ella, you need to prepare yourself for this. I fully expect the judge will deny Matthew bail. There have been too many cases of affluent or influential people being treated differently by the judicial system. From what I have learned about the judge, I believe that he'll make an example of him."

Casey looked at Ella, appearing to try to read her reaction. "Hon, I need you to be strong no matter what happens. Can you do that for Matthew and me?"

"Yes, I will," Ella promised.

"Okay," Casey replied as she nodded her head. "Let's go do this."

Ella felt her legs go weak when she stepped out of the car, so she leaned on Casey for support walking into the building. When they entered the courtroom, Casey showed Ella where to sit behind the defense table. Ella was surprised at the courtroom. She had never been in one before, and the only reference she had were the courtrooms she saw on *Law & Order*. The spectator seats were individual chairs rather than benches, and the jury seating was to the left instead of the right. The room itself had beautiful woodwork, with the imposing judge's desk at the front of the room. The prosecutor was already seated at her table, writing on a legal pad.

The side door opened, and Matthew walked out, wearing an orange jumpsuit and ankle shackles, with a chain around his waist and a jailer by his side. Ella caught her breath when she saw him, and she noticed how his face lit up when he saw her. He looked so pale and gaunt after just two days in the county jail. He mouthed, "I love you," to her, and she mouthed it back to him. Matthew sat next to Casey, and Ella saw Casey lean close to Matthew to whisper to him. He nodded his head and looked back at Ella and smiled; he was happy with her choice of attorney.

"All rise," yelled the bailiff. Ella followed the direction given and saw the judge walk into the room. He looked like a judge, clean cut with gray hair, his black robe flowing as he walked. Ella thought he had a kind face, for which she was grateful because this person would be instrumental in determining Matthew's and Ella's fate.

Casey was right; the hearing was quick. The prosecution argued Matthew had the means to flee, and he posed a threat to Adrienne and Ava. The thought of Matthew posing a danger to anyone, let alone Ava, seemed ridiculous to Ella. She asked for remand because Matthew had the means to pay almost any bail set by the court. Casey made rebuttal arguments that Matthew was an upstanding citizen who owned his own business, had no criminal record, and was willing to surrender his passport. Still, the judge's decision was swift – bail denied. Matthew looked back at Ella one more time before the jailer grabbed his arm and led him out of the room.

Ella stood watching Matthew leave the room, not taking her eyes off the door until there was no visible sign of him. Casey walked back to Ella and said, "Ella, I am going to meet with Matthew. I need time to visit him alone so I can hear his side of the story."

"But I want to talk to him," Ella argued.

Casey put her arm around Ella's shoulder as she said, "Hon, I have to talk to him alone first. There may be something he wants to tell me in private. I promise I will come to get you as soon as I can."

"Okay," said a defeated Ella. "I just need to touch him."

"I know," Casey said in an understanding tone. "The jailer will take you over to a waiting area until you can see Matthew."

Ella reluctantly followed the jailer over to a waiting area. The jail itself was part of the same building, so it was a short walk. She let her imagination run wild as to what Casey and Matthew were discussing. What if Matthew was confessing to her? How would Ella ever know the truth?

She thought back to another time in their life when Matthew made an uncomfortable confession to her. They had been dating for about two months, and Ella was blissfully in love. Matthew had surprised her one day, appearing at her door at 2:00 in the afternoon on a Monday. That was out of the ordinary for him; Matthew was dedicated to his work and rarely took time off. Ella started to say, "What a nice surprise," but the look on his face made her stop before the first word left her mouth.

Matthew pulled Ella to him, hugging her tightly. "I love you so much," he said.

"I love you too," said Ella.

"We have to talk," Matthew said with his lips against her hair. "Something has happened."

Ella's heart began to pound, and all her fears came racing to her mind. *He's going to leave me*, she thought. *I should have known I could never have a man this wonderful.*

Matthew released Ella from the hug and grabbed her hand to lead her to the living room. They sat on the edge of the sofa, knee to knee so that they could look directly into each other's eyes. "I love you," Matthew said again, "I never thought I could love someone as much as I love you." He trailed off and said, "I don't know where to start."

"Please tell me," Ella implored. "You're scaring me."

"Do you remember me telling you about Adrienne Griffin?" he asked.

Ella nodded, "Yes, the one you went to high school with that had a crush on you?"

"Yes, that's her," Matthew answered. He lowered his eyes and whispered, "She's pregnant, and the baby is mine."

Ella felt the room start spinning. "You cheated on me?" she cried.

"No, no, never," he said. "It was before we met. There was one drunken night, and it just happened. Honestly, I don't even remember it."

"I don't understand," Ella said. "Are you in love with her? Are you going to marry her?" She buried her face in her hands and began to cry.

Matthew put his arm around Ella's shoulder, but she took her hand and pushed him away. He put his arm at his side and begged, "Please, Ella, I don't love her, and I definitely don't want to marry her. I love you and only you."

"What do you expect me to say?" asked Ella. "What about the baby?"

"I want the baby in my life," Matthew answered honestly. "If I have a child, I need to be part of that child's life. I can't run away from my responsibilities."

"I know you can't," Ella replied. "You're not that kind of person. But what does this mean for us?"

Matthew placed his hand under her chin and lifted her face to his. "I was hoping you would help raise the baby. You will be an amazing stepmother."

Ella thought about what Matthew was suggesting. Would she be a good stepmother? Her mother had done so much damage, and she did not want to perpetuate that cycle. She looked at Matthew's face; he had tears running down his cheeks, and he was looking at her with such hope. Ella loved him so much that she needed him in her life, and he had not cheated on her, so she made a decision that would determine both of their futures. "I'll stay and help you," she said softly.

She saw the instant happiness spread across Matthew's face. Suddenly, he started fumbling in his pockets and pulled out a box. He moved from the couch to the floor and got on one knee. Ella knew what was happening, but she could not believe it. He was proposing to her.

"Ella," he said, "you are my everything. Will you please marry me?" Matthew opened the box to reveal a fantastic pear-shaped diamond ring.

"Of course," Ella yelled. "I love you." She placed her hands on the sides of his face and pulled him in for a deep kiss.

"I have to put the ring on you," Matthew said, laughing. He took the ring from the box, his hands visibly shaking, and placed the diamond ring on her finger. "I am the luckiest man alive."

The emotional roller coaster Ella experienced had taken its toll, and she collapsed into his arms, kissing him deeper than she ever had before. Their emotions turned into passion, and they made love for the first time right there on the sofa. Ella had been intimate with other men, but she had never had the connection and fireworks she felt with Matthew. Making love to him was the most sensual and unforgettable experience of her life.

After he fell asleep, she lay there thinking about all the changes in her life while holding up her hand to admire her new ring. She had the perfect fiancé, and soon they would have a child they would both love. The only thing that worried Ella was Adrienne. How would she feel about another woman helping to raise the baby? Matthew had never had a bad word to say about Adrienne. He said he felt sorry for her because she'd had a hard life, but he didn't seem to have any interest in her romantically. Ella could only hope for the best.

Casey's voice brought Ella back from her memory. "Ella," Casey said, "you can see Matthew now."

Ella exhaled and followed Casey down the hall to a small meeting room. Matthew was sitting at the table, still in the orange jumpsuit, but minus the shackles. He stood and rushed toward Ella when she entered the room, wrapping her in an embrace. "My Ella," he cried, "I love you, I love you."

"I love you too," Ella said as she kissed him over and over. "I have missed you so much."

"I am so sorry for everything," Matthew apologized. "You shouldn't be going through this."

"I will go through anything with you," Ella replied.

Casey cleared her throat. "We have limited time, and we need to clear the air. Matthew needs to tell you something, Ella."

Surprised, Ella extended her arms to create space between herself and Matthew. "Tell me what?"

"Ella, Matthew, sit down," commanded Casey. "I know this is awkward, Matthew, but I have to stay in here with you, and you need to tell her."

"I know," Matthew said ashamedly. "Ella, I need to tell you why I failed the lie detector test."

11

Chapter 11

Ella read Matthew's body language and heard the severe tone of his voice, and she immediately knew this explanation was one she did not want to hear. Over five years ago, Matthew had to tell Ella about the impending arrival of Ava, but she had turned out to be a blessing in disguise. This was not going to be the same outcome. She held her breath and waited for words that were sure to cause her unimaginable pain.

Matthew looked down at his hands rather than in Ella's eyes. When he started speaking, his voice was soft, and Ella had to strain to hear him over the sound of her pounding heart. "Ella," he began, "I love you, and I never want to hurt you, but something happened, and I didn't tell you. Do you remember when you were in Minneapolis and we were talking on the phone? Ava interrupted to say she forgot her teddy bear at Adrienne's, and I had to go get it so she could go to sleep."

Ella nodded silently, not wanting to say anything that would stop his confession. Matthew continued, "When I got there, Adrienne was home alone, and she said Jake was out of town. She told me the water softener needed salt added to it and asked if I would go into the basement and add it for her. I didn't have a choice since she could barely walk, and I would have felt guilty if I didn't help her. So, I went downstairs and added the salt. When I got back upstairs, she asked if I wanted some lemonade. I don't know why I said yes, but I did. I mean, the basement was so hot, and the thought of cold lemonade sounded so appealing."

Matthew stopped for a moment as if he was choosing his following words carefully; he swallowed hard and said, "I don't know how it happened, but we ended up in bed together." Matthew lifted his gaze briefly and looked at Ella, begging her with his eyes to forgive him.

Ella lifted her chin to move her eyes away from his. "You had sex with her?" she questioned softly, even though she already knew the answer.

"Yes," he said, as his eyes filled with tears. "I honestly don't know what to say to you. We were drunk and I remember Adrienne fell and I went to help her, and..."

"Please don't say anything else," Ella screamed.

"I wanted to tell you, but Adrienne said we had to promise never to tell you or Jake. She said Jake would hurt himself if he found out."

"Is it supposed to make me feel better that you wanted to tell me?" Ella asked sarcastically. "It's so considerate of you to think of my feelings after having sex with another woman."

"Ella," he begged, "I swear I didn't want it to happen. Adrienne told me the teddy bear was in her and Jake's bedroom and told me I could get it after helping with the softener soft. If only I had left instead or told Ava she would have to spend one night without her bear. That stupid teddy bear!" he yelled as he slammed his fist on the table. "That dumb thing was a reminder of what happened, so I went to the store and bought Ava a new one, hoping she wouldn't notice it wasn't the same bear. I brought the old one into the house and hid it in the closet. I was going to burn it, but I never got a chance before I was arrested."

"Adrienne!" Ella exclaimed. "How could you cheat on me with her? Of all people!" She then remembered another reason to be angry and said, "This was the night I was out of town for my charity meeting?"

Matthew nodded and Ella became angrier at his acknowledgment. "I tried to call you for hours that night and you told me your phone was dead."

"I don't have a good reason for you. All I can do is tell you that it wasn't and isn't something I want."

"Oh my God," Ella yelled. "Where was Ava? Did you leave her alone?"

"No, of course not," Matthew said. "I had to take her with me. We walked over to the house together and she was sleeping when I came up from filling the water softener."

"Did you send her those text messages?" Ella asked, taking him by surprise.

"Yes," Matthew admitted. "But I swear it was only because I wanted to tell you the truth, and she didn't want me to."

Casey interjected, "Ella, that's the reason the lie detector test showed deception. It's not because he killed Jake. They asked him if he had any sexual relationship with Adrienne, and he answered no. Any answer on the test that shows deception will cause the police to use that in their investigation, even though it's not admissible in court."

"That makes this a good thing?" Ella said as she turned her sarcasm toward Casey. "He's not a murderer, but he's a lying cheater. That's just great news."

"Ella," Matthew said, "please."

"No," she said quickly. "I need some air, and I need to not be by you right now."

Casey stood and said, "I'll drive you back to the hotel."

Ella shook her head, saying, "No, I will walk back. I want to be alone."

"I understand," Casey said. Matthew started to argue, but Casey silenced him by placing her finger to her lips.

As Ella stood at the door about to leave, Matthew said, "Ella, I love you." In the years Matthew had been saying those words to her, Ella always responded with, "I love you too." However, this time, she walked through the door and closed it behind her without saying a word.

The air that hit Ella in the face when she exited the police station was welcome. She stood there for a moment with her eyes closed, breathing in the scents of the flowers and freshly mowed grass. Her life had been as close to perfect as possible just a few days ago, and it was all falling down around her.

"Mrs. Dalton," she heard a strange voice say. She opened her eyes to see a young woman briskly walking toward her.

"Mrs. Dalton," she heard again. Ella did not want to speak to anyone, especially a random stranger. She thought about the incident in the shopping center and couldn't face a heckler on her own, so she began walking briskly in the opposite direction. The footsteps were getting closer together, telling Ella the young woman was now running toward her.

"Leave me alone!" Ella yelled, increasing her own pace.

"Mrs. Dalton," the woman said again. "Please, I have to talk to you. I don't think your husband killed Jake Dwyer."

The words caused Ella to stop and turn around to look at the woman immediately. "What did you say?" she asked.

"I don't think your husband killed Jake Dwyer," she repeated. "There are things about Jake that you do not know."

"Who are you?" a suspicious Ella asked. "I've never seen you before."

The young woman replied, "We don't know each other, but my name is Justine. I'm sorry to surprise you like this, but I saw online about your husband's hearing and I took a chance you would be here. Can we go somewhere to talk? It's important."

Ella looked around the parking lot; it was just the two of them. Ella reasoned that if she wanted to hurt her, she would choose a better location to approach her than somewhere full of police officers. Ella walked back toward Justine and studied her. She had shiny, sleek, black hair and luminous, flawless skin. Justine appeared to be a person she could trust, but Ella didn't have much faith in her instincts at the moment. The young woman looked so desperate, though, and Ella decided she needed to hear her out. "Where do you want to talk?" Ella asked.

"My car is right over there," Justine said. "Would you like to get some coffee?"

"No public places," Ella answered, thinking about her own need to avoid people and the risk of leaving with a stranger. "Can we talk by your car?"

"Sure," said Justine, "it's right over here."

The two women stood by Justine's vehicle, Ella ensuring to stay on the side closest to the building in case she needed to make a speedy getaway. She began the conversation by asking, "Why did you say that Matthew didn't kill Jake? What do you know?"

Justine turned and fixated her gaze on her car windshield and replied, "I need to tell you a story, but I need to tell it in my way and at my pace. Can you listen to my story and not ask any questions until I'm finished?"

Ella nodded to indicate her agreement, and Justine continued, "About five and half years ago, I was home from college to visit my father. He insisted I needed to go out and have fun, so he forced the daughter of one of his friends to take me out with her. We ended up at a bar downtown, and the daughter and her friends deserted me, leaving me at the table by myself. I sat there alone until a nice couple came up and introduced themselves. They seemed so sweet – they were newlyweds. They offered to buy me a drink because they said I looked sad, but I said no because I didn't drink. The woman told me she wasn't drinking either because she was pregnant and asked if they could buy me a pop instead."

Justine paused and seemed to be forcing herself to continue. "That was the last thing I remember," she said. "I woke up on their couch the following day with no memory of the night before. The lady told me I had gotten drunk, and they took me home with them to keep me safe."She took a deep breath and continued, "I don't drink, so I knew something wasn't right, and I needed to get out of there. She offered to drive me home, but I grabbed my things and ran out the door."

She turned her gaze away from the windshield and looked at Ella, who had already deduced the couple's identity. "It was Jake and Adrienne, wasn't it?" Ella asked quietly.

Justine brushed away the tears that had started to fall down her cheeks. "Yes," she said quietly. "I ran from there and used my cell phone to call my dad. He had been out looking for me all night and was so worried. I couldn't bring myself to tell him anything happened because I didn't want him to blame himself for forcing me to go out that night. So, I told him I slept on a friend's couch. I never reported Jake to the police, and you're the first person I've told."

She buried her face in her hands and began sobbing. "I know they assaulted me," she said. "When my dad brought me home, I felt disgusting and had to shower immediately. I took off my clothes and noticed the blouse I was wearing under my sweater was mis-buttoned. And it seemed like I had been,

I don't know quite how to describe it, but almost like I had been cleaned with a disinfectant."

Ella felt the empathy wash over her, and she reached out to place her hand gently on Justine's shoulder. "I'm so sorry," she said.

She looked at Ella and wiped the new tears away. "Don't you see? If they did it to me, they probably did it to someone else. What if someone got their revenge on Jake?"

Ella didn't want to ask the next question, but she felt she had to. "Do you know who killed him?" she asked.

A slight smile appeared on Justine's face. "Do you mean did I kill him?" she asked with raised eyebrows. "No, I didn't kill him, and I don't know who did. But, no matter who did it, I would like to shake their hand. And that woman is evil personified. She has to be stopped."

An uncomfortable pause followed, and Ella felt the need to change the direction of her questions. "Do you remember anything other than waking up on the couch?" she asked.

"Not really," said Justine. She appeared to think for a moment before adding, "But for some reason, I remember a teddy bear that appeared to be watching me."

"A teddy bear?" Ella questioned.

"Yeah," said Justine. "For some reason, I kept seeing that teddy bear when I closed my eyes."

A realization came to Ella. *Could it be Ava's teddy bear?* she thought. Ava wasn't born when Jake and Adrienne victimized Justine, but Ella remembered Ava telling her it had been Jake's bear when he was a child.

"Oh my God," said Ella. "Did Jake say anything about it being his teddy bear?"

Justine shrugged her shoulders. "I don't think so, but anything is possible."

Ella looked directly at Justine and said, "My stepdaughter has a stuffed teddy bear she takes almost everywhere. She told me it belonged to Jake when he was little. I wonder if that's what you saw."

"It could be," Justine reasoned.

"If it's that teddy bear," said a disgusted Ella, "he let Ava carry that thing around."

Justine nodded and added one final thought, "Mrs. Dalton, I think they're both evil. I don't know your husband, but there could be other people out there like me."

"Call me Ella," she replied before a sudden realization hit her. What if Matthew and Adrienne had conspired together to kill Jake so they could be together? Ella had always felt the sweet persona put forth by Adrienne was a charade. Now she had someone else standing beside her who also believed she was capable of horrible deeds. Ella knew she had to find the truth, even if it meant her husband was not only a cheater, but a cold-blooded killer.

12

Chapter 12

The realization that Adrienne had most likely helped Jake commit assault and that her own husband had slept with someone capable of such evil made Ella feel physically sick. She braced her hand on the car for support and vomited in the parking lot. When she lifted her torso back up, Justine looked at her with concern and confusion. "Are you alright?" she asked.

"No," Ella replied succinctly. "I think Adrienne is involved in Jake's murder somehow, but what if Matthew helped her?"

"What?" asked a surprised Justine. "Why do you think that?"

"Adrienne and Matthew slept together," Ella told her without hesitation. "What if they wanted to be together and killed Jake?"

"I'm sure it's more than possible," Justine answered honestly. "But what do we do with that information?"

"I need to speak to our lawyer immediately," Ella replied as she dug her cell phone out of her purse and called Casey.

"Ella," Casey exclaimed with noticeable worry in her voice. "Where are you?"

"Still in the parking lot," replied Ella. "Listen, there's something I need to do, but can you give Matthew a message for me, please?"

"Certainly," said Casey.

Ella thought back to leaving the room without returning Matthew's declaration of love, which she felt was hollow. "Tell him I intend to find out the truth, no matter what," she whispered.

"Hon, you can't put yourself in danger or jeopardize the case," Casey said. Then she audibly exhaled and added, "You need to think about what this can mean for Matthew"

For some reason, she felt it necessary to keep Justine to herself for the moment. Although she could help Matthew's case, she wanted to do some investigating herself. If he had been involved with Adrienne, she wanted to protect her from him. "I am thinking about what this can mean for Matthew," said Ella. "But I also need to think of myself. I need to be sure Matthew is innocent, because, if he's not, I could be in danger."

"Ella, please, I can help you. Let's work on this together."

"Not right now, Casey," Ella answered. "I do need a favor though. Can you do what you can to get me back into the house? I can't stand living in the hotel anymore."

"You must be reading my mind," replied Casey. "I am on my way to meet with the prosecutor's office now to request discovery. I will get the house released. Trust me."

"Oh, I do," Ella said. "I know you're just protecting Matthew. Believe me, I want him to be innocent more than anything. I'll call you soon; I promise."

Ella ended the call with Casey and immediately dialed another number. "Hello," said the voice on the other end.

She didn't bother with the standard phone etiquette of saying hello back. Instead, she said, "I have some new information and need to talk to you right away."

"Ella, is that you?" asked Agent Dale Williams.

"Yes, it's me," she replied. "I am asking for a meeting, but I want to meet with you someplace where we're not being recorded. Will you meet me at my hotel?"

"You know I can't do that," replied Dale. "If you have something to tell me, come in and we'll meet with the DA."

"Dale," Ella stated, "you know I wouldn't be asking if this wasn't extremely important. Please, do this as my friend and not as an officer."

"Okay," a reluctant Dale replied. "I will meet with you if you agree that if I decide the information is important, you will come back to the station and put it on the record."

"Agreed," said Ella. "Room 215."

"I know," Dale replied in a teasing tone. "I'll be there soon."

Ella looked over at Justine and said, "Let's go."

"Who was that?" Justine asked.

"An old friend," said Ella. "Who just happens to be one of the detectives on this case."

Justine couldn't hide the surprise from her face. "You want to talk to a detective alone? Are you crazy?" she questioned.

"No, I think we can trust him," Ella replied.

"I hope you're right," Justine said as she started the car.

Ella and Justine sat at the end of the bed in the hotel room, waiting for the knock on the door to announce Dale's arrival. When they heard it, they looked at each other for strength before Ella went to the door to greet Dale. He walked through the door quickly, indicating that he did not want anyone to see him entering the hotel room of the wife of a charged murderer.

Dale might be uncomfortable, but no one would know it. His presence in the room was commanding. If Ella didn't know him, she would most likely be too intimated by him even to speak. But she did know him, and this experience seemed to make her stronger each day. In a very un-Ella-like manner, she initiated the conversation. "Dale, this is Justine..." she trailed off because she realized she didn't know her last name.

"Rivera," Justine interjected as she extended her hand to shake Dale's. "My name is Justine Rivera."

"It's nice to meet you," Dale said as he accepted her extended hand.

"Dale," said Ella. "We need to talk to you about Adrienne and Jake and some things they have been doing that may have caused someone to kill Jake."

He scratched his head as if deciding whether this conversation was a good idea. "Can we sit down and talk?" he asked.

"Yes," Ella said as she motioned for Dale and Justine to help her set up chairs around the small table in the room.

After they were seated, Dale set down the coffee he brought with him, looked at Ella and Justine, and said, "You first."

Ella nodded at Justine, who proceeded to recount what she had been subjected to at the hands of Jake and Adrienne and why she felt sure they had done the same thing to other women. Dale listened intently and asked hopefully, "Did you report it?"

Justine shook her head and answered, "No, I was so traumatized at the time, and I didn't think anyone would believe me. And I didn't want to cause pain for my family." She began to sob as she added, "I wish I had reported it. If I had, then it could have stopped them from hurting the next person."

Dale raised his eyebrows and asked, "Who did they hurt next?"

"We don't know, but there must be others," Ella reasoned. "What if a victim or one of their family members got revenge?" Ella looked at Dale to try to read his reaction but only saw a blank expression. She continued, "If anything, it shows that Jake would have other people who would want to hurt him."

Dale rubbed his eyes and said, "But, Ella, what about the gun, the bloody shirt, the text messages, and the failed lie detector test? If someone else did it, how do you explain that?"

"I can't explain it all yet," Ella said as she sat back, momentarily defeated. "But I believe there's something to this. There's more to this story, and I think you think there is too."

Dale gave her a half-smile. She had always been good at reading his emotions. He took a deep breath and said, "You're right. Something weird is going on."

Ella's face brightened, and she leaned toward Dale again, clutching his hands in hers. "Please, Dale, tell me what you're thinking," she begged.

She could see the internal conflict on Dale's face as he struggled with whether to reveal what he knew. "Ella," he said, "before I tell you anything, I need your word that you will not use this against me. I'm already being questioned about my impartiality in this case. If I give you information, my credibility is shot."

"I promise not to say anything," Ella said sincerely. "Justine and I only want the truth. She deserves justice, and so does Matthew."

Dale looked sympathetically at Justine, and Ella knew he was feeling empathy for her. Dale had always stood up for the underdog in high school, and he hated bullies. Adrienne and Jake were bullies, and Dale knew it.

She said, "Dale, you're a good man and a smart, honest police officer. I know you would never want to see the wrong person convicted and sent to jail."

He nodded and agreed, "No, I would never want to send an innocent person to prison." His eyes darted between the hopeful faces of Ella and Justine, and he said, "All I can tell you is that I'm still investigating. All the evidence points to his guilt, but I won't be happy until I am one hundred percent certain."

Ella couldn't breathe when she heard those words. She had believed Dale suspected something, but hearing him say it gave her hope, which she hadn't had since this began.

"Look," said Dale. "Your attorney will find out everything anyway. She's meeting with the prosecutor's office now to obtain the evidence. Just go through everything."

"I understand," Ella said. "Can I ask you a question?"

"Sure," Dale replied.

"Do you trust Agent Ulrich? She doesn't seem to like me very much."

Dale sat back and suddenly remembered something, "I know why she doesn't like you," he said. "Did you start seeing Matthew while he was dating Adrienne and threaten to ruin him if he didn't marry you?"

"What?" Ella exclaimed. "Absolutely not. Adrienne and Matthew had a one-night stand, and I didn't meet him until after that."

"Well, that's the story Layna was given, and she must have believed it," Dale explained. "Her husband left her for another woman, and she doesn't have any compassion for anyone who cheats."

"Who's Layna?" asked Ella.

"Sorry," Dale apologized, having realized Ella had never heard the agent's first name. "Layna is Agent Ulrich,"

Ella couldn't hide her dislike for Agent Ulrich in her facial expression. Dale saw this and added, "Ella, Layna is a good cop, and she's a good person. Trust me. She's just being taken in by someone she feels sorry for, but she'll see through her in time."

"I don't trust her," Ella said emphatically. "But I do trust you."

Dale picked up his coffee and swallowed the last of it before putting the cup back on the table and saying, "We'll figure this out, Ella. You will get justice." Then he turned to Justine and told her, "And so will you."

Dale stood, and Justine stood at the same time. "Thank you," she said as she hugged him. "If I had known I could have spoken to someone like you, I would have reported it when it happened."

He gently pulled away from Justine's hug and started to walk toward the door, but something was wrong. His balance appeared to be off, and he was struggling for breath as he tried to walk.

"Are you okay?" asked a concerned Ella.

"Yes, I'm fine," Dale reassured her. "I stood up too fast. It happens from time to time." He nodded back to Justine and then hugged Ella to him, "When this is all over, you and I need to talk," he whispered in her ear.

"Yes, we do," she whispered back.

Dale made his way out the door, but something about his gait still seemed off to Ella. She was worried about him, so she pulled back the curtains she had purposely left shut in the few days she had been staying here to watch him as he made his way to his car. It was evident to her that something was wrong, and she was about to run from the room to stop him from driving when he collapsed.

"Call 911," Ella screamed at Justine as she ran to help Dale.

13

Chapter 13

"Dale," Ella repeatedly yelled as she ran toward his motionless body. When she reached him, she dropped to her knees, picked up his head gently, and held his face next to hers. She could feel his breath on her face. The relief washed over her – he was still alive. Ella stroked his hair gently while saying, "Hold on, Dale, hold on." She could hear sirens in the distance, telling her help would soon be there. The wait was unbearable, but finally, the ambulance pulled into the parking lot, and the EMTs sprinted into action. Someone touched her shoulder and said, "Ma'am, we'll help him from here."

Ella reluctantly released Dale and stood back so they could take the actions necessary to save his life. "Do you want to ride with us?" asked an attractive, blonde EMT. Ella nodded and jumped into the back of the ambulance for the ride to the hospital. She sat on a side bench and held Dale's hand while they inserted an IV and pushed oxygen into his lungs. "Are you his wife?" asked the blonde EMT.

She was still confused and looked at the EMT in shock. "Am I his wife?" she repeated.

"Yes," said the EMT, "are you his wife? He's wearing a wedding ring."

"No, I'm not his wife," Ella replied. She had never noticed Dale wore a wedding ring. Her problems had encompassed her, and she had not once asked Dale about his personal life.

"Do you know who he's married to?" asked the EMT.

"No, I don't. I'm sorry, um," said Ella, attempting to read the EMT's name tag.

"Julie," interrupted the EMT. "My name is Julie. We need to reach his family."

"His name is Dale Williams," Ella said. "He's an agent with the Minnesota Bureau of Criminal Apprehension. If you call the police station, they can help you."

"Thank you," Julie replied as she picked up her radio to relay the information to another person who could locate Dale's family.

The ambulance pulled into the hospital's ER entrance, and the EMTs again jumped from the vehicle, removed Dale, and rushed him inside. Ella followed as closely as she could, but they stopped her once the gurney went through the doors to the treatment area. Julie stayed behind and told Ella, "Please talk to admissions. This is as far as I can let you go."

"Is he going to be alright?" Ella asked with begging eyes.

Julie looked at her and said sympathetically, "There's nothing I can tell you right now. You'll need to wait for the family to arrive, and they can talk to the doctors."

Ella nodded and proceeded to do as instructed. There wasn't much information she could provide to admissions other than Dale's name and date of birth. She didn't even know his home address. The admissions clerk didn't look surprised when Ella couldn't answer the most straightforward questions. After providing all the information she could, the clerk told her to sit in the waiting room if she wished to stay.

Ella sat on an uncomfortable seat. The chairs were not meant to be used for long periods. She thought about the last time she had been at a hospital and the chair she had sat in on that night. The chair was extremely comfortable and made for people who needed to wait for an extended amount of time. She remembered someone coming to move her from the comfortable chair into a private room to wait for the doctor to tell her the news she expected to hear.

The doctor had used the kindest words he could to explain that her mother had died despite their best efforts. He said to her, "Your mother was an amazing woman. I worked with Lillian on the hospital board, and she was so generous with her time and money. I'm so sorry for your loss."

Ella thanked him for his kind words and asked if she could stay in the private room for a moment by herself. "Of course. Take as long as you need," the doctor said, and he left the room to allow her to mourn her loss in private. She fell back into the chair, trying to will herself to cry, but the tears would not come. If anything, she was more angry than sad. Her mother's death was preventable.

She ran her hands through her hair, thinking back to the conversation she and her mother had with the oncologist just a few days ago. Her mother had asked Ella to go with her for support, and Ella happily agreed. She had a complicated relationship with her mother, but Ella loved her, and she wanted to be there for her when she heard the results of her biopsy.

As usual, her mother looked amazing when Ella picked up her for her appointment—dressed in her latest designer outfit, stiletto heels, makeup that made her appear twenty years younger, and her blonde hair perfectly styled. Only her mother could turn a visit to an oncologist into a social event.

Ella held hands with her mother while the oncologist gave them the news. "Lillian," he said, "the biopsy showed that the tumor is cancerous. The good news is that it is treatable." Ella felt her mother's grip on her hand tighten as the doctor explained the course of treatment included a double mastectomy followed by rounds of chemotherapy. "You can survive this," the doctor told her.

The elation Ella felt at the doctor's assurances that her mother would defeat the disease was short-lived. Her mother was silent on the drive home, and Ella did not want to push her into discussing the diagnosis. When they arrived at her mother's house, Ella started to open her door to go inside with her and offer any comfort she could. "What are you doing?" snapped her mother.

"I thought I could go in with you, and we can discuss plans for your surgery," Ella answered.

"I'm not having surgery," her mother scoffed. "There is no way I am letting them cut me apart and deform my body. And, before you even say anything, I won't do chemotherapy either. I will not lose my hair."

Ella was shocked. "Mother," she said, "you have to do the treatment so you can live. I want you to be here for your grandchildren."

Her mother looked at Ella with disdain. "Grandchildren?" she said sarcastically. "What are the odds you'll ever find a husband and have children? How many times have I told you that men are not attracted to girls like you? Men don't marry redheads. No one wants a redheaded child."

"I know you're in shock, so I will leave you alone to think about this some more," Ella said while holding back tears from her mother's attack.

Her mother exited the vehicle without another word, and that was the last time Ella had spoken to her. A few days later, she had received a call from the hospital that her mother was there, and Ella needed to come immediately. One of her mother's maids had found her unresponsive. She had taken multiple sleeping pills rather than face the treatment for her cancer. Her mother had allowed vanity to rule her life, and she had allowed it to rule her death.

Ella thought of the complicated relationship she had with her mother and the effect it had on her. She made it apparent that Ella was a disappointment to her, starting with the fact that Ella had inherited her father's red hair. "Red hair is so unattractive, Ella," her mother told her. "Why don't you dye it blonde?"

"But, Mother, you married a redhead," Ella pointed out to her.

"Do you think I married your father for his good looks?" she asked incredulously. "I married him despite his looks. Which is precisely why you need to hope you find a young man willing to make the same concession for you."

Her relationship with her mother had been the main focus in her sessions with Dr. McGregor. "Why do you think your mother treated you this way, Ella?" asked the doctor.

"Because I'm so ugly and stupid," Ella replied truthfully. "She was embarrassed by me."

"Why do you choose to believe that? I don't think you're ugly or stupid, Ella," the doctor told her reassuringly.

"My mother was so smart and beautiful," Ella replied.

"Ella," the doctor began. "You strike me as a very intelligent young woman.

You're also lovely, not only outside, but inside as well. You have an amazing capacity to love, and you care so much for other people. Those traits alone make you a beautiful soul."

Wanting to believe the doctor's words but still hearing her mother's voice echoing in her head, Ella replied, "I don't know, Dr. McGregor."

The doctor shifted in her seat. "Okay," she said. "Let's go in another direction. Tell me what you remember about your father."

Ella could feel the smile on her face as she remembered her father. "He was brilliant and very successful, which is why my mother married him," Ella said. "I thought he was extremely handsome, funny, and sweet."

"Were the two of you close?" asked the doctor.

"We were," Ella replied. "My father never wanted to leave me behind, even when my mother wanted to go on trips to exotic locations."

"Interesting," the doctor stated. "Do you think it's possible your mother was jealous of the closeness you had with your father? You already stated that you look more like him than your mother, and if your father loved you, maybe she was threatened by that."

"I can't imagine my mother being jealous of anyone, let alone me," Ella replied.

"Maybe you should think about that, Ella? It's possible your mother was projecting all of her insecurities onto you," the doctor stated.

"I guess it's something to think about," Ella stated.

"Ella, I want you to do something for me before our next session," Dr. McGregor told her. "I want you to write down something each day that you like about yourself."

"I don't think I can do that," Ella stammered. "I would have no idea what to write down."

"It can be anything," replied the doctor. "You can write down that you like your penmanship if you want. The purpose of the exercise is for you to realize that you do have admirable qualities."

"Are you Ella?" a male voice asked, bringing Ella back from her memories.

Ella opened her eyes to see another man she did not know. She marveled at how she had met more new people in the past few days than she had in the past few years. "Yes," she said.

"I'm Noah," he said, "Dale's husband."

"Dale's husband?" she repeated in a shocked voice.

"Yes, his husband," he chuckled, "I guess that you didn't know about me."

"No, I didn't," she answered truthfully. Everything suddenly made sense to Ella. Why Dale was never interested in her and never used her feelings to take advantage of her. *No wonder he had fought to maintain their friendship*, she thought. *Maybe I was the only person he trusted.*

"I'm sorry," she added, "I have had a lot of my mind the last few days." She rolled her eyes at her comment. Here she was, complaining about her problems, and the man standing in front of her had plenty of his own. "How is Dale?" she asked.

"They said it's touch and go right now," he answered while holding back tears. "He has a blood clot that cut off the blood supply to his brain. They might have to push thrombolytics to dissolve it if the other treatment doesn't work."

"I'm so sorry," Ella told him. "I don't know what happened. He seemed fine until just a few minutes before he collapsed."

"It's not your fault, Ella," Noah told her. "If I know Dale, he could have been standing there with a severed arm, and he would have told you he was fine."

Ella chuckled as she said, "Dale was always the macho man."

"He still is," Noah answered and took a drink of his coffee.

She studied Dale's husband. He has striking blue eyes, with extremely long, dark eyelashes that complemented his sandy blonde hair. Even though he was now sitting, she guessed him to be well over six feet tall, with a swimmer's build. She felt self-conscious sitting next to a man who was so attractive.

He must have sensed her studying him because he asked, "Sizing me up?"

Ella smiled, "Of course, what else do you expect me to do?"

Noah turned his head toward Ella and said, "I've been sizing you up too. You have no idea how nervous I was to meet the infamous Ella."

"The infamous Ella?" she asked.

"Yup," said Noah. "Dale has been talking about you for years. He said you were his best friend in high school and the sweetest person he had ever met. I hope you know how much you mean to him, Ella."

Ella felt instant guilt. She had let her selfishness interfere with what Dale had been trying to tell her when she ended their relationship. He wasn't in love with her, but he loved her and needed her friendship. "He must have felt so alone when I broke off contact with him," she said more to herself than Noah.

"I won't lie," Noah replied. "It did hurt him, but he always loved you. He had been talking about calling you right before all this happened."

"I'm a horrible person," Ella said. "He needed me, and I let him down."

"You're not a horrible person," Noah assured her. "You were young, and so was he. Dale was having a hard time back then being honest with himself, so how could he be honest with you?"

Ella felt another presence standing over them. "Noah," said Agent Ulrich, "can I talk to you?" She looked directly at Ella and added, "In private."

Noah followed Agent Ulrich to another section of the waiting room. Ella observed the agent, whose first name she now knew was Layna, put her hand on Noah's shoulder and begin talking to him quietly. She would glance at Ella from time to time to ensure she could not hear what they were saying. Ella could tell the conversation was causing tension for Noah, and he became animated when responding to Agent Ulrich. He looked at Ella and shook his head at whatever the agent had just told him.

Noah ended the conversation and sat down beside Ella again. "What's going on?" she asked.

"She doesn't trust you," he answered bluntly.

Ella was tired of being a friendly little introvert. She pointed at Agent Ulrich and yelled at her, not caring who heard, "Just for the record, Adrienne never had a relationship with Matthew. I never broke up anything."

"That's what they all say," Agent Ulrich said, smirking at Ella.

Noah looked over at the agent and was about to speak when the doctor came out to talk to him. Noah looked at Ella and said, "I need to go with him. You don't need to stay – it's going to be a long night."

Ella nodded and hugged Noah. "It was an honor to meet you," she told him.

"I'll be praying for Dale."

"Thank you," Noah replied. He turned, and his long legs carried him quickly across the room where he disappeared through the double doors.

Agent Ulrich stared at Ella from across the room. "Why don't you just leave?" she asked.

"I don't have a car with me, and I left the hotel so fast I forgot my cell phone," Ella answered truthfully.

For the first time, Ella saw the agent's face soften. "I'll give you a ride to your hotel," she said. "It's on the way to the station."

"I'd rather walk," Ella replied only because she would never allow herself to be alone with this woman. She angrily left the waiting room with the agent following her when she saw a familiar Mercedes pull into the parking lot. Casey was here to save her.

Casey rolled down her window and smiled at the agent. "Thank you so much, Agent Ulrich, but I will take care of my client from here."

Agent Ulrich looked at Ella and then at Casey, shrugged her shoulders, and said, "Whatever."

"I'm so glad to see you, Casey," Ella exclaimed. "How did you find me?"

Casey answered as she handed Ella her phone. "When you didn't call me back, I went to your hotel room and met a lovely young woman named Justine. She gave me your phone and told me what happened."

Thankful to Casey for saving her from a long walk back to the hotel, Ella said, "You saved me."

Smiling at her client, she replied, "That's what I do."

"Do you mind if we don't talk on the drive back to the hotel?" Ella asked. "I have a lot to process."

"No problem," Casey said. "Why don't you play a game or something to take your mind off things." She then quickly added, "But stay off your social media accounts."

Ella nodded. She didn't want to play any games but noticed a pop-up about an email from a genetic ancestry site on her phone screen. She had forgotten all about sending in her DNA to the site. Her mother had never discussed their ancestry, and she was anxious to learn about her heritage and if she carried any medically concerning genes. Ella had been so excited to try it, and she had talked Matthew into sending in his DNA and Ava's. She opened the notice, anxious to find something to take her mind off everything else for just a moment.

She looked at her ancestry first, a mixture of Eastern Europe and Great Britain. There were also matches to potential relatives already appearing. So many cousins she had never heard of or met. Next, she pulled up Matthew's matches and saw the names of his cousins and the uncle he hadn't talked to since his parents died. Ava's matches were next, but her results confused Ella. Why would all of Ava's relatives be different than Matthew's? She should have some of the same relatives since he was her father. Concerned, she looked at the health traits section for Ava. She scanned them until she saw something. Ava showed a high risk for hemochromatosis, having two abnormal HFE genes. Ella went back to Matthew's results and noticed he did not carry an abnormal HFE gene. She quickly went to Google to look up this disease she had never heard of before. According to what she found, a person can only develop hemochromatosis if they inherit two abnormal HFE genes, and only one abnormal HFE gene can be inherited from each parent. If Matthew didn't have an abnormal HFE gene, he couldn't have passed it to Ava.

Ella covered her hand with her mouth to stifle a scream. She removed her hand and placed it on Casey's arm. "Casey," she said with an unbelievable calm, "Either the DNA results are wrong or Ava is not Matthew's biological daughter."

14

Chapter 14

Casey almost lost control of the car after hearing Ella's words, "What did you say?" she asked as she regained command of the vehicle.

"I sent our DNA to one of those online sites a few weeks ago, and the results are in," Ella explained. "Ava has something called hemochromatosis, but Matthew isn't a carrier. It would be impossible for Ava to have two of the genes if Matthew is her biological father."

"Did Matthew have a paternity test done when she was born?" Casey inquired.

Ella shook her head, "No, he took Adrienne at her word. She told him there was no way anyone but him could be the father. Matthew has a brilliant mind, but he lacks street smarts and he thinks she is an honest person."

"That certainly sounds suspicious," Casey replied. "I had a feeling there was something off about this case. Adrienne had to know Matthew wasn't the father or at least that there was a chance he wasn't the father."

"I can't believe this," Ella said. "This is going to be hard for Matthew to hear, but I know it won't change how he feels. He loves that little girl so much."

"Look," said Casey, "let's go up to your room and discuss this more. This is a huge piece of evidence, but there are some questions I need to ask you. I received the evidence from the prosecutor, and there are other things I want you to review and give me your opinion on."

Ella and Casey walked into the hotel room to find a nervous Justine pacing. "Thank God," she exclaimed. "Is Dale okay?"

"He's stable right now, but it's touch and go," Ella replied. "There is a blood clot blocking flow to his brain, but they're cautiously optimistic that it will dissolve."

"Well, that's somewhat good news, I guess," said Justine. She looked over at Casey and said, "Hello, we didn't have time to have a proper introduction earlier. My name is Justine Rivera."

"Casey Klein," she replied. "It's a pleasure to meet you." She smiled at Justine and then turned her attention to Ella, "Can I talk to you in private for a moment?"

Ella followed Casey into the bathroom, out of the hearing range of Justine. "Are you sure you want to discuss this in front of her?" Casey asked.

"She's helping me," Ella replied. "She knows things about Jake and Adrienne that neither Matthew nor I do."

She could see the doubt on Casey's face, so Ella continued, "Listen, I will talk to Justine and see if she's comfortable telling you her story." She looked Casey directly in the eyes and said, "She has a purpose here."

"Okay, if you trust her, I will trust her," Casey replied.

"Stay here for a moment," Ella told her. She left the bathroom to talk to Justine, who agreed to share her story for the third time that day, and she entered the bathroom to speak to Casey. Ella waited patiently while Justine told Casey the horrible truth about the type of person Jake had been and Adrienne still was.

Casey emerged from the bathroom, wiping away her tears with a tissue, followed closely by Justine. She looked at Ella and said, "I have something I need you to see." She walked across the hall to her room and returned with stacks of documents that she dropped on the hotel room table. "This is everything I received from the prosecutor today. There's something that is bothering me, and I want to see if my suspicions are correct."

Casey rifled through the papers with the adeptness of a seasoned attorney. "Here it is," she exclaimed. "They gave me copies of the text messages that Matthew sent to Adrienne. Matthew admitted sending them, but he said they're being taken out of context."

Ella gingerly accepted the paper Casey was handing to her. She wasn't sure she had enough strength to read these for herself. It was hard enough to hear Agent Ulrich read them to her. Ella lowered her eyes to begin reading, and she could understand Matthew's point of view. If he and Adrienne had been drunk when they had slept together, the guilt must have been eating at him.

"What else do they have?" Ella asked.

"Something fishy is going on," Casey said. "I do believe your husband has been set up. It's all too convenient. I haven't known Matthew very long, but he strikes me as an intelligent person, and only a stupid person would consent to his home being searched and being questioned without an attorney. All of the evidence was practically gift wrapped for the police."

"Do you think this has something to do with Ava's paternity?" Ella questioned.

"I don't know," Casey answered truthfully, "but we need to find out."

Justine looked between Casey and Ella and asked with concern, "What is going on with Ava?"

Ella looked at Justine because they had never discussed Matthew's daughter. "How do you know about Ava?" she asked quizzically.

Justine appeared to be embarrassed by Ella's question. "I have been following Jake and Adrienne on social media for years," she replied sheepishly. "I wanted to find out everything about them, so I created a fake account, and, as far as I know, they had no idea it was me."

Ella's ears perked up. Justine's cyberstalking might be what they need to take their next steps. "Justine," she said, "I am going to tell you something, but you have to promise me you will not tell anyone. I don't want this to get back to Matthew until I can tell him."

"I swear," Justine promised.

"We have reason to believe that Ava is not Matthew's biological daughter, and Adrienne has been lying to him for over five years," Ella told her.

Justine nodded and said, "Wow, what a bitch. But I must admit, it doesn't surprise me. She's not exactly an honest person."

"No, she's not," Ella agreed. "We have to figure out a way to find the other man Adrienne was seeing when she became pregnant. He might have information about her or people that could be helping her."

"Do you know any of her family members?" asked Casey. "They might know who she was seeing then."

Ella shook her head, "The only family member I have ever heard mentioned is her mother, and she passed away before Ava was born."

Justine piped in, "Her mother isn't dead. I know exactly where her mother is."

"She told Matthew her mother died," a shocked Ella said. "Are you sure?"

"I'm positive," Justine replied. "I have researched this woman for years, and I probably know more about her family than I do my own. Her mother was in the Minnesota Correctional Facility in Shakopee for a little over five years. After she was released, she stayed in Shakopee."

Ella couldn't believe what she was hearing. Adrienne's mother had been in prison and was not dead. "Why was she in prison?"

"Drugs," Justine replied. "From what I found, her mother had left this part of the state and moved outside of Mankato about ten years ago. She got caught selling meth and was sent to prison."

"Any idea if they had a good relationship?" Casey asked.

"I don't know," Justine replied. "But, I would guess not since Adrienne is telling people her mother is dead."

"We need to drive up to Shakopee and visit her mother," Ella stated.

"Wait just a minute," Casey replied. "I have investigators for this type of thing. Let me send someone to talk to her."

"No," replied Ella. "If she's been in jail, she probably doesn't trust attorneys. She might open up more to Justine and me."

Casey started to argue but stopped herself and instead said to Ella, "Okay, you visit the mother. You can do that tomorrow, and I will go to the jail and question Matthew about the time frame of Ava's conception."

Ella opened her mouth to speak, but Casey cut her off. "I will be careful not to reveal anything to him, but, Ella, he has a right to know."

"I know he does," she replied, "but not right now. He's been through so much already, and I don't want to push him over the edge."

"I understand," Casey said. "It will be better if he learns it from you anyway."

The room grew uncomfortably quiet, and Casey sensed her opportunity to change the subject. "Ella, there are other things I want you to look over before we call it a night." She pulled out a picture and showed it to Ella. It was a white polo shirt with the name of Matthew's business and his name embroidered on it. It also appeared to be covered in bloodstains.

"Is this the shirt they found at our house?" Ella asked.

"Yes," Casey replied, "is it Matthew's?"

"It looks like Matthew's," Ella replied. "He has so many of these shirts because this is what he wears when he works onsite at a job."

"They sent it out for DNA testing," Casey said. "They're testing the blood to verify it's Jake's, but they're only planning to test for the perpetrator's DNA on the inside of the shirt. They think the name of the business and Matthew's name, plus verification of his DNA on the inside, proves it's his shirt."

"What do you think?" Ella asked Casey.

"I think the blood is Jake's, and the shirt is Matthew's," she replied with blunt honesty. "However, I want to do our own DNA testing."

"Testing for what?" Ella asked. "If it's Matthew's shirt, won't that testing hurt him?"

"Not necessarily," Casey answered. "I want to test it for touch DNA around the neck and arm areas. If it's not Matthew's DNA on those areas, it could mean someone else was wearing it when Jake was murdered." Casey paused before adding, "I need your permission to request that test because it is expensive."

"Spend what you need to," Ella said without hesitation. "If someone else killed Jake, then that person needs to be brought to justice."

"Guys, if Matthew didn't do it, and someone is going to all this trouble to make it look like he did, who and why?" Justine asked as she placed a hand on each of their shoulders.

Ella looked at Justine and then at Casey. "I honestly don't know," she said.

"We know that Adrienne isn't physically capable of committing the murder," Casey chimed in. "There's no way she could have gotten to the clearing with her walker."

"That's true," Ella replied, "and the only reason she would want Jake dead is to free herself for Matthew. Framing him would not benefit her."

"I think we're back to someone that Jake and Adrienne assaulted. If that person thought Matthew and Adrienne were having an affair, they could have killed Jake and framed Matthew," Justine reasoned.

"It's a possibility, I guess," said Ella.

"Anything is possible," Casey said as she looked at them both with seriousness in her eyes, "You both need to watch your backs. If someone is framing Matthew and they think you're on to them, they might come after you or anyone else in their way."

"Oh my God," said Justine. "What if that's what happened to Dale? If he was getting closer to someone, what if that person tried to hurt him?"

Ella frantically searched for her phone and called the phone number Noah had given her before checking on Dale. "Please answer," she said as the phone rang.

"Hello," said Noah.

"Noah, it's Ella. How is Dale?"

"They airlifted him to Sioux Falls. I'm driving there now."

"Noah," she replied, "I know we don't know each other very well, but I need you to listen to me." She took a deep breath and continued, "My lawyer and I think there's a possibility that someone is framing my husband and that Dale figured that out. We think someone might be trying to hurt him."

There was no response from Noah, but Ella could hear him breathing. "Noah, are you there?"

"I'm here," he finally answered. "Layna thinks the person trying to hurt him is you."

"I know she does," Ella replied. "Please, believe me, Noah. I would never hurt Dale."

"Ella," he stated, "I don't know why, but I do believe you."

"Thank you," she cried. "I only want Dale to be okay. Please tell the doctors to look for anything suspicious."

"I will," Noah said. "Thank you."

"Noah, I do love Dale. He was always my best friend," Ella told him.

"You can tell him that when he wakes up," Noah said with his voice full of optimism. "I'll call you if there are any updates."

"Thank you so much, Noah. I can see why Dale loves you." Ella said.

"I see why he loves you too," Noah replied. "Goodbye."

"Dale is being taken to Sioux Falls," Ella told the others after she hung up. "The doctors don't know yet what caused the clot."

Casey nodded and said to Ella, "There's nothing else we can do tonight. Why don't you go home and get some rest."

"I can't go home," Ella said. "They won't let me."

"The house is released," Casey replied with a smile. "You can go home."

Ella hugged Casey, "Thank you," she cried. She turned to look at Justine and said, "Want to come with me? I could use the company."

Justine smiled at Ella, knowing she didn't want company as much as she wanted an early start to visit Adrienne's mother. "I would love to," she said.

15

Chapter 15

Justine appeared to know the direction to the home Ella shared with Matthew. "You don't need directions?" Ella asked curiously.

"No," Justine said sheepishly. "I told you that I was doing online investigating, so I know exactly where Adrienne and Jake live."

Ella gave her an understanding nod and then saw the house come into view. She had always loved this house and the property that surrounded it. It allowed her the anonymity and isolation she desired while giving Matthew the woods and acres of land he desired. Their home was perfect, aside from the fact that their closest neighbors were Adrienne and Jake.

Justine pulled up to the gate, and Ella used the app on her phone to open the gate. As the car wound up the spiral drive, fear griped her that the house would no longer be their home. Would her feelings toward the house change due to the intrusion by multiple strangers? When the car stopped, Ella turned to look at Justine, "Would you mind waiting here for a moment? I want to look around first."

"Of course," Justine replied as she stared at the house. "You know, I've always wanted to see the inside of this house. I would drive by it from time to time and wonder about the people who lived here. The house looks so loved."

"It was," Ella said wistfully. "I hope it still is." Ella opened the car door, strode up the walkway, and placed her key in the lock to open the door. She turned on the first light she found and was surprised by what she saw.

Everything looked the same. The officers had not turned the house upside down; in fact, it looked like no one had been in the house at all. She calmly walked from room to room, inspecting for damage as she went. The house was intact, but her feelings toward it were not. When they built their home, they decided to make it a place where everyone could feel comfortable. Having grown up in a sterile home, where she never felt like she belonged, Ella wanted warmth in her house. The floor plan downstairs was large and open, with beautiful dark hardwood floors, vaulted ceilings, and large, overstuffed furniture complementing the farmhouse decor. She had let Matthew design the kitchen because he enjoyed cooking and she detested it. He kept the decor similar to the rest of the house and installed a large island with a granite top, white cupboards, and the same hardwood used in the rest of home. Ella had insisted on a large number of bedrooms because she envisioned a large family someday. Looking around, she saw all the furniture and decorations she and Matthew had picked out so carefully together and they no longer gave her comfort. They had decided not to hire a decorator because they wanted the house to reflect their personalities, and she loved everything they chose. But any attachment she had toward those items no longer existed. The most important part of the house was missing – Matthew. The house was still here, but the reason she loved it was gone. Ella wondered if they would be together again. Even if he was innocent of Jake's murder could she ever forgive him for his betrayal?

She steeled herself and walked to the door to wave to Justine to come in, and Justine eagerly jumped from the car. "Wow!" she exclaimed when she went through the door. "It's even more beautiful than I thought it would be." She looked at Ella, who was watching Justine in wonder. "Ella, she said, why don't we just get a good night's sleep and worry about Adrienne's mother when we see her tomorrow?"

"But I want to try to figure out if we're missing anything," Ella argued.

"I know you do," said Justine, "but you need some rest. I say we get some sleep and get on the road for Shakopee early tomorrow morning. If we stay up all night, we'll be falling asleep on the drive."

"I guess it makes sense," Ella replied. "We need to be strong when we face

Adrienne's mother tomorrow."

"Even if she's addicted to meth, she still has to be better than Adrienne," Justine said. Ella looked at Justine, saw the smile on her face, and let out a loud laugh. Before they knew it, they were both doubled over with laughter, barely able to breathe.

After catching her breath, Ella said, "Thank you. I needed that."

"Anything I can do to help," Justine said. "Do you want me to sleep on this couch?"

"Oh, my goodness, no," Ella replied. "This house has seven guest bedrooms, and you can have your pick."

Justine ran toward the open, spiral staircase. Her enthusiasm for choosing her room was like that of a toddler whose parents had just told her to pick out which room she wanted in a new home. She stopped on the third step, turned around to look at Ella, and said, "Come on. You need to go to bed, and I'm not going until you do."

Ella wordlessly followed Justine up the stairs and smiled when she decided which room she wanted after a brief debate with herself. "Goodnight," she said to Justine as she hugged her. "I don't even know how to begin to thank you."

Justine hugged her back tightly and replied, "Stopping Adrienne is all the thanks I need. Goodnight." She released Ella and jumped over the threshold into 'her' room.

Walking through the door into her and Matthew's bedroom was surreal. Ella had spent nights here alone before when Matthew traveled for work, but this was different. There was a genuine risk that Matthew would never be in this room or this bed again. Even if he didn't kill Jake, could she ever forgive him for having sex with Adrienne? She lay on the bed without pulling back the covers or changing her clothes and thought of the day she and Matthew moved into the house.

Matthew told Ella he wanted to show her the grove while the movers were bringing in the furniture. "You have to see it," he said.

"Don't you think we should stay here with the movers?" questioned Ella.

"No, they have it under control," Matthew replied as he pulled on her arm to move her toward the door. "I want you to see it. It's perfect for me to use as a running trail. Please, please, please."

"Okay, okay," Ella laughed.

"Great!" Matthew exclaimed as he took her hand and led her down the path to the wooded area between their home and Adrienne's. "Look over here," he said. "Think of what we can do with this. We could build a play area for Ava."

Ella glanced in the direction of the house they had built for Adrienne and Jake. "Are they moving in today, too?" she asked.

"Yeah," Matthew replied, "but I don't want to talk about them. I want to focus on my beautiful, amazing wife."

He could not contain his excitement as they reached the clearing leading into the grove; Matthew started to pick up his pace until he was almost jogging. "Look at the path that goes through here. This will be perfect for running. I'll be surrounded by nature on both sides." He closed his eyes to take in the smells and sounds around him, and Ella stared at the man she married. She didn't know how she managed to be lucky enough to find him.

"I love you," she said. Matthew turned to her, opened his eyes, and replied, "I love you too." He smiled and pulled her into the trees. "I have one more thing to show you, but you have to close your eyes."

Ella obliged the whim of her husband and closed her eyes. Matthew stood beside her and wrapped his arm around her shoulder, gently guiding her to what he wanted her to see. "Open your eyes," he said.

Opening her eyes, she saw that Matthew had cleared a spot in the woods and created a picnic for them. The obligatory blanket was on the ground, and the picnic basket sat on the edge of the blanket. Ella stood there with her mouth slightly open, amazed again at the wonder that was her Matthew. "I can't believe you did this," she said.

"You deserve nothing but the best," he told her as he lifted her off her feet and pulled her in for a deep kiss. At the end of the kiss, he winked at her and said, "After we eat, I thought we could christen the woods."

"Why should we wait until after we eat?" Ella replied playfully.

"I love you so much," Matthew replied as he moved his face toward hers for another long kiss. He gently removed her clothes and made love to her on the blanket he had so carefully laid out earlier. When they finished, they lay naked in each other's arms, admiring the nature around them.

"Look," Ella pointed excitedly, "it's a bald eagle."

Matthew sat up to get a better view of the majestic bird. "It's a whole family," he exclaimed. "Wow, I've never seen one that close up before."

"Me either," Ella replied. "They're beautiful. It looks like their nest is right there."

"Well, that decides it," Matthew said. "We're not touching these woods. They will stay just as they are so our eagle family can enjoy their home."

Ella nodded, and then a smell caught her attention. "Do you smell smoke?" she asked Matthew.

Matthew raised his nose into the air and took in a deep breath. "I do," he replied, 'but it's probably just someone burning leaves or something." He turned to Ella, obviously not worried about the faint smell of smoke, and said, "Are you hungry, or should we christen this place again?"

"Well, I'm not hungry," she replied as she placed her hand on the back of Matthew's head to pull him down to her. They were again lost in each other, neither of them noticing Jake putting out his cigarette, watching them from behind the trees, making plans for Ella.

Justine softly knocked on Ella's door, causing Ella's eyes to spring open. "Ella," she said, "are you awake?"

Ella rubbed her eyes and picked up her phone to look at the time. It was 6:30 AM. She couldn't believe she had managed to sleep for five whole hours. "I'm up," she said groggily.

The doorknob turned, and Justine walked into the room. "I'm going to take a shower. Do you want to leave around 7:30?"

"That works," Ella replied. "I will take a shower and meet you downstairs."

"Sounds good. I can't wait to use that shower," she said as she bounced out of the room.

Ella thought the same thing. After using the hotel shower for the past few days, her shower sounded very inviting. She made her way to the bathroom and let the hot water flow over her from every direction, trying her best to let it wash away her problems.

Justine was already downstairs when Ella made her way to the kitchen. There was a little spring in her step due to her ability to finally change shoes. Gone were the uncomfortable slip-on shoes she had grabbed on her way out the door on Saturday. In their place was a comfortable yet stylish pair of shoes that matched her outfit. It made her feel better, just a little more human than she had felt yesterday.

"Let's hit the road," Justine said. "It will take a few hours to get there. I already made coffee if you want to grab some to go."

"You read my mind," Ella told her as she reached in the cupboard for a travel mug. After filling her cup, she turned to Justine and said, "Well, let's do this."

The drive to Shakopee may seem long to people outside of the Midwest, but a two-and-a-half-hour trip was nothing to a Minnesotan. Matthew and Ella had made this drive many times. They took Ava to Valley Fair, the Mall of America, and, of course, they went to Vikings games. Normally, she would never venture to places with so many people, but she always felt stronger when she had them by her side. The few times she had to visit Minneapolis by herself for her father's charitable foundation board meetings, she hired a driver so she would not have to navigate the traffic by herself. She required all meetings be held at the hotel where she was staying so she never had to venture out. Straight from her home to the vehicle and the vehicle to the hotel. The less interaction the better.

Ella leaned her head against the window, staring at the familiar scenery as Justine drove. The motion of the car and the stress she had been experiencing overtook her, and she fell asleep again.

"We're here," Justine said.

Ella bolted awake. "I'm so sorry; I didn't mean to fall asleep," she told Justine.

"It's okay," Justine replied. "I'm happy you were able to get some rest."

The dilapidated house stood before them. Ella had never seen a home like it before. It appeared to have been painted white at one time, but now only a few flakes of the white paint remained on the wood siding. The windows were covered in ripped plastic, apparently put there years ago in an attempt to keep out the cold Minnesota winter air. Some of the windows were covered in plywood due to what she assumed was the broken glass. Addiction had a grip on this home and the people in it. What if Adrienne's mother was still making meth? They couldn't risk going inside a structure like that. The house intimated her instantly, but she didn't feel the typical anxiety setting in. Her newfound strength was helping her through this. "What do we do now?" she asked Justine.

"I guess we just have to go knock on the door ask for her," Justine explained.

Ella realized she didn't even know Adrienne's mother's name. "What is her name?" she asked.

"Stella Griffin," Justine replied.

"What if she refuses to see us?" Ella inquired. "What do we do then?"

"We'll have to leave and figure out another way to delve into Adrienne's past," Justine said succinctly.

"Just in case, I brought something to convince her," she replied as she patted her purse with the crisp one hundred dollar bills she brought with her.

Ella and Justine began to walk toward the door, but someone opened the rust covered screen door before they could reach it. "What do you want?" the woman yelled.

"We want to talk to Stella," Justine replied.

"Why?"

"Because we need to talk to her, that's why."

"Are you cops?" the woman questioned.

"No, we just want to talk," Ella answered.

The woman came through the door and stepped outside, and Ella knew instantly this person was Adrienne's mother. They looked similar, except for the age difference and the obvious toll the drug use had taken on Stella's face. She could almost be Adrienne's grandmother. Stella stopped and stared at the two young women standing in her yard. "Have a seat over there," she said as she pointed to the plastic patio tables and chairs.

"Stella," Justine said as she and Ella sat in the dirty chairs. "Please join us. We just want to talk."

She shuffled toward them, wearing ripped jeans, a dirty white t-shirt, and no shoes. "Do I know you?" she asked as she sat down.

"We've never met," Justine replied, "but we know your daughter, Adrienne."

The recoil from Stella was instant. "Adrienne?" she questioned. "How do you know that bitch?"

Any fear Ella had that Adrienne's mother would protect her were gone with those words. She found her confidence and said, "My husband is Ava's father."

Stella's yellowed eyes filled with water. "Ava," she said. "The only good thing either of us has ever done." Stella turned to Ella and said, "So, you're Ella, huh?"

"You know about me?" she asked in a surprised voice.

"Yeah, I know about you," Stella said as she looked Ella up and down. "Adrienne brought Ava to meet me once and told me all about you and how you stole the love of her life."

Ella shook her head. "I didn't steal anyone."

"Relax," Stella replied. "I learned a long time ago never to believe anything that comes out of that girl's mouth."

"Can you tell us about Adrienne?"

"What do you want to know?" she asked as she lit up a cigarette.

"We want to know if Adrienne was seeing anyone other than Matthew when she got pregnant with Ava," Ella replied bluntly.

Stella laughed loudly, which led to her coughing, the kind of deep cough only smokers get. "Don't tell me your husband was too dumb to get a paternity test? She actually convinced him he's the father?"

For some reason, Ella felt the need to defend her husband to this woman. "Matthew is very trusting, and he thinks all people are honest."

"Then he's a fool," Stella said bluntly. "Sounds like he deserves her."

"What do you want?" Justine asked Stella. "It seems to me that you want something in exchange for information on Adrienne."

Stella looked at Justine and said sarcastically, "Well, aren't you the smart one." She turned away from Justine and directed her follow-up comment at Ella, "I want money obviously, and I know you have it. Adrienne told me all about you." Stella smiled, showing Ella the effect meth had on her teeth.

She had to turn away from the smile. "Whatever you want. Just tell us who Adrienne was seeing."

"First things first there, Missy," Stella said. "You got a money transfer app on that fancy phone of yours? You go put money in my account, and then we'll talk."

"I'm not transferring you any money," Ella said. "I will give you cash, but I'm not transferring anything from my account to yours."

"Cash works just fine for me," Stella said as she reached out her hand anxiously. Ella took five hundred dollars from her purse and handed it to her.

After exchanging the money, Ella said. "Your turn."

"You want to know who Adrienne was seeing then? It would be a shorter list if I told you who she wasn't screwing around with. I know of at least three guys she was messing with when she got pregnant." Stella again darted her eyes between Justine and Ella before landing on Ella. "And none of them were your husband."

"What do you mean?" Ella asked.

"Adrienne chased after that guy for years, but he wasn't interested in her. She thought he was her golden goose. One night, she got drunk, called me, and told me the whole story. They never had sex. She got him drunk, took him home, and tried her best, but he passed out. She kept trying even after he passed out, but she couldn't get him to, shall we say, rise to the occasion. That didn't stop Adrienne from telling him they did, though. When she got pregnant, she took it as a sign that they belonged together." She looked directly at Ella again and added, "But by then he had already met you. Holy shit, does she hate you."

"I know that," Ella replied.

"Yeah, yeah,' Stella said as she waved her off. "Adrienne hasn't come to see me in years and doesn't care if I live or die. She was messing around with some married guy. He fixed her car for her; she couldn't pay him, so they worked out an arrangement. That's the only one whose name I know. Go find yourself a guy named Rob Hauen in Marshall. He's a mechanic and owns Hauen's Auto Repair. My money is on him to be the father."

Ella's head was spinning. Not only was Matthew not Ava's father, but Adrienne knew he wasn't. She was using them all for money. A small part of her was happy to know Matthew didn't have sex with Adrienne, but she was mainly devastated because of the pain this could cause her husband. No matter what the DNA said, Ella knew Matthew would still love Ava as his daughter. Even so, she dreaded having to tell him.

"You know that girl lives and breathes for sex," Stella said without prompting. "I don't know if she's addicted to the actual sex or the power it gives over the guys she lays. Did you know that she slept with her stepfather just to get back at me? That's why we stopped talking. I know she blames it all on me and tells everyone what a terrible mother I was, but she was a terrible daughter." Neither Justine or Ella replied, so Stella continued. "She lost her virginity when she was thirteen years old to some horny fourteen year old kid covered in pimples. My God, once she had sex, she never wanted to stop. After him, it was one boy after another. I finally had to move us to a new town so she could escape her reputation. That's when she met Matthew and decided he was the one she wanted."

"She's been trying to trap him since high school?" Ella asked.

"Yep," Stella replied. "Matthew didn't know about her reputation and she wouldn't date anyone in that town so he would think she was a good girl. That didn't stop her from going to other towns and finding random guys to screw though. That kid was stupid enough to believe she was a virgin and saving herself for marriage."

"You're saying Matthew thought she was respectable?" a perplexed Ella asked her.

"Yes, he did. She thought he was the one that could make her respectable. She never thought for one minute that spreading her legs for any guy that asked is what caused all her problems. For some reason, she thought that kid was all she needed to feel respectable."

"Thank you for your help," Ella said to Stella honestly. "We really have to get back on the road."

"You don't seem like a frigid bitch to me," Stella told her. She leered at Justine and smiled again with her rotten teeth. "You know, I'm about to get sent back to prison. If you ever get sent up, look me up because you and I could be good friends."

Ella saw Justine visibly shiver at the thought, and she placed a reassuring hand on her back to steer her away from Stella and back to the car. "What do we do now?" Justine asked.

"I guess we stop by Marshall on the way home and pay a visit to Rob Hauen," Ella replied.

16

Chapter 16

While Justine drove toward Marshall, Ella sat in the passenger seat and did a Google search for Hauen's Auto Repair in Marshall. She found the listing easily and saw it had an average review of less than two stars. Most of the reviews focused on the owner and how he disrespected his female customers. No wonder Adrienne was obsessed with Matthew – every other man in her life seemed to have severe personality disorders.

Ella's phone began to ring while she was still reading the reviews, causing her to jump. She could see Justine lean over to try to read the name on the caller ID. "It's Noah," she told Justine, who flushed and sat back in her seat.

"Noah," Ella answered, "how are you? How is Dale?"

"He's hanging in there," Noah said with a sigh. "Ella, I have to tell you something. They've run so many tests, and, well, they found something."

Ella's heart began pounding loudly, and she could see her shirt move with each pump. "What did they find?" she asked in a whisper.

"A genetic issue called Factor V Leiden, which most likely caused the blood clot," Noah replied. "No one was trying to hurt him. It was a natural occurrence."

"Are you sure?" Ella asked. "I think Dale knows Matthew didn't kill Jake, and whoever did could be trying to stop him from finding out the truth."

"Look," said Noah, "I know you don't trust Layna, Agent Ulrich, but she is a good friend of Dale's. She knows about the test results and now she knows you never tried to hurt him."

Ella's felt a little smug knowing the disapproving agent had been proven wrong, "Well, that's good at least."

"Yes, it is," Noah answered. "I told her that Dale trusts you, and if he trusts you, I trust you."

"Thank you," Ella replied. "I don't mean to sound like I'm disappointed that someone didn't hurt Dale. Please understand that I care about him and I was convinced someone had hurt him to cover up what they did to Jake."

"I know. You're a good person, Mrs. Ella Dalton," Noah told her. "I'm going back to Dale's room now, but I'll call you if anything changes."

"Be careful," Ella told him.

"You too," Noah replied.

Justine looked at Ella, her eyes full of questions, imploring Ella silently to tell her what Noah had said. "Dale is doing better," she told her. "But his test results show no one was deliberately trying to hurt him. He has some genetic disorder, which probably caused the blood clot."

"So, that clue helps us not at all," Justine said with exasperation. "I feel like we're going around in circles."

"Well, maybe we can turn a corner soon," Ella said as she pointed out the windshield. "There's Hauen's Auto Repair."

Justine parked in the tiny parking lot, reached under her seat, and pulled out a small revolver. Ella was shocked to see the gun and asked, "What is that for?"

"I'm not going in there without protection," she said. "Who knows what that guy is capable of, and I am not going to be anyone's victim again."

"Are you sure that's necessary?" Ella asked her.

"Don't worry," Justine replied as she placed the small gun in her handbag, "I have a concealed carry permit, and this will stay in my purse as long as he behaves himself. Are you ready?"

"Give me a moment," Ella told her. She could feel her anxiety rising and needed to complete the 5-4-3-2-1 method before facing the man who could be Ava's biological father. After feeling her breathing return to normal, Ella told Justine, "Okay, I'm ready."

Ella and an armed Justine walked through the front door, the reindeer bells alerting the employees to their arrival. A man who looked to be in his mid-fifties appeared. He was balding and had a giant beer belly. His work shirt was tucked into his pants, and Ella saw suspenders holding up his too small slacks. His large stomach made the suspenders necessary as the waistband of his pants was sitting under his belly. Ella hoped with every fiber of her being this man was not Ava's father. She searched his shirt until she saw a name sewn into the right-hand pocket. It read 'Rob'.

Rob looked at Ella and Justine and let out a low whistle. "What brings you fine ladies here today?" he asked. "Does your car have a boo-boo?"

Ella felt immediately repulsed by this man. How could he be the father of such a sweet, adorable little girl? It didn't seem possible.

"Do you know Adrienne Griffin?" Justine asked bluntly.

The question caused Rob to take a subconscious step back. "Are you from the state?" he asked.

"No," Ella said as she took over questioning from Justine. "We just need some information about Adrienne Griffin. Her husband was recently murdered."

"Are you cops?" he asked.

"We're not cops," Ella said. "But we need your help."

"If you're not cops, then I got nothing to say," Rob told them. "You can see yourself out, and I'll enjoy the view as you leave."

"Listen, you piece of crap," Justine said, holding her pointed finger inches from his face.

Sensing the need to diffuse the situation, Ella put her hand on Justine's arm and pulled it down. She wasn't about to start a physical confrontation, but she was tired of being nice. "How about we leave here and go visit your wife? I'm sure she would be very interested in hearing about Adrienne," Ella told Rob. "And, after we're done talking to your wife, we can talk to the Secretary of State about your questionable business practices."

Rob held up both hands in front of him, "Slow down there, sweet cheeks," he told her. "There's no reason for anyone to get hostile. I'm sure we can work out some type of arrangement. If you want to know what happened between Adrienne and me, I can certainly show you."

The leer he gave her when he said those words made Ella's stomach turn. "Do you talk like that to your daughter?" she asked sarcastically.

"What daughter?" he asked. "I only got sons. When I plant my seed, I grow boys."

"Does the name Ava mean anything to you? She was born about nine months after your arrangement with Adrienne," Ella stated, using air quotes when she said the word arrangement.

"Hold on; you're not putting any kid on me," he exclaimed. "There ain't no way I'm that kid's father. Is that what Adrienne told you?"

"Yeah, she wants to get her hands on all this," Justine said sarcastically, gesturing with her arms at the rundown storefront.

"I don't like you," Rob told Justine. "Someone needs to teach you some manners."

"*Pendejo*," Justine said back to him.

Rob looked at Justine with complete confusion, "Say what? Speak English."

"Why did you say you can't be her father?" Ella asked, once again trying to create calm.

"Because I never had what you decent folk would call conventional sex with that woman. We had an arrangement to pay off her car, and our arrangement was strictly oral," he said with a wink.

"Yuck," Justine said loudly.

"Maybe you should try it," a defensive Rob said to Justine, "you might like it."

"Just stop with all the stupid sexual comments," Ella told Rob. Neither of us has the slightest bit of interest in you. We just need you to answer another question, and we'll leave you in peace."

"What do you want to know, sweetheart?" Rob asked as he lifted his gigantic stomach on the counter to lean closer to Ella. He slowly opened his mouth and rubbed his tongue over his lips. Ella was afraid she would become physically ill if she had to spend any more time with this sorry excuse for a man.

"Do you know who else Adrienne was seeing then?" Ella asked him, eager to get the answer and leave.

Rob stroked his chin, pretending to be thoughtfully thinking. "I might. What's in for me?"

Ella pulled a hundred-dollar bill out of her wallet and handed it to Rob. "This is all I have with me. Take it, or the next thing I do is call your wife."

"Okay," said Rob. "She had a guy with her when she came to pick up her car. He dropped her off, and she called him Christian."

It wasn't much information, but it was better than nothing. Ella refused to thank this man, so she turned to leave and motioned for Justine to follow her.

"I might have written down his license plate number," Rob yelled behind her. "If you can magically find another hundred dollar bill in that fancy purse of yours."

Ella reached into her bag, pulling another crisp bill from her wallet. "Give me the license plate number, and I will give you this."

Rob reached under the counter and produced a recipe card holder from which he pulled an index card. "Here it is," he said to Ella while waving it in the air. "Come and get it."

Justine grabbed the hundred dollar bill from Ella's hand and started walking toward Rob to retrieve the paper. "No, no, no," said Rob. "I'm only giving this to Red."

Ella reluctantly took the money from Justine, walked over to Rob, laid the bill on the counter, and grabbed the index card. Rob rubbed his thumb on Ella's hand and said, "I really am a nice guy."

She grabbed the card away from him. "You're disgusting," she said to him as she quickly turned away and ran toward the door Justine was holding open for her. Before exiting, Justine turned back to Rob and flipped him off.

They ran to the car, locked the doors, and sped away as fast as they could. "What a piece of shit," Justine declared.

"I need to take a shower. Or three," Ella stated as she hugged her knees to her chest, struggling to breathe. She closed her eyes in an attempt to recover from the anxiety-inducing confrontation she had just endured.

Justine pulled the car to the side of the road and reached for her phone with shaking hands. "What are you doing?" Ella asked.

"Reporting him to the state," Justine replied. "That guy is a sexual predator, and someone needs to stop him."

"I understand why you feel that way," Ella replied, "but can we please drive home so we can find Christian?"

"That's under control," Justine said and pressed the call button for one of her contacts. "Hey, girl, how are you?" she said to the person she called. Justine paused while the other person talked and then said, "I need to ask you a favor. Can you look up a license plate for me?" She paused again before saying, "Great." Justine read the plate number to the person and waited for a few moments before stating, "Christian Swenson, got it. Address?" Justine typed the address into her vehicle navigation and told the person, "You're the best. Talk to you soon."

"Do I even want to know?" Ella asked.

Justine looked at Ella and shrugged, "I have a friend who's a skip tracer. Easy enough to find someone with a license plate number."

"Where does this Christian Swenson live?" Ella asked.

She smiled and replied, "Mankato. We can track him down yet today."

Ella grew nervous again. Rob was so disgusting. It was clear Adrienne didn't have high standards as long as she got something in return. She was relieved that Rob could not be Ava's father, but how bad was Christian Swenson going to be?

The drive from Marshall to Mankato was relatively short, and they sat in front of the house purported to belong to Christian Swenson in about two hours. It was a small house but nicely maintained. The people who lived here must have some compassion because they obviously cared for this home. Ella saw Justine reach for purse, which still contained the revolver, and she stopped her. "How about I go in alone this time," Ella stated rather than asked.

"You don't want me to come with you?" she asked in a shocked voice.

"I think this is something I need to do on my own," Ella explained. "Why don't you use this time to report that creep?"

"Are you sure?" Justine asked her. "You didn't seem to handle the last one very well."

"I'm sure," Ella replied. "I have a feeling this man won't be like the last one."

Justine patted her purse and said, "Come get me if you need me."

"I will," Ella promised. She exited the car, walked to the front door, and rang the doorbell. She could see inside the house from the small window in the door, and she saw a man, who appeared to be in his forties, walk toward the door. He was dressed casually, in jeans and a t-shirt, had salt-and-pepper hair, and a handsome face. She could see him look through the window of the door to determine who was ringing his doorbell.

He opened the door, looked at Ella, and declared, "You're Matthew Dalton's wife."

Ella was surprised that he knew her. "Have we met before?" she asked.

"No," he sighed, "but I have heard many stories about you. Please come in."

She looked back toward the car and saw Justine watching her with concern. She gave Justine an upward head tilt to tell her that everything was okay and entered the home of Christian Swenson.

He gestured toward a chair for Ella to sit down, and she obliged. "What do you want to know about Adrienne?" he asked.

Ella was taken aback by his bluntness. "Were you seeing her when she became pregnant?" she asked.

"I was," he answered truthfully. "Broke up my marriage and ruined my family because of my stupidity."

"I don't know how to ask this gently, so I will just ask," Ella replied. "Are you Ava's father?" she asked.

Christian shook his head, "No, I'm not."

"Pardon me for being blunt, but how do you know you're not?" Ella asked.

"Because I had a vasectomy after my youngest daughter was born sixteen years ago," he said without hesitation.

Ella's heart sank again. She was convinced identifying Ava's father was the key to finding out who killed Jake. How was she ever going to find him now?

"But I think I know who Ava's father is," he told her.

The words caused her to start, "Who?" she asked.

"My son," Christian replied.

17

Chapter 17

Ella looked at Christian with surprise and asked, "Did you say your son?"

"Yes," he said with a bowed head. "Connor Swenson."

"I don't understand," Ella said. "Wouldn't he be too young to be Ava's father?"

"Not for Adrienne," Christian declared. "For you to understand this, I need to explain what happened between Adrienne and me. I know your husband is charged with killing Adrienne's husband, and I want to help you. Every part of me believes there is more to the story. Maybe helping you will allow me to free myself from some of my guilt."

Ella nodded her intent to be quiet and listen to his story.

"Connor was only sixteen when I started my affair with Adrienne," Christian said. "I don't know what I was thinking. Her car had broken down, and she was stranded on the side of the road, so I stopped to help her. She was crying that she didn't have any money to pay for a tow truck, and I foolishly took pity on her. I paid for the tow to a repair shop in Marshall and offered to drive her home, even though it was two hours out of my way. The affair started that night. She initiated it, but I should have been strong enough to tell her no."

He shook his head in disbelief before continuing, "There was something about her that seemed so wounded, but at the same time she was so seductive.

I felt like I had to protect her and eventually I became addicted to her. Before I knew it, I was paying for her rent and giving her money every month to pay her other bills. When I finally came to my senses, I broke it off with Adrienne, hoping to keep my secret and save my marriage and family. Adrienne was furious, and she screamed that she would make me pay for leaving her."

Ella could sense that Adrienne had kept her word to make him pay. "What did she do?" she asked.

"First, she took all the pictures she had of us together and showed them to my wife. She even sent her receipts to show all the money I had given her. My wife kicked me out, and my kids refused to talk to me. My entire life fell apart." Christian shook his head and said, "I probably deserved it; I know I deserved it, but Connor didn't."

He had to pause to collect himself before continuing, "Next, she set her sights on Connor. Adrienne sent me pictures of the two of them together along with a mocking message daring me to come find them. Wanting to save my son, I tracked his cell phone, and I caught them together in his car. To this day, I don't know how she approached him or where they met, but they were in his car having sex. I confronted them, and Connor yelled at me that I was a terrible father and that he never wanted to see me again. Adrienne sat there with a smirk on her face and gloated."

"Why didn't you press charges?" Ella asked. "Isn't that statutory rape?"

"That's what I thought too," he answered. "But the age of consent in Minnesota is sixteen. There was nothing I could do legally. I tried to call my wife and tell her what was happening, but Connor told her I was lying about him being with Adrienne, and she believed him over me. Not that I could blame her."

"Where is Connor now?" Ella asked.

"I don't know," he answered tearfully. "He never spoke to me again. The only thing I know is that he left town right after his eighteenth birthday."

"Why do you think he's Ava's father?" Ella inquired.

"Adrienne called me about two months after I caught her with Connor," Chris explained. She told me she was pregnant, and she tried to convince me the baby was mine. I knew it couldn't be mine, so my next thought was that it was Connor's. Adrienne was furious that she wouldn't get any money out of me because she knew she wasn't going to get any money from Connor."

Christian broke down, looked at Ella, and said, "I'm so sorry for everything I did. If it weren't for me, Connor would have never met her."

A knock on the door broke the tension, and Ella could see Justine looking through the door. "That's my friend," Ella told him. "It looks like she's ready to go."

Ella stood to leave, and Christian grabbed her hand. "I never changed my phone number, just in case Connor wanted to call. She kept messaging me and sending me pictures of you. So many comments about how evil and ugly you were and how she couldn't believe Matthew wanted to marry you. Promise me you'll be careful. I think she's a sociopath, and I know how much she despises you. She thinks you stole her life."

"I will," Ella promised as she went to the door to meet Justine. She looked back at Christian and asked, "Does Connor know Ava is his daughter?"

He shook his head, "I don't know, but I doubt it. If he knew he had a child, he would want to be part of her life."

Ella and Justine were again seated in the car on their last road trip of the day. "Do you think your skip-tracing friend can help find Connor?" Ella asked.

"I can ask her," Justine said. "He might be hard to track down, though. We don't know anything other than his name, and it's a common name. Would he be about twenty-one or twenty-two now?"

"My guess is that he's twenty-two," Ella replied.

"I'll call her tomorrow," Justine said. "She would have left work for the day already."

Lost in her thoughts about Ava and the boy who most likely fathered her, Ella turned her head to look out the window, even though it was dark, and she couldn't see anything. No matter how this turned out, she must ensure that Ava was safe and part of Matthew's and her lives. She thought back to her favorite day with Ava.

Shortly after Ava's fourth birthday, she was with Ella and Matthew for her regular visitation. While they were eating dinner, Matthew's work phone rang. After he hung up, he said, "A client has a virus on their PC. I have to go help them quick. Will you two be okay without me?"

Ava and Ella looked at each other, smiled, and yelled, "Girl's night!" simultaneously.

"I'll take that as a yes," Matthew laughed. He kissed Ava and then Ella, telling them he would be back as soon as he could.

The evening was fun, but Ella wasn't sure who had more fun, she or Ava. They made cookies, taking turns to steal a bite of the batter and pretending to be caught by the other, and each of them ending up covered in flour. After taking a necessary bath, they settled on the sofa to watch a princess movie, singing along with the songs. Ella looked over at Ava while the film was playing and could see her eyelids getting heavy. She turned off the movie and said, "Okay, time for bed."

"But I'm not tired," Ava protested in a sleepy voice.

"You might not be tired, but I am," Ella told her while she extended her arms over her head to exaggerate a yawn. "Can you go to bed so I can go to bed?"

"I guess, but only because you're tired," Ava said as she lifted her arms, indicating to Ella that she wanted to be carried upstairs.

She brought the sleepy Ava to her bedroom and lay her down on her bed. "I'll get your pajamas."

"Don't forget Teddy," Ava instructed her. "I can't sleep without Teddy."

"We must have left him downstairs," Ella told her after scanning the room and not seeing the stuffed bear. "You change into your PJs, and I'll get Teddy."

Ella found Teddy on the downstairs sofa, caught between two cushions, and quickly ran back upstairs. When she entered Ava's room, she was sitting on her bed, now wide awake. "Teddy," she exclaimed.

"Okay, you have Teddy, so now it's time for bed," Ella said.

"But I'm not tired," Ava replied.

Ella pulled back the covers on Ava's bed, trying to come up with a plan to return Ava to her sleepy state. "Why don't you tell me about Teddy," she said. "How did you two meet?"

Ava's face brightened, "He was Daddy Jake's," she replied as she hugged the bear close to her. "Daddy Jake said Teddy was his best friend when he was a little boy. He told me that Teddy has special powers to watch over me."

"He sounds like an extraordinary bear," Ella said. "It was nice of Jake to give him to you."

She nodded enthusiastically, held Teddy out in front of her, and said, "He is. I love him so much."

"It looks to me like Teddy is tired," Ella cajoled. "I think he wants to go to sleep."

Ava turned serious, looked at Ella, and asked, "Can I tell you a secret, Ella?"

"Sure," Ella told her. "You can trust me."

"I wish you were my mommy," Ava said with downcast eyes.

Ella's breath stopped because she had to think about how to reply. "Honey, you know I'm not your biological mommy, but I will always be here for you when you need me."

"Can I call you mommy?" Ava asked earnestly.

"Of course," Ella said with joyful tears. "If that's what you want to call me."

"I do," Ava said. Then she lowered her voice to a whisper and added, "But not when my mom is around. She won't like it."

"It will be our secret," Ella promised.

"Goodnight, Mommy," Ava said as she kissed Ella goodnight. "Can you sleep with me?"

"Of course," Ella said before she hugged Ava to her. "I love you."

"We're home," Justine said. "Can you do the gate code again?"

Justine's words pulled Ella back to the present. For some reason, she felt trepidation about letting Justine back in her home. She had let her stay the night before, but that was before the events of the day and her new knowledge that Justine carried a gun. Ella forced her concerns to the back of her mind and opened the gate.

"I think it's best if we just go to bed and get some rest," Ella said. "After everything that happened today, I am exhausted."

"Okay," Justine said with a shrug.

When they walked into the house, Ella observed Justine's reaction to the house again. Last night, she thought it was cute how excited Justine was about the house, but now it was unnerving her. She looked at Justine and knew she had to talk to her.

"Justine," she began, "can I ask you something?"

"Sure," she answered.

"Did you bring the gun inside with you?" Ella asked.

She averted her gaze and said, "I did. I'm sorry, but I feel safer when I have it with me."

"I would feel safer if you left it in the car," Ella told her.

"Are you scared I'm going to do something to you?" Justine asked incredulously.

"A little," Ella answered honestly. "You didn't tell me about the gun last night, and you seem a little too excited about being in my house."

"I would never do anything to hurt you," Justine said in a choked voice. "I'm sorry if I'm making you uncomfortable. I never meant to. I will leave if you want me to."

"It's not that I want you to leave," Ella told her. "But I need to know what your intentions are."

"My intentions?" Justine asked. "I don't have any intentions toward you. The only thing I intend to do is help you prove your husband's innocence and stop Adrienne."

"How do you intend to stop Adrienne?" Ella asked in a voice barely above a whisper, scared of the answer.

Justine sat on the couch and put her head in her hands. "I don't know anymore," she cried.

Ella sat beside her and rubbed her arm gently. "Tell me what you're thinking, Justine."

Raising her face, Justine looked squarely at Ella and said, "I planned to kill myself."

"What?" Ella said as she pulled away from her. "Did you plan to kill yourself but killed Jake instead?"

"No, I promise I didn't kill him," Justine declared. "I had planned to kill myself, but I'm Catholic, and suicide is a mortal sin, and I would never be able to ask for forgiveness." Justine broke into full sobs and continued, "If I killed myself, they would win, and they could go on hurting other women. When I say I want to stop Adrienne, I swear I only mean that she belongs in jail." Justine looked at Ella with pleading eyes, "I could never hurt anyone."

"Have you ever talked to anyone, like a therapist or a priest, about what you went through?" Ella asked her.

"No. We could never afford a therapist. I wasn't comfortable talking about it to our priest."

Ella felt guilty for doubting her new friend. She couldn't imagine the trauma Justine had been through and then having to face it all by herself. "When this is over, I want to introduce you to an amazing therapist. I would be happy to pay for it."

Justine gave Ella a stunned look. "I couldn't ask you to do that."

"You didn't ask," Ella told her. "No one should have to endure what you have alone."

"Can I confess something to you, Ella?" Justine asked her.

"Of course," Ella told her. "I am here for you."

She took a deep breath and began, "My mom died when I was three years old, and I don't remember her. You're what I always envisioned my mom was like. I mean, I know you're way too young to be my mother, but you are such a good person. Having a mom like you could have made such a large difference in my life." She paused, looked at Ella, and said, "That's why I was so excited about staying in this house with you. My dad was a good dad, but he worked so hard to try to make ends meet. My two sisters and I had to share a tiny bedroom, and the thought of that big bed and room all to myself, well, it made me feel like I was experiencing the life I fantasized about when I was a little girl."

Ella was silent because she didn't know how to respond to what Justine had revealed. The silence continued until Justine told her, "Did you know I had a full scholarship to college?" Ella shook her head, and Justine continued, "I was so determined to make a better life for myself and my family. I worked as hard as I could all through school and earned that scholarship." Stopping to catch her breath, tears now running down her cheeks, she continued, "I quit college after what they did to me. There was no way I could face living in a dorm around all those students." Justine looked squarely at Ella when she said, "When they did that to me, it felt like they stole my future. So, I can leave if you want me to, but please know that I truly want to help you, Matthew, and Ava."

"No, you don't need to leave," Ella told her, now overwhelmed with emotion.

Justine gave her a half-smile, reached into her purse, and pulled out the revolver. Ella held her breath until Justine said, "Here, I don't want this anymore. I've been using it as a crutch for too long."

She reluctantly took the gun from Justine. "I'll hold onto this for now," Ella told her as she carefully placed the revolver temporarily into her own handbag.

The sound of the gate buzzer caused them both to jump. Ella looked at the security camera and saw Casey, so she opened the gate to let her in.

"Where have you been?" Casey yelled as Ella opened the door for her. "I've been calling you, but you wouldn't answer your phone."

Ella rolled her eyes at herself and replied, "I turned off the ringer when I was talking to Christian and forgot to turn it back on."

"That's not important; the question was rhetorical," Casey told her. "I have some big news."

18

Chapter 18

Ella's heart skipped, and the exhaustion from the day seeped away, "What happened?" she asked Casey excitedly.

"They found new evidence," Casey replied breathlessly. "Before they released the house back to you, they got a tip and did a cursory check of the woods. You won't believe what they found."

"For God's sake, Casey, tell me," Ella said with exasperation.

"I'm sorry," she replied. "They found a homemade silencer made out of a water bottle with a fingerprint on it." Casey paused for dramatic effect and added, "It's not Matthew's fingerprint."

Ella's mind raced, and she asked, "What does that mean?"

"Well, it means reasonable doubt about Matthew's guilt is creeping into the minds of the police," she replied. "You'll never believe who found it."

"Who?" Ella asked.

"Agent Ulrich," Casey replied. "From what I heard, she was pretty excited when she found it, but her excitement died when she was told the fingerprint didn't match Matthew." She looked at Ella and added, "She also found the fingerprints you gave and compared them to try to find a match, thinking you helped him."

Ella looked at Casey, remembering she had been fingerprinted when she was at the police station. "Boy, she must really hate me," she said as Justine came to stand by her side.

Casey laughed and said, "I would have loved to see her face when those fingerprints didn't match either you or Matthew."

The thought of Agent Ulrich standing there with a confused look on her face did make Ella smile momentarily, but her focus swiftly turned back to her husband. "But what does this mean for Matthew? Will they let him out of jail?"

"No, not yet," Casey said. "But we have a much better chance of getting bail for him. I'm going to file for a new hearing based on new evidence."

Ella cupped her hands over her mouth and nose and said, "I can't believe this. This proves someone set Matthew up, but who?"

"Slow down," Casey told her. "They won't see this as proof that Matthew was framed. If anything, they might assume he had an accomplice."

Ella realized Casey had not heard the events of her and Justine's day. "Casey, we think we found Ava's father," she blurted out.

"What?" Casey said with surprise. "Who is it?

"His name is Connor Swenson," Ella told her. "He was only sixteen years old when Adrienne started sleeping with him." She paused and added, "The only problem is that we have no idea where he is."

"I'll get my investigators to start looking for him right away in the morning," Casey said authoritatively.

"There's no way I'm going to be able to sleep tonight. I can't wait until morning; I have to help Matthew now," Ella said determinedly to Casey and Justine.

"There's nothing we can do tonight," Casey said.

"Maybe we need to search the house," Justine said. "If they missed the silencer in the woods, what if they missed something in here?"

Casey looked at Justine and Ella and said, "It's not a bad idea."

"What if we find something that implicates Matthew?" Ella asked.

"I guess we'll deal with that when, and if, it happens," Casey stated.

Slapping her hands together, Justine said, "Well, let's get started."

Ella, Casey, and Justine climbed the stairs to begin the search for anything that could help prove the truth. "I'll start with the hall closet. Justine, you take that room, and Casey, you take that one," Ella directed as she pointed at the bedrooms.

Casey and Justine left for their respective search locations, and Ella opened the door to the hall closet. It contained everyday household items, extra blankets, pillows, and sheets. There was one item that caught Ella's eye, their wedding album. She wasn't sure how it ended up in this closet, but she couldn't resist the pull to open it and look at the pictures. They had a small wedding; neither Matthew nor she had any living parents. Matthew had an uncle, but he didn't speak to him anymore. When she started planning the wedding, she knew she didn't want anything ostentatious. That wasn't her style or Matthew's. She laughed to herself, thinking of her trying to throw a big wedding with several bridesmaids; she didn't even have any friends or family to fill the maid of honor role. The justice of the peace's wife and son had to do the honor of witnessing the vows. Even though it wasn't a society page wedding, it was the best day of Ella's life. She ran her finger lovingly over Matthew's face in the picture of them smiling at each other."

"Soon," she said to the picture. "We'll have the answers soon."

"Ella, come here," yelled Casey from the other room, bringing her back from her wedding day memories. She jumped up, running to the room to join Casey. When she entered the room, she saw Justine sitting on the floor with a box open in front of her. There sat Teddy.

She saw Justine look down at the bear and shudder. "Are you okay?" she asked her.

"I think so," Justine said. "That - that bear looks familiar. I think it was in the room when Jake and Adrienne..." Unable to finish her sentence, Justine jumped up and ran from the room. Ella could hear Justine in the bathroom become physically ill.

"Okay," Casey said. "What is it about this bear?"

"It's the bear Justine remembers from the night Jake assaulted her," Ella replied. "It's also the bear Matthew went to get from Adrienne's the night they slept together."

Ella stared at the bear. Hating it for what it represented, but wondering why someone as unsentimental as Jake would hold on to a childhood toy.

"What if he hid something in it," Casey said as she picked up the bear from the box and examined the body. "I don't see anything to show it's been sewn up or that there's anything inside it."

Ella reached for the bear, taking it from Casey's hands to examine it for herself. She had seen the bear so many times before but never really looked at it. Every instinct she has was telling her there was something wrong with this bear. Ava had taken Teddy with her everywhere, insisting she had to hold onto the bear because Jake made it clear only she had permission to play with Teddy – no one else.

She turned the bear, the light catching the plastic eye of the bear just right, and Ella saw it. Her eyes grew large, and she grabbed Casey's shoulder. "Casey, look at its eyes," she exclaimed.

Casey stood from her location on the floor to get a closer look at the bear. "Is that a lens?" she asked.

"It looks like one," Ella said. "Oh my God! He was recording us. Jake told Ava the bear had special powers to watch over her."

"He might not have been recording you, Ella," Casey said gently.

Understanding what Casey was inferring and worried she would have to join Justine in the bathroom, she asked quietly, "Do you think what he did to Justine is on here?"

"Unfortunately, there's only one way to find out," Casey said, taking the bear from Ella's hands.

"He recorded me?" a soft voice asked from the doorway.

Casey and Ella turned to see Justine, her face drained of all color and her hands shaking as she brought them up to her mouth.

"We don't know, honey," Casey told her. "But I have to look to see if there's evidence on here."

"Please don't make me look at it," Justine begged as she crumpled down to the floor.

Ella sat by her on the floor and wrapped her in a hug. "You don't have to watch anything, Justine."

"I don't want anyone to see that," she cried.

Unable to imagine the pain and humiliation Justine must be feeling, Ella did the only thing she could, which was to hug her tighter. She looked at Casey for help.

Casey knelt down by Justine and said, "I am so sorry, but I have to look at it. If there's anything on it, we'll turn it over to the police, and no one else will see it. This is necessary to bring Adrienne to justice for what she did to you."

Justine didn't answer, and she curled on the floor into the fetal position. Ella looked at Casey and said, "I think it's better if I look at it."

"No," Casey said firmly. "You don't want to see whatever may be on here."

Ella stroked the sobbing Justine's hair. "Would you prefer I look at it?" she asked.

Justine's scared eyes looked at Ella, and she silently nodded her approval. "Please watch over her," she told Casey as she took the bear and went to her bedroom to view its secrets in private.

Alone in her bedroom, Ella extracted the camera from the bear and hooked it up to her laptop for playback. Matthew knew everything about computers, and he had taught her as much as he could, so figuring out how to play the footage on the camera was easy for Ella. The hard part was willing herself to press play.

Taking a deep breath, she downloaded the video and pressed the button, steeling herself for what she was about to see. The video started, and Ella could tell she was looking at Jake and Adrienne's bedroom. At first, no one was in the room, but then she saw Jake coming into the room backward. He had his hands under Matthew's arms and was carrying him. Then Adrienne came into view, carrying Matthew by his legs. The two of them brought him to the bed and laid him down. They were talking to each other, but the video had no sound. She steadied her gaze, determined not to miss anything. Adrienne and Jake were both animated, waving their arms as if they were arguing. Jake picked up Adrienne and tossed her onto the side of the bed opposite Matthew. Adrienne pointed at Matthew's feet, and Jake pulled off Matthew's shoes and socks. Jake appeared to be arguing with Adrienne again, but she must have won because he grudgingly left the room, slamming the door behind him. It took all of Ella's strength to watch Adrienne sitting next to her husband on that bed. Adrienne removed her clothes and then removed Matthew's, her hands rubbing over his body as she did.

Ella had to stop the video to gather herself. That son of a bitch let Ava love and hug this bear, and he knew he was using it for his disgusting crimes. What kind of sick person would do that? Maybe it would be better to have Casey watch the remainder. *No*, she thought, *I have to watch this so I know exactly what happened.* She couldn't spend the rest of her life wondering. She pressed play again, reminding herself that her husband appeared to be a victim. Adrienne played with Matthew, trying to force him to get an erection, but it didn't work. Ella smiled to herself; even when he was unconscious, Adrienne couldn't force Matthew to have sex with her. She was still trying when Jake came back into the room, again waving his hands; he appeared to be yelling at her. Jake went around the bed and pulled Adrienne up by her arm. She slapped him and stomped out of the room. Jake walked to the teddy bear, pressing something to turn it off.

She was so happy to discover that Matthew had not had sex with Adrienne and so angry with Jake for giving Ava the bear that she momentarily missed the enormous red flag in the video. Ella heard the door open slightly, and Casey peeked into the room.

"I'm sorry, but Justine wants to know if you saw her," Casey explained.

"No," Ella said, "it was a video of Adrienne trying to assault Matthew."

"Trying?" Casey said with a raised eyebrow.

"Yes, trying," Ella replied. "Matthew is unconscious, obviously drugged. She tried but failed to do what she wanted."

"Matthew will be so happy to know he didn't betray you with Adrienne," Casey said. "Um, I found something else in the box with the teddy bear."

"What was it?" a surprised Ella asked.

Casey wordlessly handed Ella a pink piece of paper with a woman's name and phone number written on it, along with the words, "Call me."

"Who is Jessica?" Ella asked, now wondering if her husband was having an affair with someone named Jessica.

"The only way to find out is to call the number," Casey stated.

Ella picked up her phone and dialed the number. She heard a voicemail message informing her Jessica was not available right now. Without thinking, she left a message telling Jessica that she was Matthew Dalton's wife and to call her as soon as possible.

After leaving the message, a realization hit Ella hard. "Casey," she said, "didn't Matthew say he thought he slept with Adrienne about a week ago?"

"Yes, why?" asked Casey.

"Because Adrienne has been claiming for months that her MS is so bad that she needs to use a walker and that she would soon need a wheelchair, but she was walking in the video with no issues," Ella replied. "She was able to help Jake carry Matthew."

19

Chapter 19

Adrienne stood in her kitchen, drinking coffee and leaning against the counter for support. Jeff came up behind her, wrapped his arm around her waist, and kissed her on the cheek. "I love you," he told her.

Rolling her eyes, she wondered how much longer she could tolerate Jeff. She wanted to tell him he was boring, and she needed a man who could give her real sex, not the vanilla type he gave her. But she needed him for now, so instead, she turned her head, smiled at him, and replied, "Love you too."

"What are your plans for the day?" Jeff asked her as he poured himself some coffee.

"I'm exhausted," she replied. "Can you take Ava and do something? I need my rest."

Jeff's disappointment was apparent. "I was hoping the three of us could do something together, like a family."

"How do you think it will look if I go on a family outing with my murdered husband's brother?" Adrienne asked without attempting to hide her irritation at the question she considered beyond stupid.

"That's probably true," Jeff said dejectedly. He looked at Adrienne with hope in his eyes and said, "Can I ask you a question?"

"I suppose," she said with shrugged shoulders.

"When this is over, I want to adopt Ava," he declared. "If Matthew is convicted, we can have his parental rights terminated. I love Ava, I love you, and we can be a real family."

Adrienne stared at Jeff blankly, her mouth slightly hanging open. She had plans for her life, and they certainly didn't include Jeff. At a loss for words, she muttered, "Jeff, no."

Jeff held up his hands to stop her argument. "I know it seems sudden, but you know I want to protect you and Ava."

"Why do you think I need you to protect me?" she asked defensively.

"Because of everything you've been through," he replied. His eyes filled with tears, which instantly disgusted Adrienne because she didn't think a real man should cry. "You know my dad hurt my mom repeatedly, and I can't stand seeing a man hurt a woman. So many men have hurt you. I would never hurt you."

"Look," she answered, sensing she needed to appease Jeff to keep him under her control. "I understand, but I can't talk about this right now. Once Matthew is convicted, and this is behind us, then we can talk about it." She looked at Jeff, feeling no empathy for what he had experienced as a child or what he was experiencing now. Forcing herself to be nice to the weeping mess in front of her, she hugged his head to her breasts. "We'll be a family, Jeff, I promise."

Jeff lifted his head away and looked up at her face. "I love you so much."

Desperate to change the topic, Adrienne said quickly, "Ava is waiting for you out in the yard. Can you take her to Sioux Falls to go shopping?"

"Of course, my darling," Jeff replied. "Do you want us to bring you back anything?"

"No, you go have fun. I'll see you later, and we'll have some fun of our own," Adrienne said with a wink.

Jeff smiled at her and said excitedly, "I'll see you tonight."

Once he left, Adrienne lay on her couch. Jeff had satisfied her needs the first time they had sex, but she had been so horny anyone could have accomplished that. The thought of more sex with Jeff made her stomach turn. Jake had been so forceful and so fit. Jeff was so bland, and he was definitely not a hard body. *Maybe if he spent more time at the gym and less time at church, he could tighten up into my desired physique*, she thought.

Adrienne found herself thinking about her young lover, Connor. She had been furious with Christian for leaving her, not because she loved him, but because he paid her rent and gave her money. He had even given her money to pay for her car repair at Hauen's Auto Repair, but Rob offered her an alternative, so she took it. She would never turn down an opportunity, even if it were as disgusting as Rob Hauen. She used the money he had given her to buy new clothes and to have her nails done.

Christian's wife was the first contact she made when he left her. Adrienne stopped her as she was leaving her place of employment, giving her the pictures she had taken of the two of them in bed together. She did not care about the pain she saw on his wife's face. She only cared that Christian paid dearly for walking away from her. The satisfaction she received from learning that his wife was divorcing him was short-lived. She wanted to hurt him as deeply as she could, and she knew nothing would hurt him more than losing his child to her.

Adrienne did her research about the age of consent and knew Christian wouldn't be able to do anything to her for having sex with a sixteen-year-old. It had been easy enough to arrange a meeting with Connor. She followed him one day to learn his route home from school, and the following day she was on the side of the road with a flat tire. Most men will stop to help a damsel in distress, and Connor was no exception. Adrienne was pleasantly surprised at how handsome he was, and he was obviously attracted to her. She used all her tricks to make Connor feel special, rubbing his arm, telling him how strong he was, thanking him for saving her. Her attention caused him to blush repeatedly. In no time, they were driving his car to a secluded location. He had been a virgin when he met her, which made it more exciting for Adrienne. It wasn't hard to convince him to have sex with her. All it took was her hand in a particular location, and he was all hers. Connor was already furious with his father for cheating on his mother, and it was easy for her to ruin their relationship irreparably. She knew Christian would try to tell Connor that Adrienne was the other woman, but she had convinced Connor that she had no idea he was married and that she was the one who ended it when she had discovered that fact.

She missed Connor and wanted him with her instead of Jeff. True, she had started sleeping with him only to get revenge on Christian for dumping her, but Connor was enthusiastic and willing to learn new things. He hadn't been a skilled sexual partner when she met him, but he had developed into the best one she ever had. Even better than Jake. Adrienne knew precisely where Connor was after he disappeared from his mother's home, and she continued sleeping with him even after she married Jake. If Connor had not been so young, she would have preferred to marry him instead of Jake. He would have been the better husband, but Adrienne needed someone to support her, and a sixteen-year-old couldn't do that. They had last seen each other the night before Jake's murder. They had sex for hours. His young body had so much more stamina than Jake's. Remembering Connor's body against hers caused Adrienne to ache for him, and she reached for her phone. She put the phone down, realizing it was too risky to see Connor. *Soon*, she thought to herself, *I'll have him with me again.*

She turned her thoughts to Jake and the day he found out about Connor. He had caught them together in the bed she and Jake shared. He had been furious, but Adrienne quickly pointed out that Jake was having sex with other women. "But you wanted me to," Jake argued unsuccessfully.

Adrienne knew Jake would never leave her; he wouldn't be willing to give up the expensive house and monthly child support checks because his wife enjoyed having sex with another man. After that, Adrienne didn't bother to hide her relationship with Connor. She invited him over when Jake was home, taking him into the bedroom, leaving Jake fuming in the living room.

Sometimes she would finish with Connor, send him on his way, and pull Jake into the bedroom for another round. Even though he was angry, Jake would perform for her. He was desperate to please her, and that made the sex that much better for Adrienne. After one of those days, Jake sat up in bed and told Adrienne a secret. "I saw Matthew and Ella having sex in the woods on the day we move into the house," he told her.

"And?" Adrienne asked. "That was years ago."

"I want her," Jake answered bluntly. "She's going to be my next target."

Adrienne bolted upright and dug her fingernails into Jake's arm. "Are you crazy?" she yelled at him. "If you do anything to her, we lose everything."

"But I want her," Jake whined. "She won't know anything happened. Please, I can't stop thinking about her. I'll be careful."

"No," Adrienne told him emphatically. "Not only would you be risking everything for one night, but I would never forgive you if you had sex with her."

"Why do you care?" Jake asked. "You have a boyfriend."

"Because she stole Matthew from me," Adrienne answered. "I will not allow you to have sex with her. If you do, this marriage is over, and you're on the street."

"If you kick me out, I'll tell Matthew the truth about Ava and that you don't actually have MS," Jake threatened.

Adrienne gave Jake a smug smile. "Why do you think I offered to record your dalliance with the college girl? Did you honestly believe it turned me on?" Seeing the bewildered look on his face, she continued, "You're so stupid. I only suggested we pick up a woman so I would have something to hold over your head."

"But, but you were into it," Jake stammered.

"Was I?" Adrienne said with a wrinkled nose. "Think about it, genius. I did it once and then told you that you were on your own."

"The girl will say you were in on it. You will get charged too."

"Do you think I'm stupid?" she asked him. "I knew that once you recorded it that you wouldn't be able to stop. You should really use a stronger password on your cloud account. A password of my name and our anniversary was pretty easy to guess. All of your recordings are now saved in a secure location and will be turned over to the police if you don't do as I say. Sadly, the recording of the pretty college girl was destroyed."

"I can't believe this," Jake said while shaking his head.

"Well, believe it," Adrienne answered. "You and I both know the cops will believe me and not you. You're the one on the recordings, not me. You don't even know that girl's name and you'll never find her." She grabbed Jake's chin with her hand and turned his face toward hers. "I am the boss, and what

I want is all that matters. And what I want is to have you and Connor satisfy me whenever and wherever I say. Do you understand me?"

"Yes, I understand you," Jake said as he nodded his head.

"Good," Adrienne said as she kissed Jake on the end of his nose. "I don't care what woman you have sex with, as long as it's not Ella. Keep doing whatever it is you've been doing, as long as I come first."

Jake fell back into the bed, turning away from Adrienne, but she grabbed his shoulder and turned him toward her. "You said you saw Ella and Matthew on the day we moved into this house?" she questioned.

"Yeah," Jake answered with a smile, obviously thinking about Ella in her glory.

Adrienne nodded her head and pursed her lips. "So, when you came back to the house that day after going out for a cigarette, you threw me on top of the kitchen island and screwed me raw."

"Oh yeah," Jake said.

"Were you fantasizing about her while you were doing me?" she screamed at him.

"What if I was?" Jake said fearlessly. "You can't tell me you don't fantasize about Matthew when you're with me."

Furious, Adrienne told him, "I want you now." She didn't need him at that moment, but she wasn't about to be a stand-in for Ella, and her anger made her want to exert her power over him.

Resigned to his arrangement, he complied and rolled toward her. "As long as you keep me happy, you'll be happy," she told him as she wrapped her legs tightly around his waist.

"Oh, Matthew," she moaned as she forced him inside her.

The sound of the door opening brought Adrienne back from her memories. Jeff and Ava were home, arms full of shopping bags. Ava excitedly came over to her mother to show her the new toys Uncle Jeff had bought for her, but Adrienne brushed her off. "It's been a long day, Ava. You need to go to your room and go to bed."

"Now?" Ava cried.

"Yes, now," Adrienne ordered.

"Okay," a sad Ava replied and shuffled off to her room.

"Are you feeling better?" Jeff asked her.

Adrienne reached up for him. Thinking of Connor and Jake had aroused her, and Jeff was her only option, so he would have to do. "I need you," she whispered to him as she pulled his body on top of hers.

"Here?" Jeff asked. "But Ava is down the hall."

"Yes, here," Adrienne stated firmly. "I need you right now, and I want to do it here. Don't worry; Ava will be fine." She began rubbing him, and all of Jeff's arguments disappeared. When Jeff entered her in his dull, predictable way, his flabby stomach hitting against her taut one, she closed her eyes and fantasized about Connor and Jake.

20

Chapter 20

Adrienne woke up in Jeff's bedroom, realizing that he must have carried her to bed after their night of disappointing sex in the living room. He was not in bed with her, though; instead, she found a note stating he was taking Ava out for the day so she could rest. She carried her walker out to the kitchen, knowing no one was there to see her walking without it, finding another note from Jeff. This note stated he had left muffins and juice for her breakfast. *He might suck at sex,* she thought, *but at least he took Ava off her hands again.* She looked at the muffin sitting on the counter and threw it in the trash. No way was she eating anything that would cause her to gain weight and get a body as bad as Jeff's.

She poured coffee and went over to her usual spot on the couch. Ava's teddy bear was also sitting on the sofa; she must have forgotten to take it with her. Adrienne stared at the bear, wondering why Jake had been so obsessed with keeping his childhood toy. But Ava loved it, and it kept her busy, and that was good enough for Adrienne. She sank back into the cushions and thought of her daughter.

When she first found out she was pregnant with Ava, she had no intention of completing the pregnancy. Adrienne had never wanted to have children. She wasn't interested in the effect a baby would have on her body and her social life. Her first thought was to try to blackmail Christian for money, but his revelation about his vasectomy meant he wouldn't give her anything. Since

Christian wasn't the father, she knew Connor must be. Knowing Connor had no money, Adrienne remembered the drunken night she spent with Matthew. She had convinced him they had sex that night, even though Matthew was too drunk to perform. Matthew made good money, and he was in love with Ella, who had serious money. If she could convince Matthew that the baby was his, he would pay her a large amount of child support.

She called Connor to tell him she was pregnant but said Matthew was the father, embellishing their night together to imply that Matthew had taken advantage of a drunken Adrienne. Connor had immediately wanted to confront Matthew for taking advantage of her, but she had assured him she would handle Matthew. She had to lie to the young man because if Connor knew the baby was his, he could ruin all her plans for easy money.

After ending her call with Connor, she called Matthew, telling him she had to speak to him immediately. He didn't want to see her because he was dating Ella, so she blurted out her news. "I'm pregnant," she cried.

Matthew was silent for what seemed like minutes. "Is it mine?" he asked finally.

"Yes," she lied. "I haven't been with anyone else."

"If the baby is mine, I will take care of it," Matthew replied.

"What about your girlfriend? Will she understand?" Adrienne asked.

"She will," Matthew told her. "She loves kids, and this happened before we met." As if to reassure himself, he repeated, "She will understand."

Adrienne's main goal was to secure a comfy future for herself, but she had secretly hoped Matthew would offer to leave Ella and marry her. She had wanted him since she met him, but he had never been interested in her. "I was hoping we could be a family," Adrienne told him.

Matthew let out a large sigh, telling her, "But I don't love you, Adrienne. I love Ella."

"I understand," Adrienne sobbed. "I just want my child to have a family and a good childhood. Not like what I had."

"Adrienne, I promise you that the baby will have a great childhood. Once you get to know Ella you'll see how amazing she is," Matthew said with so much love in his voice that Adrienne wanted to vomit. "I will talk to Ella, and we'll make a plan to take care of this baby together. Think about it; this could be the luckiest baby ever, having three parents to love them."

Although she knew she was lying to him, Adrienne rubbed her eyes, still feeling slighted by Matthew. "But Ella has so much money. What if my child prefers your lifestyle to mine? I can't give them everything you can. I need to be the best mother I can be, but how can I do that if I have to work all of the time to support the child?"

"You and the baby won't want for anything," Matthew promised. "I just want to be a part of my child's life."

"Do you promise?" Adrienne asked.

"I promise," Matthew said. There was a long pause before he added, "But I think a paternity test is needed."

"If you think that is best," Adrienne told him. "You are the father; I know that for a fact. Matthew, you know I was a virgin before our night together. Now I can't give myself to my husband on our wedding night."

Feeling guilty, Matthew said, "I want to be there for you and for our child."

"Our child?" Adrienne asked hopefully.

"Yes, I believe you, Adrienne. I was just...never mind. It's going to be fine. I don't need a test."

"Okay," Adrienne told him between fake sobs. "Go tell Ella and let me know what you plan to do."

She had secretly hoped that when Matthew told Ella, she would be unwilling to help raise another woman's child, and Matthew would come back to her. It hadn't worked out that way, but at least she got a big, expensive house to live in for free, a new SUV, and $10,000 a month in child support. Adrienne had not wanted Ava, and she couldn't believe how painful it was giving birth. She thought women who did this willingly were crazy, but she was happy to have her little gold mine as long as she didn't have to take care of her much. As she grew, Ava spent more and more time with Matthew and Ella, which was fine with Adrienne. They had taught her how to walk, talk, and even potty trained here, but they never threatened to lower her child support payment. She was free to spend her days and nights with Connor and Jake. She saw Ava as strictly a means to an end. Once she had real money, she planned to hire a full-time nanny to take care of Ava or send her off to boarding school. There was no need for her to ever be bothered with caring for her daughter again.

That's why she was so worried after Ava's fourth birthday party and the blowup that had occurred between her, Jake, Matthew, and Ella. She knew they had taken it too far, and Matthew was going to push for full custody, meaning she would be forced out of her house and lose the monthly payment. Before Matthew and Ella arrived at the party, she had been thinking about Matthew's body and how he had never been interested in her sexually. Whenever she was feeling that way and Matthew was around, she would find excuses to touch him. It had never worked, but her confidence in her ability to seduce men gave her the courage to try. It didn't matter to Adrienne that there were children present; she wanted her hands on Matthew, and she used any excuse to touch him. Jake had been drinking, and he was watching Ella. He was staring at her in a creepy stalker way. When Ella bent over to pick up Ava, Jake started to reach his hands out to grab her backside but saw Adrienne watching him and pulled his hands back before he made any contact. Adrienne looked at Matthew and knew he had seen it too, and there was no way he would accept Jake attempting to touch Ella.

The confrontation between the two couples came quickly after Matthew saw that. After a furious Matthew and Ella left, Adrienne berated Jake for his stupidity. "You were all over him first," Jake exclaimed.

"He tolerates me touching him because I'm the mother of his child," she told him. "He will never tolerate you trying to put your hands on his wife. You screwed us. He's going to try to take Ava away from me."

"No, he won't," Jake replied, trying to hug her.

"Yes, he will. He thinks he has to protect Ava and Ella, and that means getting them both away from you," she said, pushing him away. Her hands were shaking, and she said, "We have to come up with something to change his mind."

"What are you thinking, babe?" Jake asked her.

Adrienne waved him off while she paced the room, thinking deeply. A smile spread across her face, and she said, "I got it."

A few days after the birthday party, Adrienne called Matthew in tears, begging him and Ella to come to talk to her. She had something important to tell them. Matthew was reluctant, but Adrienne turned up the waterworks, and he finally agreed. He and Ella would come to talk to her, but only if Jake had not been drinking. And she had to promise that Jake would not come near Ella.

"He won't; I promise," Adrienne told Matthew. "Thank you so much for agreeing to see me." She hung up the phone, wiping away her manufactured tears, and turned to Jake. "Get ready to put on the performance of a lifetime," she told him. "They're on their way."

When Ella and Matthew came to meet with them, she was proud of Jake for the first time. He performed wonderfully, making Matthew and Ella believe her multiple sclerosis diagnosis. She was worried for a moment when Matthew said Jake had to attend Alcoholics Anonymous, but her steady hand on his arm convinced him to maintain his calm.

After Ella and Matthew left, promising not to push for Ava's full custody, Adrienne and Jake celebrated by having sex on the floor. When they finished, Jake laughed and mimicked Adrienne, "Please don't take my daughter from me."

Adrienne wasn't angry at Jake; she thought it was funny. She replied, "That was so hard to say with a straight face. I was worried I was going to say paycheck instead of daughter."Adrienne hugged herself, so proud of her plan to fake having multiple sclerosis. To her, it was the perfect ruse because she could use a flare-up as an excuse when she needed it, and when she wanted to have fun, she could say she was in remission.

The two of them lay on the floor, satisfied in their deception, thinking their worries about losing their free ride were behind them.

Jake and Adrienne's belief that they had Matthew and Ella firmly where they wanted them disappeared a few weeks before Ava's fifth birthday. "That bitch!" Adrienne yelled as she hung up the phone.

"What's the matter, babe?" Jake asked her.

"That was Matthew," she explained. "Ella sent Matthew's and Ava's spit into one of those ancestry sites to have their DNA tested."

"So?" Jake said while shrugging his shoulders. "Who's that going to hurt?"

"It's going to hurt us," she replied bluntly. "What do you think is going to happen when Little Miss Perfect gets Ava's DNA results, and they don't match Matthew's?"

Jake shrugged again, and Adrienne became visibly frustrated with him, "Don't be stupid," she yelled. "Do I have to spell it out for you?" Jake continued to look at her blankly, so she added, "When she gets Ava's DNA, she'll figure out that Matthew isn't Ava's father."

"Don't worry about it, babe," Jake told her. "You said Matthew is the kid's father."

Adrienne stared at her husband, wondering how he could be so obtuse. "I lied," she replied sarcastically. "She's not his daughter. Our gravy train will come to an end."

"Crap," a now comprehending Jake replied. "What are we going to do?"

"I don't know yet, but we have to do something," a desperate Adrienne answered. She looked at Jake's blank expression and knew she was alone in devising the plan. "I have to think," she said. She walked back toward the bedroom, and Jake followed her, but she turned her around at the door frame, using her body to block him from entering the room.

"Don't you want my help?" Jake asked.

"Right now, I need Connor," she said to a visibly angry Jake. "I'll need you later."

Jake sat on the couch, stewing when he saw Adrienne let Connor into the house, and the young man followed her to the bedroom to have sex with Jake's wife. About three hours later, he emerged from the bedroom, waving at Jake on his way out. Adrienne followed closely behind him, almost giddy when she ran up to Jake to plant a huge kiss on him. Jake pushed her away. "I guess Connor helped you," he said contemptuously.

Ignoring his attitude, Adrienne replied, "He did. It's like having endless sex with him rattled something loose in my brain, and I came up with the perfect idea." She looked at Jake and added, "Now it's time for you to help."

"What do I have to do?" an exasperated Jake asked her.

Adrienne smiled and replied, "Play the victim."

21

Chapter 21

"What?" asked a confused Jake.

Adrienne straddled Jake, kissed his neck, and told him, "I have a great idea. When this is all done, you and I won't have to rely on Matthew and Ella for money anymore."

Jake pushed her back so he could look at her face, and Adrienne knew she had piqued his interest. "How do we do that?" he asked.

"We set up Matthew and Ella and sue them for injuries and mental distress," she replied. "You just have to get a little injury."

He placed his hands on her waist and lifted her off him. "What do you mean by a little injury?"

"It won't be that bad," she told him. "Just a few punches and a little gunshot in your shoulder."

Jake let out a nervous chuckle and firmly stated, "No way."

Adrienne climbed back on Jake's lap and whispered in his ear, "I do love you, Jake. If you do this for me, we can go back to the way things were and I'll even give up Connor for you."

"Permanently?" an intrigued Jake asked.

"Yes, permanently," she replied. "I'll stay faithful to you, and you can continue to bang whoever you want."

"Can I have Ella?" Jake asked hopefully.

"Yes," she promised. "I won't stand in your way and you can do whatever you want to her. In fact, the more you do to her, the happier it will make me."

"Tell me the plan," an excited Jake told her.

Adrienne sat with Jake, laying out each detail of her plan to steal millions from Matthew and Ella. A skeptical Jake shook his head, saying, "Are you sure this is going to work?"

"Have I ever been wrong before?" she asked. "No one is better as this than I am."

Jake raised his eyebrows, showing Adrienne that he agreed with the estimation of her deceptiveness. "What do we need to do first?" he asked.

Placing her hand on Jake's shoulder, she said, "We have to find someone to beat you up and fire the shot."

"I thought you or Connor would do it," Jake replied.

Adrienne shook her head violently. "I could never hurt you like that," she declared. "Connor can't do it because we can't have him involved in this."

"Why not?" asked Jake. "I thought he helped you come up with the plan."

"He didn't come up with the plan, Jake," an annoyed Adrienne replied. "He only helped me by relaxing me."

"Whatever," Jake retorted. "Why can't he do it?"

"If he does it, then he'll hold that over me if I try to end things with him," Adrienne reasoned. "If you want me to keep banging him regularly, then I'll be happy to have him do it."

"No," Jake replied sharply. "I want him to go away."

"Then think of someone else," Adrienne instructed him.

Jake thought for a moment and said, "What about Jeff?"

"Jeff?" Adrienne asked, pretending to be shocked by Jake's choice when she had, in fact, been relying on Jake suggesting his brother. "He likes Ella, and he would never be a part of setting up her husband. He's too goody-goody."

"Let me explain something to you about my brother," Jake started. "He's a protector. If he thinks Matthew has hurt you, he will do anything he can to help protect you. Plus, he'll think he's helping protect Ella."

Intrigued, Adrienne titled her head to the side and asked, "What do you mean, he's a protector?"

"I told you that Jeff and I moved here from South Dakota to live with our uncle after our parents died, but I never told you this part. Jeff and I grew up in an abusive home, and we witnessed our father beat our mother repeatedly. Jeff always tried to protect our mom, but he was too little to do anything to our dad. One night, Jeff tried to protect her after our father backhanded her, but he was so small, and my father pushed him down. He was about to kick him when our mother jumped between them. He beat the hell out of our mother for trying to protect Jeff. Her injuries were so severe that she died from internal bleeding." Jake paused, and for the first time since she had known him, Adrienne saw tears in his eyes. "Our dad isn't dead; he's on death row. Jeff felt so guilty for not being able to protect our mother. Ever since then, he has always wanted to protect the underdog, especially if the underdog is a woman. He knows it's his fault our father killed our mother."

Adrienne did her best to feign empathy for her husband. Actually, she was using Jake's confession to her advantage. Her plan relied on Jeff's participation, and Jake had just given her the perfect opportunity. "I have an idea," she told him.

"I am not going to hit you so he attacks me," Jake stated.

"Not that, silly," Adrienne replied in a teasing tone. "What if I make him think Matthew assaulted me? Would he agree to help us set him up if he thought that I was attacked?"

"Possibly," Jake told her. "I guess the only way to find out is to ask him. Let me call him and see if he'll come over."

"No, not yet," Adrienne told Jake. "We have to make it look like Matthew attacked me; it has to be believable."

"How do you propose we do that?" Jake asked her.

Adrienne saw a new opportunity for her to bed Matthew finally. "I'll get Matthew over here by pretending to need help, use a little of your secret potion on him, and we'll put him in bed with me," Adrienne plotted.

"No, no, no," Jake said adamantly. "You don't need to have sex with him for real. You just want an excuse to screw him," he said accusingly.

"That's not true," Adrienne said in such an unconvincing way that she knew Jake didn't believe her. "Listen, I have to make Matthew think something happened. What if Jeff confronts him, and Matthew is clueless? What will happen to our plan then?"

"I suppose that makes sense," Jake reluctantly said. "But you're just going to make him think something happened, right?"

"Sure," Adrienne assured him, knowing she had no intention to keep her promise. "Nothing will actually happen."

The night Adrienne and Jake started their plan, they knew Ella was out of town for her charitable foundation, so they sent Ava off to stay with her father. She purposely forgot to pack the teddy bear in her daughter's overnight bag. Adrienne knew Ava would refuse to sleep without Teddy, and Matthew would have no choice but to retrieve the bear. They both waited nervously for Matthew's inevitable phone call, which came at 8:30. "Ava forgot Teddy, Adrienne. Can we come over quick and get him?" Matthew asked her.

"Sure," Adrienne replied easily. "I'm sure he's here somewhere. I'll look for him before you get here."

"Thanks, I'll be there soon," Matthew replied.

Adrienne disconnected the phone call, turned to Jake, and said, "You need to hide outside, and I'll let you know when he's passed out so you can come back in."

"Okay," Jake replied. He grabbed Adrienne, pulled her to him, and said, "I do love you. Don't do anything you'll regret."

She hugged him to her, saying, "I love you too, baby. When this is all over, we will be happier than we ever thought possible. Now, get your cute ass outside before Matthew gets here."

Jake tried to kiss her, but she turned her head and pointed at the back door. He slunk out the door and disappeared into the darkness. A few minutes later, the doorbell rang, and Adrienne used her walker to make her way to let Matthew and Ava in the house. "Come on in," she told Matthew cheerfully.

"Did you find Teddy?" Ava asked her.

"Yes, he's in my room. We must have left him in there when we were playing earlier," Adrienne explained.

"Do you mind if I go grab him?" Matthew inquired.

"No, but can you do me a favor first?" she asked. "Jake is out of town, and the water softener needs some salt. Could you go downstairs and add some for me?" She glanced at her walker, looked back and Matthew, and said, "I would do it, but I have such a hard time doing it myself."

"Sure," Matthew said, "no problem."

While Matthew went downstairs, where Jake had set up a heater to make the backroom extremely hot, Adrienne went to the kitchen and poured two glasses, one for Matthew and one for her. She placed the drugs into Matthew's glass and stood in the kitchen drinking the plain lemonade she had poured for herself. She poured another glass of lemonade laced with antihistamines for Ava. "Ava, come drink this, baby."

Ava bounced into the kitchen and eagerly took the glass from her mother to drink the lemonade. Adrienne was a little worried about the dose, as she had given Ava more than she normally did to ensure she fell asleep quickly. "Why don't you go lie down on the sofa until you daddy comes back? You can take your lemonade."

"Okay, Mom," Ava answered.

After a few minutes, Matthew came back upstairs, his shirt wet from sweat, "It's sweltering down there," he exclaimed. "You might want to have Jake check that out when he gets back."

"I'll be sure to tell him," she chirped. "Would you like some lemonade? You look like you can use it."

"That sounds great, thank you," he replied, picking up the glass and drinking it in its entirety in one attempt. "Can I have another glass? It was really hot down there."

"Sure", Adrienne answered, pouring more of the vodka spiked lemonade into his glass, which he again drank quickly.

"Well, I better get Teddy," he said as he started down the hall.

Adrienne had not expected him to gulp the lemonade down, and she worried that it wouldn't take effect until Matthew left, so she pretended that her hand slipped off her walker, causing her to fall to the floor. "Ouch," she cried. "Matthew, please help me up."

Matthew came running back toward Adrienne, kneeling by her side, "What happened?" he asked.

She looked at him to reply that she fell, but she saw Matthew hold his hand up to his forehead and saw his body begin to sway. He was about to pass out. She reached out as fast as she could to steady him so he wouldn't hurt himself by falling. "Are you okay?" she asked.

"I feel like I'm drunk," he said. "Was that just lemonade?"

"Oh no!" Adrienne exclaimed, "I must have accidentally used the lemonade Jake had spiked with vodka. No wonder I fell down."

"Where is Ava?" Matthew asked. "I need to take her home."

"Matthew, you can't possibly think I'm going to let you drive with my daughter when you feel like this."

"We walked here," he replied. "Adrienne, I don't feel well."

"There, there," she told him as she gently kissed him on the lips. "You'll be fine. Let yourself go to sleep; Adrienne's got you." Matthew turned his unfocused gaze toward her and closed his eyes.

Adrienne gently laid his head on the floor and went to summon Jake. She opened the back door and yelled, "Get in here."

Jake came back into the house and saw Matthew lying on the floor. "Looks like it worked," he said, pointing out the obvious.

"Grab him under his arms," Adrienne instructed Jake. "I'll grab his legs so we can carry him to the bedroom. Ava's out cold on the couch."

Doing as ordered, Jake picked up Matthew and carried him toward the bedroom. He and Adrienne laid Matthew on the bed. Becoming worried about Adrienne's intentions, Jake asked her, "You're not going to try anything with him, right?"

Adrienne rolled her eyes at her husband and said, "Would you let it go? I am only doing what I have to so this works."

Jake must have sensed an opportunity and made an argument toward Adrienne. "If you do him, then I get Ella."

A furious Adrienne turned to Jake, waving her arms angrily. "How many times do I have to hear about your obsession with that bitch?"

"I'll still come home to you, baby," Jake told her. "I'll get her once and then I'm all yours."

"I don't want to talk about her anymore," Adrienne yelled at him. "We made our agreement and I will keep it. Now, help me get him ready."

Angry, Jake picked Adrienne up and threw her onto the side of the bed opposite Matthew. "If you want him, I am done helping you."

Adrienne laughed at Jake's sudden courage. "I don't think so, sweetheart. Don't forget about a little recording of you that I possess," she threatened. She pointed at Matthew's shoes and said, "Take off his shoes and socks."

Resigned to what he had to do to avoid prison, Jake took off Matthew's shoes and socks as instructed. He looked over at Adrienne, and she was removing Matthew's shirt, licking her lips as she did. She saw him watching her and told him, "You can leave. Besides, you need to go to Matthew's shed and do your part."

"Do not have sex with him," Jake ordered one more time before he left the room.

Determined to do what she wanted, Adrienne pulled off the rest of Matthew's clothes and tried everything she could think of to coerce an erection from Matthew, but nothing worked. Frustrated, she lay back on the bed. She needed him so much; he was the only man ever to turn down her advances, and he was the one she had wanted the most.

Upon his return from the shed, Jake came back into the room, holding one of Matthew's work shirts and his 9mm weapon. Adrienne never removed her steely gaze as she purposely used her fingertip to trace the outline of his abdominal muscles, daring him to ask her if she had sex with Matthew. "You had sex with him, didn't you?" he said accusingly.

"It's none of your business," Adrienne yelled at him as she deliberately ran her her tongue over Matthew's bare body.

Furious, Jake walked to her side of the bed, grabbed her by the arm, and pulled her up. "I told you that you couldn't have sex with him," he yelled directly in her face. "If you had sex with him, I am not going through with this plan."

Jake had never refused to listen to her before, and she was not happy about his sudden courage. She looked directly back at Jake and slapped him across the face. She could see that Jake was stunned; she had never been physically violent toward him before, but she didn't want to hear one more word about Matthew. "Get over it," she ordered him before she turned and stormed out of the room.

She sat naked on her sofa, waiting for her husband to come to his senses and apologize to her. In her mind, she was in the right, and Jake was in the wrong. She could be obsessed with Matthew, but he had no right to point it out to her. A few minutes later, Jake did come out of the room, holding the teddy bear. "You need to get back in there before he wakes up, or this was all for nothing," Jake told her.

Adrienne studied her husband. He appeared to be smirking at her. "What are you smiling at?" she asked.

"Nothing," he replied. "I'm not sure when he'll wake up since I don't normally use it on someone his size." Jake handed her the teddy bear and disappeared out the back door.

She watched her husband leave, wondering why he looked so pleased with himself. Adrienne considered following him, but she heard a groan coming from the bedroom and hurried back. She picked up the shirt Matthew had been wearing, briefly holding it to her face to breathe in his scent, then threw it under the bed. Adrienne threw the shirt Jake had taken from Matthew's shed on the floor where the rest of their clothes were strewn, set the teddy bear on the dresser, lay down beside Matthew, and fell asleep with her head on his chest.

A few hours later, Matthew began to stir, rubbed his eyes, looked at Adrienne with confusion, and shook her awake. "What's going on?" he asked in a scared voice.

"Don't blame yourself," Adrienne told him. "Our urges got the better of us, and we gave into temptation."She leaned forward to try to kiss Matthew, but he moved further away from her.

"No, no," Matthew kept repeating. "This didn't happen. I can't do this to Ella."

Irritated to hear her rival's name, Adrienne was content to let Matthew leave. "I promise not to say anything to Ella," Adrienne said sweetly.

Matthew bolted from the bed and began to pull on his clothes frantically. "I have to tell Ella," he yelled at Adrienne.

"You can't," Adrienne told him. "If Jake finds out, he'll hurt himself. He said if I ever cheated on him with you that he wouldn't want to live."

"I have to tell her," Matthew said. "I can't lie to her."

"Please," Adrienne begged him. "Your marriage might survive this, but mine won't. Besides, why hurt Ella when you don't have to? She doesn't have to know."

Matthew stared at Adrienne, "Why don't I remember anything?"

"I don't remember anything either," she lied. "We were both drunk."

She saw Matthew's eyes darting back and forth as if trying to regain his memories of the previous night. "I remember you falling and you kissing me..." he said as he ran his hand nervously through his hair.

"Matthew, I'm sorry. We were drinking and one thing must have led to another."

"Oh my God, where's Ava?" Matthew yelled as he ran from the room. He returned shortly, grabbed the teddy bear from where Adrienne had left it and said, "She's in the living room. I'm taking her and going home."

"If it makes you feel any better, I will never say anything to Ella."

22

Chapter 22

Adrienne waited a few minutes after Matthew left the room before calling Jake to join her again. "He's gone," she told him when he answered the phone. "Your turn."

"I'll be right there," Jake replied.

"Hurry up," she commanded him. She lay back on the bed, sexually frustrated from Matthew's inability to get hard for her, waiting impatiently for Jake to return. When he entered the room, he removed his clothes and joined her.

"What exactly am I supposed to do?" he asked.

"Make it look like Matthew attacked me," she told him. "Grab my arms and squeeze hard enough so you leave bruises. Just don't leave any marks that can be seen without clothes. We can't have the cops see them when they come to question us."

Jake obliged by lying on top of Adrienne and grabbing her upper arms and squeezing, so he would leave finger-shaped bruises. All the frustration he had felt for her that day must have built up because he improvised and bit her on the shoulder. "Ouch," Adrienne screamed. "What the hell is wrong with you?"

"Sorry," Jake told her. "I guess I got caught up in the moment. Do you want me to penetrate you?"

"What do you think?" she asked sarcastically. "It has to look believable, so get in and make sure it's rough, so there are bruises on my thighs." Jake had never been a gentle lover, which was just fine with Adrienne, but this was a little rougher than even she liked it. However, she was still so worked up by touching Matthew's naked body, she climaxed easily.

When it was over, Jake rolled off Adrienne and curled onto his side. "What is wrong with you?" she asked him.

"That's the first time I didn't enjoy sex with you," he replied. "It didn't feel right."

"Well, get over it," she said with no compassion. "It's time to call your brother. Make sure he is here bright and early tomorrow."

Jake left the room to call Jeff, returning after a few minutes. "He'll be here early tomorrow morning," he told her.

"Perfect," she said as she patted the bed to let Jake know to join her again. "It's been a long time since we've cuddled, baby. Why don't you come here, and we'll hold each other all night." Jake lay down on the bed next to Adrienne, and she wrapped her arms around him. "I do love you, baby," she assured him. "This will be over soon, and it will be just you, me, and lots of money."

"I hope you're right," Jake replied as he closed his eyes and fell asleep in the arms of the woman he loved.

Adrienne was pleased the next morning when she woke up and saw the bruises on her arms and legs. They would surely convince Jeff she had been viciously attacked, invoking his protective instinct. She dressed in short shorts and a sleeveless top to ensure the bruises were fully visible. Adrienne was admiring her bruises in the mirror when Jake yelled at her to let her know Jeff had arrived.

She grabbed her walker, making her way to the living room, attempting to appear as weak as possible. Jeff looked at her, saw the bruises, and immediately jumped off his chair to help her to the sofa. He looked back and forth between Adrienne and Jake. "What happened to her?" he asked.

Adrienne lowered her head and began to sob. "It was Matthew," she cried. "He assaulted me last night."

"Did you call the police?" Jeff asked with venom in his voice.

"We couldn't," Adrienne stated. "He and Ella have so much money, so the police protect him. I want him to pay for what he did, but we have nowhere to turn."

Adrienne looked up and saw the anger on Jeff's face, and she knew she had him hooked. She gave Jake a look that let him know to proceed with the plan. "Jeff," Jake started, "this makes me so sick, especially after seeing how Dad treated Mom all those years. I wasn't here to protect her, and I feel so guilty."

"He can't get away with this," Jeff said through clenched teeth. He looked at Jake and said, "You and I need to pay him a visit."

"You can't do that," Adrienne interrupted. "If you do anything to him, you'll be arrested. He has so much power, and I can't let you jeopardize your freedom for me."

"But he can't get away with this," Jeff protested. "What if we tell his wife?"

"She won't believe you," Adrienne protested. "Even if she did, she's so concerned about appearances that she wouldn't do anything about it."

Jake glanced at Adrienne, who motioned toward Jeff with her eyes. "Jeff," he said, "I think I've come up with a way to make Matthew pay for what he did to Adrienne."

"Whatever it is, I'm in," Jeff answered quickly. "Men like that disgust me. They should be wiped off the face of the earth."

She grabbed for Jeff's hand to pull him toward her. "Thank you so much for helping me, Jeff. You're my guardian angel."

He looked at her and replied, "You're such a good person, and I have prayed for you for so long, Adrienne. If God can't take away your pain, I will. No one should have to go through what you have."

Adrienne kissed Jeff's hand. Startled, he blushed and quickly turned toward Jake. "What now?" Jeff asked.

"Explain it to him, baby," Adrienne told Jake.

Jake took a deep breath and laid out their plan to Jeff. "Matthew goes jogging almost every day through a path in woods between our houses," he explained. "We need you to come out there with us and attack me."

"Attack you?" a surprised Jeff asked. "Why would I attack you?"

"If you punch me a few times and shoot me in the shoulder, I'll tell the police that Matthew did it," Jake explained to his brother. "The police won't be able to ignore a shooting. They'll have no choice but to arrest Matthew."

"You want me to shoot you?" Jeff asked incredulously. "I don't know if I can do that."

"Quit being such a baby," Jake scolded as he looked at his wife. "I should have known he wouldn't have the balls to do it."

"Jake, please, don't be so mean to your brother," Adrienne told him before she turned her attention to her brother in-law. "Jeff, you're the only one who can help us. You're about the same height as Matthew, so the bullet trajectory and the location of the punches will make sense if you do it."

Jeff looked at his brother, not believing what he was asking him to do. "Jeff, you have to do this," Jake ordered. "If you don't, Matthew is going to get away with what he did to Adrienne. The cops won't do anything about that, but they will have no choice if he shoots me. Hospitals have to report gunshot wounds."

"Jeff," Adrienne said as she grabbed his hand again. "Matthew left his shirt here. You can wear it when you fake the attack on Jake, and we'll put the shirt on Matthew's property. They will have to arrest him."

Jeff raised his head and stared at the ceiling, "I don't know," he said.

"You said whatever it was, you were in," Jake reminded him.

"It's okay, Jake," Adrienne said, producing more fake sobs. "If Jeff doesn't want to help, I will have to live with this pain, seeing Matthew take Ava to his house for visits. Never knowing if he'll hurt her too."

Jeff started and looked at Adrienne. "Do you think he would hurt Ava?"

"I don't know," she said. "I didn't think he would hurt me, but he did. Who knows what he does to poor Ella behind closed doors."

The mention of Ava and Ella being in danger seemed to be the push he needed. "I'll help you," Jeff said quietly.

Jake smiled at Adrienne. "Maybe you're not a waste as a brother," Jake told him. "Who knew you would finally be good for something."

"I'm doing this for Adrienne, not for you," Jeff retorted.

Enjoying the animosity between the two men, but needing to steer the conversation back to her and her plan, she told him, "Thank God for you,

Jeff." She then looked at Jake and said, "Let's get started."

"We need to get everything ready for the shooting, and then plan out the attack," Jake stated.

"I don't have a gun," Jeff replied.

"We have a gun for you to use," Adrienne explained. "Jake stole Matthew's gun out of his shed after he attacked me. He keeps the gun locked up, but the combination is Ava's birthday. Jake took it because he didn't want Matthew to come back to the house and use it on me." She again turned on the flow of tears to ensure Jeff understood her level of distress.

"We have to make a silencer," Jake stated. "I learned how to make one a while ago out of a plastic bottle."

Jeff had a water bottle in his hand, and he showed it to Jake. "Will this work?" he asked.

"It should," Jake answered. "I'll be right back." He returned quickly with paper towels and gloves for the three of them to wear so that they wouldn't leave fingerprints on the silencer.

Adrienne put on her gloves and turned to Jeff, "Give me the bottle so I can wipe your fingerprints off it," she told him.

Jeff handed her the bottle and turned his attention back to Jake. Adrienne picked up the paper towels to wipe off the bottle. She had a backup plan, which neither Jake nor Jeff knew. She intended to ensure Jeff's fingerprints stayed on the bottle, so she had her scapegoat. After pretending to wipe off Jeff's fingerprints, she handed the bottle back to Jake.

"Thanks, baby," Jake told her. He and Jeff assembled the homemade silencer, and the only thing left to do was to figure out the perfect day to carry out their plan.

"Why don't you go scope out the woods and find the perfect place, baby?" Adrienne asked Jake. He looked at her, obviously unhappy with her direction. "I can't possibly get out there in my physical condition," she explained.

"Okay," Jake said reluctantly. He looked at Jeff and said half-seriously, "I guess I have to go find a place for you to shoot me, big brother."

Unaware of Adrienne's plan, Jake did as he was told. Unbeknownst to Jake, Adrienne had been secretly contacting Jeff for weeks, enticing him to fall in love with her. When she and Jake were first married, it was plain that Jeff was intimidated by her, but she needed his help to carry her plan to fruition. Jake thought Adrienne didn't know about their family history, but Adrienne had researched him before she picked him up in that bar. She was fully aware their father murdered their mother, and they moved to the area to be raised by their uncle.

Adrienne had grown tired of Jake, his obsession with Ella, and what he called his extracurricular activities. She was ready to replace him permanently with Connor. Sure that if she divorced him, Jake would spill her secrets to Matthew, she began calling Jeff when Jake wasn't around, telling him she needed his spiritual guidance. Jeff was happy to assist her in her quest to find religion, and as he grew closer to her, she laid seeds of doubt about Jake's character. She told Jeff that Jake was taking steroids, which he actually was, but she lied that the steroids had caused him to become violent with her. Adrienne's favorite role was playing the victim, and Jeff was a captive audience. She had successfully convinced him she was a good but misunderstood person and that Jake was the one with all the flaws.

Once Jake was safely out of hearing distance, she turned her attention back to her brother in-law. "Jeff, he's getting worse. I'm scared of him."

"What happened?" a protective Jeff asked her.

"He thinks I'm in love with someone else," she told him. "He said he'll kill me if I leave him."

"Are you in love with someone else?" Jeff asked hopefully.

Adrienne glanced toward the door nervously, pretending to check that they were truly alone "I am," she said as she lowered her eyes.

"Who?" Jeff asked.

"You," she answered quietly.

She saw the look of bliss that passed over Jeff's face and knew now was the time to pounce. She pulled out her phone and accessed her videos. "Jake sent this to me accidentally," she lied. "Jake is a rapist. He recorded himself attacking some poor girl." She handed the phone to Jeff and turned away. "I can't watch it again, but you need to see what he did."

Jeff took the phone from Adrienne to watch the disturbing video. She opened her closed eyes a sliver to try to gauge Jeff's reaction. He appeared to have the exact reaction she wanted. Jeff's face had turned red, and he put the phone down in disgust. "I can't watch anymore," he said.

"When I confronted him, he told me that he's done this many times. I don't know how many women he has hurt. I don't know what to do," she told Jeff.

"This wasn't the only time he did something like this?" Jeff asked with disgust.

"Not from what he told me," Adrienne stated. "That's not all." She looked at Jeff and slowly pulled back her shirt to expose the bite mark Jake had left on her shoulder. "After I confronted him, he told me it was my fault for not fulfilling his sexual desires."

Jeff shook his head in disbelief. "My brother is a monster. I can tell the girl in the video is unconscious and unable to protect herself. And then to threaten you. I can only imagine the fear you must have of him."

"I'm so sorry you had to find out like this," she told him. "You're the only one I can trust. What if—no, I can't say it because it's too horrible."

"What?" Jeff asked her. "Please finish what you were saying."

"What if Jake hurts Ava?" Adrienne howled. "I would never be able to forgive myself."

"Do you think he has hurt her?" Jeff asked.

"I don't think so," Adrienne told him. "But I think he's capable of almost anything. He told me that if I told anyone what he did to that poor girl, he would kill me just like his father killed his mother."

"Adrienne, you need to leave him," Jeff told her.

Shaking her head, Adrienne said, "That won't work. He'll still be able to hurt me. Or worse, hurt Ava."

"What can I do to help you?" Jeff asked.

"Promise to save me if he ever attacks me."

"I promise," Jeff stated in full protective mode.

She looked him dead in the eyes and decided to fuel the fire, "Do you know how he talks about you?"

"Yes, I know he's not very fond of me," Jeff replied, "but he's still my brother."

"Do you know he said it's your fault that your father killed your mother? He completely blames you."

"What?" Jeff exclaimed. "I was a kid."

"I know, sweetheart, but Jake said if you had just taken your punishment like a man that your mother wouldn't have stepped in to protect you. That's why he always calls you names like wussy boy and, and...pussy."

"I can't believe he actually blames me," Jeff said incredulously. "I know he thinks I'm a wimp, but I didn't know that was why."

"He's wrong about you, Jeff," she purred at him. "You know, it's been wonderful getting to know you over the past few weeks and I know how strong you really are. You've shown me what a real man should be like. Only a real man can treat a woman so well and protect her like you do. I wish I had married you instead of Jake."

"You do?" Jeff asked.

"Of course," Adrienne said, knowing Jeff had never been successful with women. In the time she had been married to Jake, he had not even gone on a date. "Who wouldn't want you instead of Jake? Someone who loves you unconditionally and doesn't prey on women."

Jeff recoiled at the mention of his brother's crimes, and said solemnly, "Women deserve to be protected from abusive men." He then closed his eyes and appeared to be deep in thought. After a few moments, he replied quietly, "I do promise."

"What do you promise?" Jake asked from the back door.

Adrienne and Jeff jumped because they had not heard Jake return. "He was having second thoughts, but he will help us take care of Matthew," she covered.

"Great," said an unsuspecting Jake. "I think we can do this on Saturday afternoon," Jake told them.

"That's the day of Ava's birthday party," Adrienne said.

"I know," replied Jake. "But I think we need to get this done sooner rather than later."

"I couldn't agree more," Adrienne said with a smile. "Jake can instigate a confrontation with Matthew by being inappropriate toward Ella. That way multiple people can see the altercation and will tell the cops about it. It's perfect."

23

Chapter 23

Adrienne was up early on the morning of Jake's murder to set up Ava's birthday party decorations. She had to ensure she had everything done, so it appeared she was having a normal day. Ava was excited after her party and was running around the house. Adrienne gave her an extra piece of cake, spiking her food with antihistamine so Ava would fall asleep, blissfully unaware that Jeff had been there and Adrienne had been gone. Jeff came into the room, causing her heart to skip a beat; she was moments away from changing her life.

Jake slapped Jeff on the back and told him jokingly, "Thank you for doing this, Jeff. I wouldn't trust anyone else to shoot me."

Jeff glanced at Adrienne and she knew his was nervous. She quickly said, "Let's get out there so we get it done before Matthew starts his afternoon jog. Someone will have to carry me since I can't navigate through the woods with the walker."

"I'll carry you, baby," Jake told her, flexing his steroid-enhanced muscles to show off to his brother. "Stand behind me and get on my back."

Adrienne awkwardly climbed onto Jake's back, eliciting a gaze of sympathy from Jeff, and the three of them exited the house to start their journey toward the woods.

Jake carried Adrienne quickly to the clearing he had selected the other day as the location they would use. It was the exact spot where Matthew and Ella had held their picnic, but Adrienne was unaware of that fact. She heard a noise and nervously looked into the trees. "There are bald eagles in here," she said.

"Yep," Jake replied. "There are all kinds of birds in here, eagles, hummingbirds, hawks."

"They are so beautiful," Jeff exclaimed. "But I feel like they're watching us."

"They're just dumb birds," Adrienne stated. "They can't tell anyone."

Jeff glanced up at the majestic birds one more time, took a deep breath, and said, "Let's get this over with."

Jake nodded, putting on gloves before pulling the gun and silencer from the bag Jeff had carried to the clearing. He placed the homemade silencer onto the end of the weapon. "It's ready. Put on your gloves, Jeff," he ordered.

Doing as he instructed, Jeff put on his gloves and put Matthew's stolen shirt on over his own. He took the gun from Jake, looking at his brother and then at Adrienne. Sensing he was starting to waver, Adrienne blew him a kiss behind Jake's back and mouthed "Thank you" to him.

"Make sure you hit me in a spot that won't cause too much damage," Jake stated. "I don't want to bleed too much."

Jeff nodded silently before saying, "Can you turn around, Jake? I won't be able to pull the trigger if I am looking at your face."

"Whatever," he said as he turned his back to his brother. "It's probably better if I can't see it coming anyway."

"Adrienne, you can't be that close," Jeff told her. "Let me carry you over toward the trees."

"You know your weak ass won't be able to carry her," Jake stated. "Let me do it." He shoved his brother out of his way, walked over to Adrienne, and picked her up so her legs were wrapped around his waist and they were face to face.

She looked into his eyes, gave a quick smile, and said, "Jake, I have to tell you something."

"What is it, baby?" he asked.

Now was the time to start her plan. Adrienne moved her lips to his ear and whispered, "I'm sick of you and your shrunken balls. I had sex with Connor last night and I will not give him up. We laugh about how stupid you are."

Jake stared back at his wife, unable to speak, his breathing becoming shallow.

"What's the matter?" she taunted him. "Upset that you've been replaced? By the way, you will never get Ella. I was never going to let you have her."

She saw the anger come over his face as he grabbed her by the waist and threw her to the ground. "You bitch!" he screamed at her as he clenched his fists. "You're going to pay for this."

"Jeff, help me," she screamed.

"Leave her alone, Jake!" Jeff yelled.

"What are you going to do about it?" Jake sneered as he turned toward his brother. "You're nothing but a pansy."

Jeff raised the gun. "I said to leave her alone."

Jake carefully took steps to circle around his brother until the gun was pointed directly at his face."You and I both know you won't be able to do it."

Jeff's hand trembled as he slowly lowered the gun to his side. "Please just leave her alone."

"I knew you couldn't do it," he snarled. "Once a pussy, always a pussy. Now, I'm going to do her what our father did to that cheating whore you call a mother."

Adrienne pulled her legs toward her as Jake turned in her direction. "Jeff, please." Before Jake could reach her, she heard the muffled sound of the gun firing.

The force of the blast caused Jake's blood to splatter onto Jeff, and Jake fell to the ground instantly. Jeff dropped the gun, fell to his knees beside her, sobbing voraciously. "Please forgive me, Lord. I had to; he was evil."

Adrienne sat there, breathing heavily, hardly believing that Jeff had done it, but satisfied that he had. "Jeff, don't blame yourself," she told him as she put on her pair of gloves. She placed her hands on the side of face and raised his head to look at her. "You had no choice." Jeff didn't respond to her; he was still praying for forgiveness for his sin. Irritated, Adrienne raised her voice but didn't yell, "Jeff, you have to get yourself together. You have to shoot him one more time to make sure he's dead."

Jeff broke out of his trance and looked at her. "What?"

"We can't risk that he's still alive and it would be inhumane to let him suffer."

He got off his knees to do as Adrienne instructed. He stood over his brother's motionless body, again pointing the gun at Jake's head and pulled the trigger.

"You are my hero," Adrienne praised him. "Now, bring me the gun, sweetheart."

Doing as she demanded, Jeff brought the gun to Adrienne, who removed the homemade silencer. "What are you going to do with that?" Jeff asked her.

"I'm going to destroy it when we get back to the house," she stated. Seeing Jeff's perplexed expression, she added, "I have to. Matthew wouldn't have used a silencer, and it's too risky to leave it here."

"Aren't we going to call the police?" he asked. "He was attacking you. It was self-defense."

"I know it was, but we came out here with a plan to shoot him. No one will believe us. We have to proceed with our plan and pin this on Matthew."

"Are you sure that's what you want to do?"

"I don't want to, but we have to," she explained. "This way you have protected me from Jake and Matthew. I would probably be dead if it wasn't for you." She pulled Jeff's face to hers and kissed him in a way she was sure he had never been kissed before. "I love you."

Caught in the bliss of his first real kiss, Jeff carefully removed Matthew's bloody shirt and took the gun back from Adrienne. Opening another bag, he placed the gun and bloody shirt inside.

"Take these over to Matthew's," she instructed. "Hide the gun in the safe using the combination I gave you. Then, put the shirt into the woodpile behind that garage."

"You're sure their cameras won't catch me?" Jeff asked nervously.

Adrienne nodded her head, "I'm sure. Matthew's gun safe is in the extra shed where he has his man toys, and he doesn't have any cameras on the back of that one. They only have cameras around the main house and garage. As long as you're careful to take the path I told you, the house camera won't pick you up. We just have to wait for Matthew to jog by so he doesn't see you."

"Okay," Jeff said as he picked up the bag with shaking hands. He stood in a location to hide him from anyone running down the path, watching for Matthew.

Adrienne leaned back to smell the fresh air, now mixed with the scent of recent death. When she turned her head to the right, she saw something she didn't expect. "Oh, shit!"

"What is it?" Jeff asked.

"There's a trail camera right there! It's been taking our pictures."

"I'll cut it down," Jeff said. "It will be fine."

"Are you sure?"

"Yes, it looks like a simple one. It just takes still shots." Jeff walked to the tree, pulled out his pocket knife, and cut the trail camera strap. He brought it back to Adrienne. "We'll have to keep this until we get back to the house, but I will burn it."

They sat in silence until they heard a man's voice yell, "Dammit!" Jeff peeked through the trees and saw Matthew; he had tripped over something and fallen into one of the bushes.

"There he is," he whispered to Adrienne.

Needing to let Jeff believe she could not walk, Adrienne stayed seated even though she wanted to see Matthew's beautiful form as he was running. "Is he gone?" she whispered back.

"I can't see him anymore," he told her.

"Go now," she commanded. "Good luck."

"I'll be back to get you," he promised.

"I'll be here," she replied, blowing him another kiss.

Adrienne watched Jeff disappear between the trees, running as fast as his out-of-shape body would carry him. Once he was gone from her view, she removed the silencer from the bag, stood up, and walked into the woods. She found what she felt was a good location and dug a hole, placing the silencer inside and filling in the hole. After finishing her backstabbing task, she walked back to Jake's body, stood over him, and said, "That's what you get for trying to order me around and for obsessing over that bitch. Think of how much money I will get once I sue them for your wrongful death." Adrienne hugged herself, daydreaming about the lavish lifestyle she would have. "I have special plans for your precious Ella," she whispered into his ear. "When this is over, she'll be in prison, I'll have her money, and if everything goes as planned, I'll finally have Matthew."

When Jeff returned, Adrienne was sitting in the spot where he had left her. "We need to get out of here," he told her breathlessly.

Adrienne nodded and replied, "First, we need to erase our footprints. Find a branch with leaves on it and use it to sweep them away."

Jeff wordlessly did as he was told, and cleaned up any footprints they may have left in the dirt. "Okay, let's get out of here," she stated. "You have to carry me back to the house."

He went over to Adrienne to pick her up. After a struggle, he finally managed to arrange her onto his back so that he could carry her back to the house. Adrienne was quickly irritated with the slow progress he made, having to stop to catch his breath repeatedly. "We're almost there," she encouraged him. "We have to get back soon, so we don't run out of time."

Not wanting to let Adrienne down, Jeff increased his pace, managing to get her to the backyard of her home. "Put me down here," she ordered. "We need to take off our shoes and burn them so we don't track anything into the house."

He set her down gently on the grass and removed her shoes before removing his own. "What do I do with these?" he asked.

"Place them into the bag with the other items. Then, bring me into the house so we can change clothes."

Completely out of breath, Jeff was bent over, placing his hands on his knees for strength. After composing himself, he placed the shoes into the bag, picked her up again, and carried her into the house to set her down gently on a kitchen chair. After she was seated, Adrienne instructed Jeff, "We have to change clothes. Everything we're wearing has to be burned."

"Where should I change?"

Adrienne had purposely left their replacement clothes on the kitchen table with the intention of bringing Jeff deeper under her spell. "We don't have much time, so we will need to change here." She pulled her top over her head, revealing her bare breasts. Jeff's eyes grew large as he stared at her chest and grew even larger when she pulled off her leggings to reveal she wasn't wearing any underwear.

"Jeff, you need to change and drive home now. Take my clothes and find somewhere in the country to burn everything. I'll call you after Matthew agrees to go look for Jake." Jeff did not move, unable to take his eyes off her naked body. "You have to go now, Jeff," Adrienne ordered. "We're running out of time."

Forcing himself to avert his gaze, Jeff changed his clothes before he moved toward the door and blew Adrienne a kiss from the doorway. "I'll see you soon," he told her.

"Until then," she replied, holding up her hand to pretend to catch his kiss.

24

Chapter 24

Ella and Casey were concerned about Justine's mental state. They had been monitoring her since the previous evening, ever since she had found out that Jake may have recorded her, and she refused to get up from the floor. She remained curled in the fetal position. After seeing no progress throughout the night, Ella stated, "We have to get her help." Casey agreed, and Ella picked up her phone to place a call to Dr. McGregor.

"Hello, is that you, Ella?" the doctor asked excitedly. "I have been trying to reach you."

"I know," Ella replied sheepishly, thinking of all the calls she had ignored from her doctor. "We need your help, but it has nothing to do with me. I'm here with a young woman who seems to be having a breakdown, and I am worried about her."

"May I speak to her?" Dr. McGregor asked.

"Let me ask her," Ella replied. She held the phone toward Justine and asked her, "Are you willing to talk to Dr. McGregor?" she asked her. Justine did not answer. "Please," Ella begged her. "She can help you; trust me."

Justine raised her hand to accept the phone offered by Ella. "Yes," she said to the doctor. Casey and Ella stood watching over Justine while she spoke to the renowned therapist. Periodically, Justine would reply with a yes or no answer before she held the phone up to indicate to Ella to take it back. "Here," she said.

Taking the phone, Ella said, "Dr. McGregor, what should I do?"

"She's agreed to come in for help," the doctor told her. "You need to bring her to the hospital immediately. I will meet you there."

"We'll be there as soon as we can," Ella promised. "We have to bring her to the hospital," she told Casey. "Can you help me get her to the car?"

"Of course," Casey replied. The two women gently helped Justine to her feet and supported her as they walked her to the car.

"Everyone is going to know what happened," Justine stated.

"Justine, you're so strong," Ella told her as Casey drove them to the hospital. "But no one can go through this alone. Please promise me you'll let Dr. McGregor help you."

Staring ahead blankly, Justine nodded her head. "It's all an act, you know," she said. "I'm not strong. I just pretend to be."

"You are strong," Ella reassured her. "Look how much you have helped me over the past few days. There aren't very many people who could do that. I may be too young to be your mother, but I'm not too old to be your friend."

Justine rolled her head to the side to look at Ella, "You are such a good person," she told her. "I would love to be your friend. Do you really think this doctor can help me?"

"I know she can," Ella replied honestly.

Dr. McGregor was waiting in the parking lot when Casey pulled up to the emergency room entrance. Ella waved her over, and she ran to the car. "Hello, Justine," she said. "I'm Dr. McGregor."

Justine looked at the doctor with glazed eyes, "Hello, Dr. McGregor, can you help me?"

"I will do everything I can to help you," she promised her. The doctor turned and motioned for the orderlies waiting by the door to bring over the wheelchair. They lifted Justine from the car, placed her into the wheelchair, and started toward the hospital entrance."

"Take care of her," Ella ordered Dr. McGregor.

"You know I will," the doctor replied. "Ella, I need to go take care of Justine right now, but you and I need to talk about everything you've been enduring. Promise me you'll call me."

"I promise," Ella told her. "Hopefully, this will be over soon."

The doctor looked at her inquisitively. "You seem different, Ella. Not physically different, but emotionally different."

"I think I have changed more in the past few days than I could ever imagine," she replied.

Not having time to ask her to explain in more detail, the doctor gave Ella a pat on the arm and an encouraging smile before turning to hurry into the hospital to focus on Justine. "I hope she gets the help she needs," Ella said wistfully.

"She will," Casey assured her. "She's in good hands."

Ella thought of the help Dr. McGregor had given her over the years and how far she had progressed in that time. A sense of calm washed over her because she knew Justine was receiving the best care she could.

25

Chapter 25

Adrienne was again sitting on her sofa, thinking about Jake's murder and the next steps she needed to take. There was still so much to do. She heard a car pull into the driveway, looked around to verify Jeff could not see her, and stood to look out the window. It was Agent Ulrich. The next phase of her plan was in motion.

"Jeff," she yelled after moving back to the sofa. "Someone is here."

"Who is it?" Jeff asked as he came down the hallway.

"I don't know," Adrienne said deceptively over the sound of the doorbell.

Jeff went to the door, opened the door slightly, and said, "Hello, Agent Ulrich."

"Hello, Mr. Dwyer," replied the Agent. "May I come in?"

"Of course," Adrienne said sweetly from the sofa. "It's so good to see you, Layna. Is there an update on Jake's case?"

Agent Ulrich walked into the house and replied, "Actually, there is. We found a rudimentary homemade silencer in the woods, not far from where Jake was shot." She paused before adding, "There was one readable fingerprint on it."

Adrienne saw the color drain from Jeff's face and could see his chest moving rapidly as his breathing became erratic. "I don't understand, Layna," she stated. "When was that found?"

"I found it last night," she replied. "Someone called in an anonymous tip about where we should look for it."

"I, I can't believe it," Adrienne stammered. "Does that mean someone saw what Matthew did?"

"We don't know," the agent answered honestly. "But there's a problem. The fingerprint doesn't match Matthew or Mrs. Dalton."

"What does that mean?" Adrienne questioned her.

"It means we have to rule out anyone we can, so we can find the source of the fingerprint," Agent Ulrich answered her. "I have fingerprints from you, Adrienne, but I need to get prints for Mr. Dwyer."

"Of course," a confident Adrienne replied. "We don't have anything to hide."

"Great," the agent replied as she handed her card to Jeff. "Just come to the station today and we'll get you printed and cleared. I'll see you soon."

Once the agent left the house a frantic Jeff jumped up and started pacing. "It has to be my fingerprint, Adrienne," he cried. "Neither you nor Jake touched it without gloves. I was the only one who did."

"I'm so sorry, Jeff," Adrienne replied in her sincerest voice. "I could have sworn I wiped it clean."

"What am I going to do? They're going to arrest me," he said frantically. "I thought you destroyed it."

"I didn't get a chance before the cops showed up," she lied. "But I hid it where I didn't think anyone could find it. Someone must have taken it and hidden it in the woods."

"What are we going to do?" Jeff cried. "This is my punishment for killing my brother and coveting his wife. I never should have agreed to this."

Adrienne rolled her eyes, wondering what Jeff meant by 'we' since her fingerprints weren't on the silencer. "What if you run away, Jeff?"

"No, I can't do that and leave you here to deal with the aftermath of my disappearance. What if they come after you?"

"They don't have any evidence to implicate me," she reassured him. "If you run away, Ava and I will find a way to join you later."

"No, I couldn't ask you to live the life of a fugitive. I wouldn't do that to you or to Ava."

Knowing she had no intention of joining him, Adrienne kept pushing. She needed him to disappear so he would be blamed as Matthew's accomplice and she could be with Connor. "Just pray on it, Jeff, and the answer will come to you."

"You're right," he told her. Jeff folded his hands and closed his eyes to pray for the guidance he so desperately needed. Adrienne sat there impatiently waiting for him to arrive at the epiphany she required him to have.

After what seemed an eternity, Jeff opened his eyes, "I know what I need to do," he told Adrienne.

"What?" she asked him nervously, hoping he would answer that he would disappear and her plan could move to the next phase.

"I'm going to confess," he declared.

Adrienne had to force herself to stop the smile from starting on her face; this is even better than what she wanted him to do. "What are you going to say?" she asked with actual interest.

"I'm going to tell them I found out Jake was a rapist, and I killed him because he was evil," Jeff replied candidly.

"What are you going to say about me?" Adrienne asked, her breath now coming rapidly.

"Absolutely nothing," Jeff replied. "They don't need to know anything about you. You have to stay free because Ava needs you. I'll tell them that I went to Matthew with what I knew, and the two of us plotted it together to keep Jake away from Ava, and you didn't know anything about it. If they think Matthew and I worked together, you'll still be safe."

"Jeff, you're amazing," Adrienne told him. "You really are my guardian angel."

He looked at Adrienne, gave her a slight smile, and kissed her gently. "I need to pay for what I did. Even if it was necessary to protect you, it's still a sin. Maybe we'll be together in paradise again someday," he said as he stood to leave to turn himself in to the police.

"I love you," Adrienne yelled at him as he walked out the door. After the door shut behind Jeff, Adrienne fell back on her sofa, kicking her legs in the air, unable to contain her glee. She wished Connor was with her so that they could have celebratory sex, but that would have to wait for the moment. This was even better than she had planned. Momentarily collecting herself, she reached for her phone and called a familiar number. When the person on the other end of the line answered, she said, "He decided to confess. You know what to do," and hung up the phone without a reply.

26

Chapter 26

Casey's phone rang, knocking Ella out of her peaceful trance. "Are you serious?" Casey yelled. "I'll be right there."

"What happened?" Ella asked her.

"Jeff confessed to killing Jake," she replied excitedly. "We have to get to the police station right now. It's his fingerprint on the silencer."

"I can't believe it," Ella muttered. "Does this mean Matthew can come home today?"

"Jeff claims that he and Matthew conspired together to kill Jake," Casey stated while looking straight ahead, focusing on the road.

"That's crazy," Ella shouted. "Matthew barely knows him."

"I believe you," Casey told her. "He's up to something, but I don't know what it is yet." Casey pulled up to the station, and she and Ella ran into the building.

"I want to see my husband," Ella demanded to the desk sergeant before Casey could pull her away.

"You have to calm down," she told her. "Let me find out what is going on before we decide to start screaming at people, okay?"

"Okay," she promised. "But I want to see Matthew."

"I know, hon," Casey replied. "But you're not going to accomplish that by yelling at people. Although I have to admit, it's nice to see you assert yourself."

Ella couldn't help but smile at the attorney. She trusted her more than she had ever trusted anyone, aside from Matthew and Dr. McGregor. "Just let me go back there with you," she begged her. "I'll be good."

"Okay, but you have to be on your best behavior," Casey warned her. Ella followed Casey through the doors into the building area where Dale and Agent Ulrich had questioned her just a few days ago. It seemed like forever since she was last here. Casey pointed to a seat in the hallway and said to Ella, "Wait here, and I'll be back as soon as I can."

Ella put her elbows on her knees and rested her face in her cupped hands. Just last week, this moment would have sent her into an uncontrollable panic attack, but she sat in the chair calmly, waiting for Casey to return.

"Would you like some coffee, Mrs. Dalton?" she heard a voice ask.

Raising her face from her hands, Ella saw the young officer she had first seen on the day of Jake's murder standing over her with a cup of coffee. Accepting the cup from him, she stated, "That would be great. Thank you, Officer." She paused and added, "I'm sorry, I don't know your name."Admitting this to someone had once been one of her greatest fears, and she couldn't bring herself to ask him his name on Saturday, but today she asked the question with ease.

"Benson," he replied. "My name is Officer Benson."

A chuckle escaped Ella's mouth. "My favorite show has a detective named Benson."

He smiled and nodded, "You're a *Law & Order* fan, huh?"

"Yes," she replied. Ella turned her head when she heard Casey's heels clicking on the floor. The lawyer was running toward her.

"Excuse me," Casey said to Officer Benson. "I need to talk to my client in private."

"Of course," the officer replied. "Have a good day, Mrs. Dalton." He tipped his hat to Ella and walked away.

"What did you find out?" Ella asked her.

"Well, Jeff told them that Jake was a rapist and that he admitted it to him when Jeff confronted him. He claims he tried to get Jake to turn himself in and he refused."

"What does that have to do with Matthew?" Ella inquired.

"Jeff said that he was worried about Ava's safety since she was in a house with Jake, so he went to Matthew for help," Casey stated. "He said that he and Matthew conspired to kill Jake to ensure he wouldn't hurt Ava."

"That makes no sense," Ella argued. "Matthew would have told me."

Casey took a deep breath and added, "Jeff said Matthew knew that Jake was planning to attack you."

"Me?" a shocked Ella asked. "Jake has made some inappropriate comments to me, but I don't believe Matthew ever thought he would attack me."

"Jeff said that Jake has been obsessed with you since..." Casey's voice trailed off.

"Since what?" Ella asked. "Tell me, Casey."

Casey exhaled loudly and said, "Jeff said Jake spied on you and Matthew in the woods and saw you being intimate. Ever since then, Jake has been obsessed with you. He said Jake admitted to him that you were going to be his next victim."

Ella rubbed her hands down her face. "I can't believe this," she proclaimed. "How does this keep happening?"

"Right now, it's Matthew's word against Jeff's," Casey stated. "The good news is that the fingerprint on the silencer matches Jeff. The bad news is that all of the other evidence points to Matthew." Casey paused, "There's something else I have to tell you."

"What is it?" a frightened Ella asked.

"Jeff claims that Matthew was stalking Adrienne and that she is scared of him," Casey told her.

"But we have proof that it was Adrienne who assaulted Matthew," Ella replied.

Casey smiled. "Exactly," she said. "I have Agent Ulrich waiting down the hall. She wants to see the recording."

"Gladly," Ella replied.

She followed Casey down a hall into the same room she had been in when undergoing the interrogation. Ella sat at the table, smugly looked at Agent Ulrich, and said, "I have something you need to see."

"I know you don't like me, Mrs. Dalton," the agent told her. "But I'm just doing my job. If you have evidence that proves Miss Griffin committed a crime, I will review it and treat it the same as any other evidence."

"It's not that I don't like you, Agent Ulrich," Ella told her. "It's that you formed an opinion of me based on the lies of another person, and no matter what I said to defend myself, you were unwilling to listen."

"Fair point," she replied. "But you need to understand that I listen to untruths and half-truths every day, so I usually know how to determine when someone is lying."

"Well, you didn't this time," Ella retorted. "Look, maybe we can talk when this over to clear the air, but at this moment, the only thing that matters to me is Matthew. You need to see this."

Agent Ulrich nodded, and Ella played the video she had downloaded from the teddy bear and transferred to her phone. She could see the agent's eyes glaring at the screen as she witnessed the attack on Matthew. When it was over, she looked at Ella and said, "Well, if you'll excuse me, I need to send someone to arrest Miss Griffin for sexual assault."

"Did you notice how well she was walking, Agent Ulrich?" Ella goaded her. "This occurred when her MS was so bad that she needed a walker to move. Isn't that why you ruled her out as a suspect in Jake's murder? Because she wouldn't be able to get to the scene?"

Ella exhaled loudly because she could tell the agent was reevaluating her belief in Matthew's guilt. Finally, things were starting to go their way. Before she could thank the agent for listening to her, the door swung open. Another officer was standing in the doorway. "Layna," he yelled. "You need to come quick."

Agent Ulrich jumped up from the table and ran out of the room. "What is going on?" Casey yelled.

The officer looked at Casey and Ella. "You need to stay here. Do not leave this room," he ordered.

"Well, I'm not just going to sit here," Casey asserted. She pulled out her phone to place a phone call.

"Who are you calling?" Ella asked.

"One of my connections," Casey told her with a wink. "I have more than one way to find out what is happening here." She held up her finger to Ella, indicating for her to be silent. "Hey, can you tell me what's going on? Yes, I'm here right now."

Casey hung up the phone and grabbed Ella's hands with hers. "Jeff hanged himself in his cell," she said solemnly.

27

Chapter 27

Stung by Casey's words, Ella stated forcefully, "I don't believe that he killed himself. We have to get Matthew out of here."

Casey nodded and replied, "I don't think he did either. It's a little too convenient that his confession is recorded, and right after that, he hangs himself."

"It doesn't make any sense, Casey," Ella stated. "Jeff was a decent man. Something, or someone, had to convince him to murder Jake."

"We have to find a way to prove it, though," Casey declared.

The door flew open again, and the officer who had rushed in to summon Agent Ulrich stood there. "Sorry, but you ladies have to leave. We have to clear the building of all non-personnel."

"No problem, we understand," Casey told him as she stood and pulled Ella up to join her. "Let's go out to my car, Ella."

They attempted to walk past the officer, but he stopped them, saying, "I have to escort you out."

"Of course," Casey replied.

Ella and Casey walked silently, side by side with the officer until they were out of the building.

Casey took the keys to her Mercedes, placed them in Ella's hand, and told her, "Take my car and drive yourself home. Make sure all your security systems are on and don't let anyone in the house."

"What are you going to do?" Ella questioned.

"I'm going to stay here until they let me back into the building, and I am going to get Matthew in protective custody until I can get bail and get him out of this place," she stated. "Someone got to Jeff here. They're not going to get Matthew too."

"Won't it be better if I stay here?" Ella asked.

"No," Casey replied. "We don't know who to trust, and they're not going to deal with you anyway. Your house is like a fortress, so you're much safer there."

Reluctantly, Ella took the keys from Casey. "Please be careful, Casey, and please protect Matthew," she pleaded.

"You know I will," Casey assured her.

Ella drove back to her house, carefully examining her surroundings before getting out of the vehicle. She saw nothing amiss, but she still bolted from the car and ran to her door, slamming and locking it behind her. Thinking she had left her purse in her car, she became momentarily frantic. Thankfully, she realized she had forgotten her bag when they rushed to bring Justine to the hospital, and her purse was sitting on the entryway table, exactly where she had left it.

The sound of her ringing phone broke the silence, which made her jump and knock her phone to the floor. Dropping to her knees, she grabbed the phone and looked at the caller ID. She did not recognize the phone number on the screen. Staring at her phone, trying to decide if she should answer or not, the number suddenly made sense. "Hello," she said excitedly.

"Mrs. Dalton," said the caller. "This is Jessica. Um, you left me a confusing message."

In an accusing tone, Ella asked, "Jessica, can you explain to me why my husband has your phone number with instructions to call you?"

"Mrs. Dalton," Jessica stammered, "I don't know what you're thinking but believe me, it's completely innocent."

"Then explain it to me," Ella ordered.

"I'm a wildlife photographer," she stated. "Your husband contacted me about taking pictures of the bald eagles in the woods behind your house."

Ella thought about Jessica's innocent explanation. That sounded like something Matthew would do, but she decided she needed to test the photographer further to verify the story. "When were you out there taking pictures?" she asked.

"A little over a week ago," she replied. "Your husband wanted me to take pictures of the birds so that he could surprise you with prints for your house."

Knowing the explanation make perfect sense and angry at herself for assuming the worst about her husband yet again, Ella told her, "I'm so sorry for jumping to conclusions. I've been under a lot of stress the past few days."

"It's okay," Jessica stated. "After putting up the cameras, I went out of town, so I apologize for not contacting you or your husband earlier."

"Did you say you put up cameras?" an excited Ella asked. "Like trail cameras?"

"Yes, I put up trail cameras," a chagrined Jessica replied. "Sorry I didn't ask for Mr. Dalton's permission before I did, but he left after showing me where the eagle nest was, and there are so many other interesting bird species out there I wanted to capture. Did you see the hummingbirds?"

Ella began to cry, but they were tears of joy. "I'm sorry, Mrs. Dalton," a confused Jessica said. "I didn't know it would upset you that much."

"I'm not upset, Jessica," Ella replied. "You don't know it, but you might have saved my husband's life."

"I don't understand," Jessica stated.

"Did you say you were in town?" Ella asked.

"Yeah, I was just going to get groceries since I have nothing in my house," Jessica answered.

"Can you come out to my house and show me where the trail cameras are?" Ella implored. "It's a matter of life and death."

"Can you please explain how my bird pictures—" Jessica started, but Ella cut her off.

"I will explain once you get here," Ella told her. "Please, this is extremely important."

"Okay," Jessica replied. "I should be there in about fifteen minutes."

Ella's heart was racing as she dialed Casey's number, but there was no answer. She left a message telling Casey to call her immediately and stood by her front door waiting impatiently for Jessica to appear.

About twenty minutes later, the buzzer for the front gate sounded, and Ella answered it eagerly. "Jessica, is that you?" she asked.

"Yep," Jessica replied.

Ella immediately pressed the button to open the gate for Jessica, slung her purse over her torso, and went outside to meet her as she drove up. She walked to the driver's side of the car, and Jessica rolled down the window to talk to her. "I am so happy to see you," Ella told her.

"Are you going to explain what is going on?" Jessica asked.

"Can I explain it on our way to the cameras?" Ella asked. "We can't waste time."

Jessica seemed to be questioning whether she should follow her or not, but she did get out of her car and start to walk beside Ella. "You have to slow down," she stated because Ella began running to the woods.

"I'm sorry," Ella told her. "You do deserve an explanation. I don't know any way to say this other than just to say it. On Saturday, my husband was arrested for murdering someone on this trail."

Her words caused Jessica to stop walking immediately. "Your husband murdered someone, and you think I'm going to follow you out there. Are you crazy?" she asked.

"Please," Ella begged. "Matthew is innocent. I know he's being framed, and I think your cameras might have recorded the real killer." She could see the young woman's understandable hesitation, but she needed to know what was on those cameras. Ella grabbed Jessica's hand and said, "You met my husband. Did he seem like the type of person that could commit murder?"

"No, but that's what they always say about murderers," Jessica countered.

"You were in the woods with him by yourself. Did he ever try to hurt you or make you feel uncomfortable?" Ella asked pointedly.

Jessica looked at her feet and replied, "No, he never said or did anything inappropriate."

"Then please help me," Ella begged her. "I think your cameras are what we need to solve this."

"Okay," Jessica replied. "But people know where I am."

"Thank you, Jessica. You can be the hero in this story," Ella told her.

The two women continued walking to the woods, and soon they came to the location they needed. The yellow police tape that had been on the trees now lay on the ground, ripped and tattered by the strong Minnesota winds. "Where are the cameras?" Ella asked her.

"Up here by the tree with the bald eagle nest," Jessica replied.

"You can stay here if you want," Ella told her.

Jessica shook her head. "No, I need to show you. I hid them very well. Apparently, I did quite a good job since the police never found them."

Ella followed Jessica into the woods, looking wistfully at the clearing where Matthew had so carefully laid out their picnic. Where the blanket had lain, there was now a dark stain from Jake's blood. "Up here," Jessica said, pointing at the trees ahead.

"One camera is up pretty high in the trees because I wanted to get a view of the inside of the nest. That one probably won't help you," Jessica stated. "But I hid one back here to get a view of them by the ground."

Ella followed Jessica to an area beyond the clearing and watched her pull back some branches to reveal there was no longer a camera. "Where is it? It wasn't listed as evidence when Casey was given discovery," stated a quizzical Ella.

Jessica shrugged. "Maybe the person who committed the murder cut it off; I didn't have it locked."

Her hope to clear her husband was gone, and she felt her heart sink. "All of the pictures are gone?" Ella asked her, afraid of the answer.

"Whoever took them probably thinks so," Jessica replied as she held up her phone, "but they would be wrong. The cameras I use send the pictures to the cloud. Let's see what's on there." She pushed buttons on her phone and logged into her cloud account. "Found them."

"Can you find the pictures from Saturday afternoon?" Ella asked her.

"Sure, as long as they didn't cut it down before the murder," she replied. "So that you know, this camera takes still shots; it doesn't record. But it's motion-sensitive, so if someone was out here moving around, it should have gotten them on camera."

Ella nodded her head, saying a silent prayer that Jessica would find the pictures that could prove Matthew's innocence.

"Holy shit," exclaimed Jessica. "You have got to see these."

She looked over Jessica's shoulder to view the images. Ella saw the photos she had prayed for right there before her eyes. Jessica handed Ella the camera, showing her how to navigate between the pictures. There were so many pictures capturing them in the act; a picture of Jake, Adrienne, and Jeff huddled together; a picture of Jake with his back turned to Jeff; a picture of a menacing Jake standing over Adrienne; a picture of Jeff pointing the gun at Jake's head; a picture of a dead Jake lying on the ground with Jeff standing over him; pictures of Jeff leaving with a bag in the direction of Ella and Matthew's home. But the image that caught Ella's attention was the one of Adrienne, standing over Jake's body, smiling.

Ella thrust the phone back at Jessica and placed her hand over her mouth. "Oh my God," she said. "This proves that Matthew is innocent."

"I can't believe it," Jessica said. "What are you going to do now?"

Her thoughts immediately turned to Ava, who was alone with Adrienne. Jeff was no longer there to protect her, and Ella knew she had to get Ava away from her mother. "You have to show the lead lead detectives the pictures," a desperate Ella said as she dug Agent Ulrich's business card from her purse and handed it to Jessica. "Call her and tell her what we found. Don't give those pictures to anyone but Agent Ulrich. No matter what they say."

Jessica nodded and started to run out of the woods but looked back toward Ella. "What are you going to do?" she asked her.

"I have to save my daughter," Ella said.

28

Chapter 28

Ella raced down the path and through the woods until she saw Adrienne's house come into view. She had been allowed back into her home around the same time Ella was allowed back in hers. She had to get Ava out of there without raising Adrienne's suspicions. Ella now knew the level of violence Adrienne was capable of, and she had no intention of letting her hurt Ava any more than she already had. She stopped to catch her breath and clear her head. Ella knew Adrienne wasn't going to allow her to walk in and take Ava away. She knew Matthew would not want her to face Adrienne alone, but she also knew he would not want Ava to spend one more moment with someone capable of doing what Adrienne had done. Ella could only think of one idea to convince Adrienne to release Ava to her, and she wasn't confident that it would work. But she had to try, so she approached the front door and rang the doorbell.

Adrienne was not expecting company, and the sound of the doorbell startled her. Her walker was in the living room, but she was in her bedroom. She had to sneak down the hall to ensure no one would be able to see her walking without assistance. Peeking her head around the corner, she could see Ella at the door, and she was unhappy about it. Ella had never come to her home without Matthew, and if she was here, then Adrienne knew she had an ulterior motive. Carefully, she reached around the corner to grab her walker and make her way to open the door to her arch-nemesis.

"What do you want?" she snarled at Ella the moment she opened the door.

"Adrienne," Ella said excitedly. "Did you hear the news?"

"What news?" Adrienne questioned. The last news she heard had been that Jeff committed suicide, and she no longer had to worry about him implicating her in Jake's murder.

"Jeff confessed!" Ella exclaimed.

"So?" Adrienne asked sarcastically. "That doesn't mean Matthew is innocent."

"Well, that's not what the police think," Ella lied. "They're releasing him tonight. Can I please take Ava home with me so she's there to surprise Matthew when he gets home?"

"She's sleeping," Adrienne snapped at her.

"Please, Adrienne," Ella implored. "It will mean so much to Matthew to have Ava there when he gets home."

Anxious to hear the real reason for Ella's visit, Adrienne decided to play along with Ella's blatant lie. If Ella were here by herself under any other circumstance, she would slam the door in her face, but tonight she stepped back so Ella could enter and said, "Come on in, and I'll check on Ava and see if she wants to go."

"Thank you, Adrienne. Matthew will be so happy to see Ava," Ella told her as she cautiously stepped inside the house.

Ella heard the door slam shut behind her, causing her to turn quickly and see Adrienne standing in front of the door, arms crossed. "Is something wrong?" Ella asked nervously.

"You're lying," Adrienne declared. "There's no way they're letting Matthew out of jail tonight."

Looking down at her hands because she had never been able to look someone in the face while lying, Ella asked, "Why do you say that?"

"Because I have had to bail Jake out of jail before, and they don't just let someone out. Jake was only there for a DUI, and there was a ton of paperwork to be completed before they let him out. I would imagine that it's quite a bit more complex to have an accused murderer released." Adrienne said smugly. "Now, why don't you tell me why you're really here trying to steal my daughter?"

"I don't know what you're talking about, Adrienne," Ella stammered, still unable to look her in the eyes. "Can I just take Ava home for the night so she can see her father?"

"What do you know?" Adrienne asked in an accusing tone.

"I know that Jeff confessed," Ella stated. "That's all."

"You're a terrible liar, Ella," Adrienne told her. "You know how I know you're a terrible liar? Because I'm a good liar."

"I think it's best if I leave now," Ella said. "Please get Ava so I can take her with me."

Adrienne laughed at Ella's request. "Ava isn't going anywhere," she stated. "Besides, I fed her full of antihistamine, and she's not going to wake up for a while."

"You drugged her?" Ella asked in horror.

"I had to," Adrienne said. "She always wants and needs attention, and I don't have time for that. Besides, she's fine; it's never hurt her before."

Mortified, Ella thought of the little girl asleep in the other room, viewed as such a burden by her own mother that she resorted to drugging her. "Look, I'll carry her out. Would you please let me take her home with me? If you don't want her to bother you, I'll take her home, and you can be free to do whatever you want," Ella begged.

"No, I don't think so," Adrienne said. "I think it's time for you and me to have a heart-to-heart. What do you say; should we have a nice girl chat?"

"I need to get home. Everyone is expecting me soon," Ella lied.

"You're lying again," Adrienne chided her. No longer attempting to hide that she could walk without assistance, she went into the kitchen and left her walker behind. "Sit down, Ella, let's talk," she said from the other room.

Ella stayed where she was, unwilling to sit down but also unwilling to leave Ava behind. Adrienne came out of the kitchen and walked toward her. She pulled a large butcher knife from behind her back, pointed it at Ella, and told her, "I said, let's have a heart-to-heart. Sit down, bitch."

No choice but to do as instructed, Ella sat down on the closest chair, adjusting her purse so it sat on her lap. "What do you want to talk about,

Adrienne?" she asked in a frightened voice.

"I want to know why you think you're so much better than me," Adrienne told her. "Why do you think you're so perfect, beautiful, and smart but think I'm a dumb, disgusting whore?"

"That's not fair, Adrienne. I don't think that about myself at all," Ella said truthfully.

"Oh, please," Adrienne scoffed. "You're Little Miss Perfect. Everyone loves you. Matthew loves you; Ava loves you, and even Jake, well, I wouldn't call it love, but he wanted you."

"No, I am far from perfect," Ella replied. "I have a lot of problems."

Adrienne thoughtfully considered Ella's words. "You know what? I think you're right, and you're not Little Miss Perfect. If you were the sweet, meek thing you pretend to be, you would have done the honorable thing and stepped aside when Matthew got me pregnant. Don't you think, Ella?" Adrienne said to her.

"I'm sorry you were hurt, Adrienne, but that's not my fault," Ella told her. "Matthew and I love each other."

"A good person would have given us a chance to be a family," Adrienne yelled at her.

"Matthew had to consider what was best for him, not just you. You can't force true love, Adrienne," Ella replied quietly.

"No one truly loves anyone," Adrienne declared, waving the knife around wildly. "No one has ever loved me, not even my mother."

Hearing Adrienne speak about her mother gave Ella the knowledge of one thing she had in common with Adrienne. Sensing this might be her opportunity to disarm her, Ella said, "I know how you feel. My mother never loved me either."

Adrienne squinted at Ella; she didn't believe her. "So? Even if she didn't love you, she left you with a shit ton of money. I would have taken that over love any day of the week."

"I would have rather had her love," Ella replied in earnest. "Money really can't buy you happiness. It never made my mother very happy. I'm sorry for how your mother treated you, Adrienne; I honestly am. You must have endured so much pain from her failures. But they were her failures, not yours. Everyone, even you, deserves their mother's love." Even as Ella was speaking the words to Adrienne, she realized they applied to her as well. Her mother had never been loving and criticized everything about her. She was not the failure; her mother was.

For the first time in her life, Adrienne began to cry real tears. "Stop trying to psychoanalyze me, you stupid bitch," Adrienne screamed at her. "It's not going to work."

"I'm not trying to analyze you; I only want to help you," Ella told her.

Adrienne steeled herself. She wasn't about to let her loser of a mother stop her from enjoying seeing Ella squirm. "I don't want or need your help," she said firmly. "What I want to do is find out how much Matthew loves you after he finds out about your affair with Jeff."

"What?" Ella yelled. "I barely know Jeff."

"That's not what his suicide note says," Adrienne said in a mocking tone. "Do you want me to read it to you? I think it's really quite well written."

"No one will believe that," Ella said.

"Of course they will," Adrienne chuckled. "They've believed everything else I've fed them so far." Adrienne placed her hand under Ella's chin and looked into her eyes. "When I started this whole thing, my goal was to hurt you as much as possible. The best way I could think to do that was to frame you for Jake's murder and take Matthew away from you, just like how you took him away from me. But I knew Jeff would never help me frame you, so my second thought was I could frame Matthew and still take him away from you. Plus, I get to hurt Matthew for rejecting me every time I threw myself at him. Putting Matthew in jail and taking your money seemed to be the best way to hurt you both, but after thinking about it, I think it will work out to have you go to jail and get Matthew for myself. I think you need to hear this," she said.

Ella shook her head, not wanting to hear the lies Adrienne had created about her, but Adrienne forcefully pushed Ella's chin away and picked up the laptop sitting on the coffee table. "This is Jeff's," she said about the computer. "What's on here is really quite intriguing. This note will be found by the cops when they get here to investigate his suicide." Adrienne smirked at Ella. "That's right. I already know Jeff confessed. I also know his confession included that Matthew and Jeff plotted together to kill poor Jake."

"Adrienne, please," Ella begged. "Think of what this will do to Ava. You can stop this, and no one has to know."

"Why should I care about what it does to Ava?" Adrienne questioned. "It's not like I even wanted her." She held her finger up to her lips to tell Ella to be quiet. "Now listen carefully because he mentions you," she said before reading Jeff's fabricated suicide note to Ella.

My name is Jeff Dwyer, and if you're reading this, I am dead. I am ashamed to admit that I murdered my brother, Jake Dwyer. My reason for the murder was one of the oldest in history – the love of a woman. I have been having an affair with Ella Dalton for over a year, and I thought we were madly in love. She told me she wanted her husband, Matthew, out of the picture so we could be together, but she didn't want to divorce him and pay him a divorce settlement. Ella didn't want to murder Matthew either because she knew she would be the prime suspect, so she concocted a plan to murder Jake and frame her husband. She thought Jake was the perfect victim because she knew Matthew was still in love with Adrienne Griffin, Jake's wife. Ella thought if she framed Matthew by murdering Jake, that would hurt Adrienne more than anything. She is desperately jealous of Adrienne because she knows Matthew married her for her money, and his heart lies with Adrienne.

I am genuinely remorseful that I agreed to this plan, but my love for Ella blinded me. Unfortunately, the silencer was found, and my fingerprint will be matched to it. I cannot live with the guilt of killing my brother, so I am going to confess. Having made my peace with God, I am ready to face my punishment. Unfortunately, I am still too much in love with Ella to tell the full truth, so I will implicate Matthew in my confession, and she'll still get her revenge on him.

However, if anything happens to me, it will be apparent that I meant nothing to Ella. Please know I would never commit suicide as that is the ultimate sin. If I die due to an accident or suicide, Ella Dalton killed me. Please make sure Ella Dalton is locked up for life, and please set Matthew Dalton free. He is an innocent man. She gave me Matthew's gun and told me to wear his shirt when I killed Jake and then placed it back in the shed once the murder was done. She told Matthew to get the gun so his hands would have gunpowder residue, and she led him to the body so he would touch Jake's body. Please, believe me, he is innocent and needs to be set free.

"You're crazy!" Ella screamed.

"Maybe I am," Adrienne said, moving closer to Ella, holding the knife close to her face. "Or maybe I am just that much smarter than you. You see, I planned to sue you for Jake's wrongful death and take most of your money while you rotted in jail, but now you know too much so you'll have to die instead. Actually, it's probably better that you die so you can't refute Jeff's letter. It still works out for me because I can sue your estate once you're dead. Even better, I can marry Matthew and have all of the money he inherits from your estate."

"Please, Adrienne," Ella begged her. "You can have my money; I just want to take Ava."

Adrienne shook her head, "No, I want you to have nothing and me to have it all, and now that includes Matthew." She studied Ella, looking her body up and down, "Where should I cut you first?" she teased her. "I was thinking your face because I hate your face."

Ella put her arms on the chair, pushing her body back in an effort to move away from Adrienne, causing her purse to shift on her lap, exposing Justine's revolver. She had forgotten that she had placed the gun in her bag last night. Ella quickly grabbed for the firearm and pointed it at Adrienne. "Get away from me," she yelled at Adrienne.

"What the hell?" a surprised Adrienne asked. "Where did you get that?"

"From a friend," Ella told her. "Now, you're going to drop that knife, and Ava and I are going to leave. Is that clear?"

"You think you won?" Adrienne sneered. "You haven't won anything."

"I know everything," Ella told her. "I know Matthew isn't Ava's father, I know you drugged Matthew, and I know you helped Jeff murder Jake."

Adrienne froze because the only two people who knew she drugged Matthew were her and Jake. There was no way Ella could know about that. "What do you mean I drugged Matthew?" she screamed.

"I know you did, you sick, twisted witch," Ella screamed back.

Furious, Adrienne yelled, "It was consensual, and he wanted me. Believe me, he wanted me bad."

"Now I know you're lying," Ella said, turning the tables on Adrienne. "Matthew has never wanted you. Do you remember Jake's teddy bear? The one he gave to Ava." She saw Adrienne nod and continued, "Well, we found a camera inside of that bear. Jake recorded the whole thing."

"You're lying," Adrienne said. "That teddy bear is here."

"No, Matthew swapped it with a new one after you assaulted him. He hid the real one at our house in a closet," Ella told her. "That's right, Matthew was so disgusted by the thought of touching you, he was planning to burn the teddy bear that reminded him of you."

"You're lying," Adrienne said again, but with much less conviction. She knew Ella was telling the truth.

"You couldn't even get Matthew to have sex with you while he was passed out," Ella derided her. "Twice you tried, and twice you failed." Ella saw the shock on Adrienne's face and decided to land the final blow. "That's right. Your mother told me about the night you claimed you and Matthew conceived Ava. I know you have never had sex with Matthew. Even drunk or drugged, Matthew has enough sense to avoid you."

Adrienne couldn't believe that Jake had betrayed her that way. "That son of a bitch!" she screamed.

"I guess you didn't have quite the hold over Jake that you thought you did, huh?" Ella mocked her. "Even he was smart enough not to trust you."

Still full of confidence, Adrienne said, "It doesn't matter. When it comes down to the wire, Agent Ulrich will believe me over you."

"Agent Ulrich has seen the recording of what you did to Matthew," Ella told her. "She's sending someone to arrest you, and they'll be here soon."

"I hate you so much," Adrienne seethed. She moved to attack Ella in an attempt to take away the gun, but she saw something out of the corner of her eye.

"What are you doing here?" Adrienne yelled at the officer standing at the doorway, pointing his service revolver at them both.

"I was sent here by Agent Ulrich to arrest you for sexual assault, Miss

Griffin," Officer Benson replied. He turned his attention to Ella, who still had the gun focused on Adrienne. "I'm going to need you to put down the gun, Mrs. Dalton. No one needs to get hurt."

Ella didn't lower the weapon but kept it trained on Adrienne. Officer Benson walked toward her cautiously, still aiming his revolver. He put his hand on her arm, gently pushing until she lowered the gun. He immediately removed it from Ella's hand and placed it in the waistband of his pants. "Are you hurt, Mrs. Dalton?" he asked in a concerned voice.

"No, I'm not hurt," Ella stated. She pointed at Adrienne and yelled, "But she killed Jake and tried to frame Matthew for it."

"I believe you, Mrs. Dalton," Officer Jensen told her. "Please sit and try to calm down. I need you to relax, so you're not a threat to me, and I can arrest Miss Griffin."

Relieved for the officer's presence, Ella did as he commanded and sat in the chair.

Officer Benson looked at Adrienne. "Miss Griffin, I am going to read your rights and place you in handcuffs. I won't have to hurt you as long as you don't resist me."

"I won't resist you," Adrienne promised him.

Officer Benson walked toward her, and Adrienne smiled and said, "I could never resist you."

Ella rolled her eyes at Adrienne's feeble attempt to seduce the young officer. "Do you think that's going to work?" she sarcastically asked Adrienne.

"I don't know," replied Officer Benson, winking at Adrienne. "It might."

"Come here, baby," Adrienne ordered him. Officer Benson grabbed her to him and gave her a passionate kiss.

"God, I have missed you," he exclaimed.

"Not as much as I have missed you," she replied as she rubbed against him. "I can't wait to ravish you. You look so damn hot in that uniform."

Confused, Ella looked at the officer and Adrienne. She had only met the officer three times previously, but she had never really looked at him. She focused on his face, realizing he reminded her of someone and that someone was asleep in the other room. Ava had those same blue eyes. "Oh my God,"

Ella said softly. "You're Connor Swenson."

Startled, Adrienne and Connor turned to Ella. "How do you know that name?" he yelled at her.

"I met your father," Ella replied. "He misses you."

"My father is a worthless piece of shit. I couldn't care less if he misses me," Connor said bluntly.

"How could I be so stupid?" Ella wondered out loud. "You're the young man she seduced when you were just sixteen."

Adrienne smiled and said, "Pretty clever, right? I told you I'm smarter than you. It took some manipulation to get him a job as a cop, but we pulled it off."

Pleased with herself, Adrienne turned to Connor. "Babe, you have to kill her. She knows way too much. Like I already explained to Ella, I'll just have to sue her estate."

"Whatever you say, babe," Connor replied as he pointed his service revolver at Ella. "Sorry to have to do this, Mrs. Dalton, but whatever my baby wants, my baby gets. I guess I came into the house and had to shoot you because you were about to kill Adrienne."

"Connor, you don't have to do this," Ella implored him. "Please, you can walk away. You haven't killed anyone."

Adrienne began to laugh hysterically. "Oh, honey," she said to Ella. "I thought you said you knew everything."

"Let me tell her, babe," Connor told Adrienne.

"Okay, babe," she replied. "I don't want to steal your thunder."

"You see, Ella," Connor paused and then added sarcastically, "is it okay if I call you Ella?" He waved his hand to indicate her answer was meaningless and continued, "Who do you think arranged for Jeff to commit suicide in his cell?"

"That's right," Adrienne said smugly. "Connor and I are soulmates. We will do anything to be together." She turned to Connor and added, "Isn't that right, babe?"

"It sure is," Connor said. "She is my everything, and I will do anything for her. It's almost finished." Adrienne cleared her throat to indicate Connor had not yet completed all she had asked. "I know, babe," Connor added. "After finishing off Ella here, I have one loose end to take care of." Turning his gaze back to Ella, he said, "Agent Williams is still alive. I thought we got lucky and natural causes would take him out, but he managed to pull through. Don't worry though, he will be joining you on the other side soon."

Trying to think of anything to stop Connor from killing her and then killing Dale, she blurted out, "Agent Ulrich is still going to arrest Adrienne for assaulting Matthew. You won't end up together."

"That's a good point, Mrs. Dalton," Connor replied thoughtfully. "But evidence has been known to disappear. Agent Ulrich never had a chance to download it from your phone, and unfortunately, your phone was ruined in the struggle." Connor grabbed Ella's phone from her purse, threw it on the floor, and smashed it with his foot. "Oops," he said.

Adrienne stood behind Connor, smirking. "I've had enough of this dumb bitch. Shoot her, Connor," Adrienne ordered.

He again raised his gun toward Ella. Suddenly a tiny figure ran across the room and flung herself onto Ella, protecting her. "Please don't hurt my mommy," Ava cried.

A disconcerted Connor lowered his revolver, unwilling to shoot the child protecting Ella with her petite body. "I don't know what to do, babe," he said to Adrienne.

Furious, Adrienne berated her daughter. "You stupid, ungrateful brat," she yelled at Ava. "How dare you call her your mommy. I'm your mother." She tried to tear Ava off Ella, but Ava would not loosen her grip. Afraid of what Adrienne would do to the little girl if she successfully pried her away, Ella wrapped her arms around Ava, holding her as tight as she could.

"No, I want Ella to be my mommy, not you," Ava sobbed.

"Fine," Adrienne said through clenched teeth. "Guess what, Ava, I never wanted you anyway. You two deserve each other." Adrienne shoved Ava toward Ella and stood beside Connor again. "Kill her too, Connor," Adrienne ordered him.

"I don't think I can kill a little kid, babe," Connor replied. "It's one thing to kill Ella. After all she's done to you, she deserves it. But what has the kid done?"

"Did you hear what she said?" Adrienne yelled at him. "She told me she doesn't want me as a mother. Well, I don't want her as a kid." She grabbed Connor's arm, trying to raise it to force Connor to shoot them both. "Do it!" she screamed at him.

Ella was frantically trying to think of something to save their lives, so she shouted out to Connor, "Do you really want to murder your own daughter?"

"What did you say?" asked a startled Connor. "That's impossible; Matthew is the father. Adrienne would have told me if I was."

"Think about it, Connor," Ella said. "You were only sixteen when Adrienne got pregnant. Do you think she would have given up the opportunity to get money from Matthew by telling you the baby was yours?"

"Adrienne," Connor whispered. "Is she my daughter?"

"Of course not," Adrienne lied. "She's Matthew's."

Connor turned away from Adrienne, walked over to Ella and Ava, and closely examined Ava's tear-stained face. "Her eyes are just like mine," Connor said.

"Don't look at me or my mommy," Ava yelled at him. "Leave us alone. You're a bad man."

"This is why you would never let me see her. Whenever I was here, you hid her away from me. How could you not tell me, Adrienne?"

"I did what I had to do to survive, babe," she told Connor. "You couldn't support a family then."

"What else have you lied to me about?" Connor said to her, still staring at Ava's face.

"Nothing, babe, I love you, and I was planning on telling you once we were rid of Jake and Matthew," Adrienne lied, quietly moving toward him. Connor sensed her movement and turned quickly to face her. He never saw the knife in her hand as she plunged it into his stomach. He clutched at the knife, stumbled over the chair, and fell to the floor.

Adrienne grabbed Connor's gun and turned her attention back to Ava and Ella. "Now, look what you did, Ella. You killed poor Officer Benson."

"You really are insane," Ella told her.

Ignoring the insult, Adrienne tilted her head, gazed at Connor's body on the floor, and said, "Now, this pisses me off. He was the best sex I ever had, and I never got to bang him one last time." Turning her attention back to Ella, she taunted her by saying, "I guess I'll have to settle for fucking your husband's brains out once he finds out about you and Jeff and how you tried to frame him, and he realizes I am the only one who's always loved him. Before you die, take a quick moment to think about Matthew on top of me, making a replacement for Ava."

"You can't honestly be willing to murder your daughter. Please, just let her go," Ella pleaded.

"Goodbye, Ella," Adrienne said, pointing the gun directly at her head. "I always hated you."

"Freeze," came an order from the doorway. Surprised, Adrienne turned toward the voice. "I said freeze," Agent Ulrich commanded her again.

"I don't think so," Adrienne told her. "You see, Layna, I always get what I want, and I want her dead." She raised the gun again to fire at Ella. Having no choice, the agent fired one shot, hitting Adrienne squarely in her chest. The gun fell from Adrienne's hand, and she dropped to the floor. She briefly reached her hand toward Ella and said, "Ella, please help me."

Ella stared at her in disbelief. How could this woman, who had tried to frame her husband, frame her, murder her, and murder her daughter, honestly think she would help her. "I'm not stupid, Adrienne," she told her. "Enjoy Hell, you psychotic bitch."

Adrienne's reached-out hand dropped to the floor, and Agent Ulrich rushed toward her, kicking the gun away from her hand. She knelt down and felt for a pulse. "She's dead," the agent told Ella. Moving toward Connor, she felt for his pulse. "He's still alive," she exclaimed and immediately used her radio to call for an ambulance while applying pressure to his wound.

"How did you know?" Ella asked her after the agent finished relaying instructions for the ambulance and backup.

"Jessica called me and told me what the two of you had found. She also told me you had come over here."Agent Ulrich shook her head. "What were you thinking coming here alone?" she scolded.

"After what Jessica and I found, I had to get Ava away from her," Ella explained. "She's my daughter."

She nodded her head and said, "I understand. I probably would do the same thing if my children were in danger."

Ella had never thought of Agent Ulrich as a person with feelings and insecurities. She had no concept of how hard it must be in law enforcement, and she felt guilty. "I'm so sorry if I ever mistreated you," she told her.

Agent Ulrich smiled at her and replied, "Thank you, Mrs. Dalton."

"Please call me Ella," she replied. "You saved our lives. We owe you everything. Thank you, Layna," calling her by her name for the first time.

"You're welcome, Ella," she replied.

While Layna focused on assisting Connor, Ella held tight to Ava, trying her best to comfort her, before glancing at Adrienne lying on the floor. Blood was pouring from her mouth instead of the verbal garbage that normally spewed from it. Her thin lips now forever closed.

Epilogue

Two months after Adrienne's death, Ella and Matthew stood in the kitchen of the home they had once loved, boxing up the last of their belongings. Three needless deaths had occurred, and neither of them wanted their daughter to grow up in the shadow of what her birth mother had done.

Yes, their daughter. After Matthew was released from prison, the three of them shared a tearful, joyful, and love-filled reunion. Ella realized she had to tell him the truth about Ava's parentage, and when she did, he reacted exactly as she expected. Matthew couldn't have cared less about genetics; Ava was his daughter, and no test would change his feelings for her. Casey quickly filed on behalf of Ella and Matthew for the legal adoption of Ava. She assured them it would be a relatively straightforward process since Ava's biological parents were dead or facing life in prison. According to the birth certificate, Matthew was still Ava's legal father; her only concern would be any claim to custody that Connor's parents could make.

Ava's biological father had survived his injuries and agreed to make a full confession and plead guilty. He admitted that he and Adrienne had indeed come up with the plan together that day in Adrienne's bedroom. Jake, sitting on the sofa, was unaware his and his brother's murders were being planned just feet from him. Jake and Jeff were never meant to survive; they were necessary sacrifices for Adrienne to have the life she craved. Adrienne had not bargained on an agent as detailed as Dale, though, and she realized he had to be taken out of the picture. Jeff was supposed to kill Dale, but before he could, fate intervened and Dale suffered his near fatal blood clot. When Jeff left her home to confess to Jake's murder, Connor knew his instruction was to murder Jeff in his cell and make it appear it was a suicide. If Jeff ran gone into hiding, they would have tracked him and killed him eventually.

She promised Connor the two of them would be together once the plan was complete, but she had lied to him too, planning to string him along while she pursued Matthew. He had been unaware of Adrienne's dream to have Matthew released from jail and Ella put there in his place. She had laid out the best plan she could, but her lies eventually caught up to her.

After finalizing his guilty plea and receiving his prison sentence, Connor asked to meet with Matthew and Ella before being transferred to the state prison. Although initially reluctant, Ella agreed to the meeting, and she was glad she did. Connor showed genuine remorse for what he had done, apologizing to them both and asking them to raise Ava to believe he was dead. He was so ashamed of what he had done, and he didn't want his shame reflected on Ava. Knowing he would die in prison and wanting what was best for her, he informed them he had signed away any parental rights he had, and he had also secured an agreement from his mother and father to sign away any claim they had. This would allow them to fast-track their adoption of Ava. Connor's mother wanted nothing to do with the child, seeing her as the spawn of Adrienne rather than Connor's daughter. Christian didn't blame Ava, but he agreed to release his rights so the little girl could grow up with the loving parents she had known since her birth. Connor also told Ella he had reached out to his father to thank him for his cooperation, and they were speaking again. "Can you believe my dad still loves me?" he asked her with tears in his eyes.

Ella hadn't thought of Christian before the meeting with Connor and, after speaking with Matthew, they agreed to take Ava to meet her grandfather. He was thrilled to meet her, and Ella and Matthew were happy for Ava to have a grandparent. The two of them bonded immediately, and Ella knew Christian would be an essential part of Ava's life.

Casey went back to Minneapolis and her law practice, but she and Ella remained friends. They would meet for dinner or lunch and discuss anything but Adrienne. During one of those dinners, Casey told Ella she was starting a non-profit to provide pro bono legal work for women who have been sexually assaulted. She would represent their interests in court. Her first case was a class-action lawsuit against one Rob Hauen in Marshall. Ella was so proud of her friend for standing up for those women. After their dinner, Ella thought of all the women Casey would help, and she was inspired.

She went home that night to tell Matthew her plans, and he backed her fully. They had placed their home for sale but contacted the real estate agent the next day to take it off the market. Ella had bigger and better plans for this house they had so lovingly built together. Her next call was to Dr. McGregor, who was surprised to receive a job offer from her patient, but quickly accepted.

"Construction company is here, honey," Matthew told her.

Ella glanced at her husband, wondering how she ever doubted him, even for a moment. "Well, let's get this started," she replied.

She and Matthew walked outside to meet the construction company, Ella giving them explicit instruction on carrying out her vision. Matthew stood by her side, smiling at the force his wife had become. She saw him watching her, smiled back at him, and said, "What are you smiling at?"

"You're amazing," he answered her. "Ava and I are so lucky to have you."

"Not as lucky as I am to have the two of you," she answered truthfully. "Thank you for letting me do this."

Ella turned back for one last look at their home. She and Matthew had decided to turn the house into a live-in treatment center for domestic abuse or sexual assault victims. Dr. McGregor would run the facility, and no one would be turned away due to their inability to pay. No one should have to face that trauma alone, and they were determined to help as many people as possible. The house where they had allowed Adrienne and Jake to live was also being converted into a treatment center for men in abusive and controlling relationships. "Women like Adrienne exist," Matthew reminded her, and Ella recognized the need to help male victims as well.

Dr. McGregor pulled up the driveway to meet Ella and Matthew for the official transfer of the property. She was ecstatic when she saw the passenger in Dr. McGregor's car. "Justine," Ella exclaimed.

Justine jumped from the car as soon as it stopped and ran to her for a hug. "How are you?" she asked Ella.

"I am fine," Ella answered her. "How are you?"

"I think I am going to be okay," Justine stated. She turned to look at the large house and added, "I'm your first resident."

"Your room is ready and waiting for you," a smiling Ella replied as she handed Justine an envelope.

"What is this?" she asked.

"Open it," Matthew and Ella said in unison.

Justine opened the envelope and began crying as she read what it contained. "I don't know what to say."

"You don't have to say anything," Ella replied before she turned to rest of the group. "Everyone, I would like present the first recipient of the Ella and Matthew Dalton scholarship."

Justine put one arm around Matthew and one arm around Ella to hug them to her. "I will make you proud."

"We know you will. Focus on getting better first. This scholarship is waiting for you when you're ready."

Ella turned to hand the keys to Dr. McGregor, knowing she, Ava, and Matthew had to be on the road soon to their temporary home. They had purchased an acreage in Duluth and were in the process of constructing another dream house, but they had rented a lake house until their permanent home was ready.

Another car pulled up the driveway, and two men exited the vehicle. "You didn't think you were going to leave without saying goodbye, did you?" a teasing Dale asked.

"How could we leave without saying goodbye to you?" Ella asked as she hugged him before turning to hug Noah.

"You know," Matthew said, "you guys could move up north with us. It would be great to have another couple to hang out with."

Dale looked at Noah, who nodded for Dale to proceed. "Well, we can't move to Duluth, but we are moving to Minneapolis," Dale said.

"Well, Apple Valley," Noah interjected.

"You are?" Ella asked. "Are you leaving the BCA?"

"I am. I accepted an offer from the FBI Minneapolis office," Dale said proudly. "It's always been my dream to work for the FBI."

Ella beamed at Dale. "I'm so happy for you," she shrieked. Turning to

Noah, she added, "Take care of him, Noah."

"You know I will," Noah replied.

"Where is Layna?" Ella inquired.

"She's on another case out of town," Dale stated. "But she asked me to tell you to take care of yourself and that she wishes you the best."

Matthew put his hand on Ella's shoulder. "We do have to leave, honey."

Sighing, Ella knew it was time to say goodbye to all her beautiful friends. For the first time in her life, she had real friends, and although they would soon be separated by distance, she knew they would remain close. She hugged each person again, telling them she loved them, before getting into the truck with Ava and Matthew for the long drive to Duluth.

Ella turned to look at Ava in the backseat. "Are you excited?" she asked her.

"I am, Mommy," Ava said. "Will I be able to make friends when we get there?"

"Of course," Ella told her. "You'll have a lot of friends."

Smiling, Ella thought how proud she was of her daughter. She had been through so much but was still a loving, caring little girl. Dr. McGregor had recommended an excellent therapist for Ava, and she was dealing with the trauma of what happened the night she lost her mother. Adrienne had never felt her mother's love, and neither had Ella, and she was determined to end that cycle with Ava. She and Matthew would always ensure Ava knew she was loved.

Ella was fully aware that she wasn't cured of her issues yet, but Dr. McGregor had recommended a therapist in Duluth, and she felt stronger than she ever had in her life. She discovered she was worthy of love, and many people did love her.

After a few hours, they arrived at the lake house. Ava had been sleeping for the last two hours of the drive, so Matthew carried her into the house before coming back to help Ella with their bags. The place they rented came fully furnished, so they had moved most of their belongings to storage, but Ella wanted one item with her. She carefully took the large print from the back of the truck, handing it to Matthew.

"You want to hang this up tonight?" Matthew asked her.

"Yes, I do," she said playfully. "They are our protectors. We're lucky we got this picture before the artist becomes too famous for us."

"It is beautiful," Matthew agreed.

Ella followed Matthew into the house, where he removed one of the large pictures from the wall and replaced it with Ella's picture. It was a beautiful print of a photo Jessica had taken of the bald eagles in their woods. "They saved us," Ella told him as he wrapped his arm around her waist. "Without them, we wouldn't be here.

Message from the author:

My lifelong dream was to become a published author. I sincerely hope you enjoyed reading the novel as much as I enjoyed writing it and realizing my dream. Now that you have finished the book, I would love if you could take a moment to share your thoughts and leave a review. Thank you so much.

Laura

Made in the USA
Monee, IL
10 March 2022

e17c56c7-d5b5-45b0-a827-7a544dd1f4a9R01